Please return or renew this item by the last date shown. There may be a charge if you fail to do so. Items can be returned to any Westminster library.

Telephone: Enquiries 020 7641 1400
Renewals (24 hour service) 020 7641 1400
Online renewal service available.
Web site: www.westminster.gov.uk

QUE

KT-420-380

Philip Tarla has worked as an advertising copywriter in his native Australia for over twenty years. He is a PEN prize-winning short story writer, and lives in Melbourne with his wife and his two sons. *The Beat Jazzle* is his first novel.

THE EVIL INSIDE

PHILIP TAFFS

Quercus

First published in Great Britain in 2014 by

Quercus Editions Ltd
55 Baker Street
7th Floor, South Block
London
W1U 8EW

A CIP catalogue record for this book is available
from the British Library

ISBN 978 1 84866 399 2
EBOOK ISBN 978 1 84866 400 5

10 9 8 7 6 5 4 3 2 1

Typeset by Jouve (UK), Milton Keynes

Printed and bound in Great Britain by Clays Ltd, St Ives plc

To Shoba and Moira.
And to Alan Pilkington who said 'you'll see'

The Danger Zone

I jumped out of the taxi onto the slippery hospital driveway.

It was still raining like Noah was in town.

'Shit!'

I slapped a fifty into the happy driver's hand, ran round to the other side of the cab and opened the door. Mia slid out – belly up, legs akimbo.

I steered her towards the entrance as she dropped small red bombs of blood every few feet.

Doors hissed and we were suddenly in the terrifying sterility of the Cabrini Emergency Department. It was unbearably white and bright, an overlit limbo. A digital desk calendar on the counter clicked over to 1.19 a.m.: 09/09/99.

There were three nurses sitting behind the admissions desk, drinking coffee. One of them was whinging about her inept husband, keeping her two colleagues highly amused. A country music song was whining on the late-night radio: ' ... and that was the tremendous Tanya Tucker with "I'll Come Back as Another Woman" – but when you're as beautiful and talented as Miss Tanya, why would you want to?'

'Excuse me,' I said. 'We need some help here.'

None of the nurses paid us the slightest bit of attention. I banged the bell on the desk. 'Hell-ooo!' I bawled.

'We'd like to help, Sir, please calm down,' Nurse No. 1 said, putting down her cup. 'Now, if you'd just like to fill out this form—'

'Fuck the form!' I frisbeed the clipboard back over the counter at her. 'My wife is pregnant and bleeding and I want some help – right now!'

The nurse rolled her eyes and made a lackadaisical announcement into a microphone. After a minute, another nurse materialized and took Mia's elbow. 'Sir, I'll take care of your wife if you take care of the paperwork,' she said, leading Mia off into the glare.

I swore again, reluctantly took the clipboard back from the desk nurse and began scrawling furiously. The other two nurses continued their conversation as if nothing had happened while I spilt the entire contents of my wallet onto the floor trying to locate the requisite health insurance and credit card details.

I finally completed the form and handed it back with a fierce 'Here.'

'Thank you, Sir,' the desk nurse said. 'Now one of these other nurses will take you down to where your wife—'

But I was already walking.

'What's wrong with her?'

Mia had her legs up in stirrups. She was hooked up to a foetal monitor and there were a couple of drips stitched into her forearm. She looked green.

'She's lost a lot of blood,' the junior doctor in blue said quietly. 'But we'll have that under control in a minute. The baby – how many weeks is it?'

Twenty-three? Twenty-five? Fuck. I wasn't exactly sure. My brain was jelly. And the ponytailed doctor looked too young to drive a car, let alone handle an emergency like this.

'I think about twenty-four weeks,' I guessed. 'Near the end of the Danger Zone.'

The doctor nodded. 'Her gynaecologist is on his way. About ten minutes.'

I held Mia's hand as they continued to take readings. I looked at the ultrasound, at the tiny being who had brought us here. It didn't seem to be moving much.

I couldn't think. I couldn't talk. I just kept wishing there was a teleportation machine that could zap Doctor Hill to us in an instant.

'Guy?' Mia said quietly. 'What'd the doctor say?' She sounded dreamy, far away.

'She said Hill's on his way.'

'Oh. Good.'

Mia was thirsty. I went out into the corridor. Two young orderlies were leaning on the water cooler, discussing the details of last weekend's Blues–Lions football final.

'Excuse me,' I said, moving in between them. The water was cool but it did nothing to slake my thirst. 'Excuse me,' I said again, refilling my cup. The orderlies finished their breeze-shooting and slow-waltzed off with their buckets and mops.

I leaned against the cooler myself for a moment, closing my eyes: trying to turn unbearable reality back into a bad but baseless dream. I tried to convince myself that with all the miracles of modern science and technology, nothing really catastrophic could happen to my wife – or our unborn child. After all, this was almost the twenty-first century. This wasn't an episode of *ER*; this was a real hospital with real medical professionals.

Like Doctor Hill.

Then he was suddenly there in front of me: bald, patient, kind – just as Mia had described him. My words spewed out in a torrent: 'Oh, Doctor Hill thank God you're here Mia's bleeding and she first started last Friday night and I'm sorry I haven't come to meet you yet but I was going to come next week and—'

Hill held up a palm. 'Please, Sir. Calm down. You must be Mr Russell?'

'Guy.' I pumped his hand, spilling Mia's water with the other.

'Now, when did Mia start bleeding this evening?'

When? When? Fucking when? Think, man, think!

'Um, well she wasn't feeling well so she went to bed early. She called out to me at about 12.30 a.m. and she was bleeding then. In fact, the sheet was all covered in blood.'

Truth be told, I was still up reading my father's old Penguin copy of *The Count of Monte Cristo* and had had a few drinks: that's why I'd had to call a cab instead of driving Mia myself.

Hill didn't say anything. We were walking quickly towards Mia's room.

He looked at me kindly. 'Why don't you wait in the waiting room down the end there while I talk to Dr Ross,' – that must have been the name of the junior doctor – 'and examine Mia.'

4

Hill's firm but gentle hand on my arm suggested I should do as he asked. He went into Mia's room and closed the door.

I don't know how long I sat in the purgatory of that waiting room. I plucked a *Gone Fishing* magazine out of the rack and flicked through it blindly. A new nurse brought me a lukewarm coffee. But she said nothing, and then walked away again.

I flipped the page and stared at an old black-and-white photo of Ernest Hemingway standing next to a shark he'd caught down in Cuba in the fifties.

Like many young writers, I'd had my obligatory 'Hemingway Phase'. Immediately after university, I hitchhiked to Western Australia and got a job on a filthy old fishing trawler called *Dirty Mary* in a windy coastal town you'd miss if you blinked. *Dirty Mary*'s captain (I knew him only as 'Olav') was a mountainous bewhiskered old Norwegian drunk whom I suspected had fled his homeland after murdering someone there.

Anyway, the naive plan was that I'd work on the boat during the day and write down my visceral and fascinating *Old Man and the Sea* type experiences at night in my cramped, smelly bolthole above the town's only hotel. The problem was, after a day hauling nets and cutting bait, I was just too damned tired to work at night.

I lasted just three months and drifted back to Melbourne with only three pages of notes and a nasty case of Hep C from drinking too much cheap Australian whisky and eating mouldy food out of rusty tin cans.

I lifted the magazine closer: *The one that <u>didn't</u> get away from Papa,* the caption read. Hemingway looked like a big fat shark himself. But despite his sunny smile, I felt as cold as an iceberg. I needed a cigarette. Or a joint. Or maybe something even stronger.

'Mr Russell?' Hill was in front of me again, trying to get my attention. 'Guy?'

'Hmm?' It was hard to refocus on reality. Light was bouncing off his pate like a laser display.

'Guy, come with me. I have something I need to discuss with you and your wife.'

*

'The thing is,' he took Mia's hand, 'we're seeing foetal distress. Low heart rate. The baby's trapped in a hostile womb.'

He could have been speaking Swahili. I stood there, paralysed and confused. Meanwhile, a nurse I hadn't seen before was plumping Mia's pillow. She was an older woman, with streaky grey-blonde hair. There was severity in her face rather than sympathy. She punched the pillow like a middle-weight.

Hill went on. 'In simple terms, your baby's amniotic sac has ruptured. That's why Mia is bleeding. And possibly why the baby's not moving. There's also meconium in the amniotic fluid.'

I wondered if Mia had mentioned to Hill about the last time we'd had sex – the Friday before.

He read my mind. 'That bleeding Mia experienced when you last had *intercourse*,' – he pronounced the word as if it were a major crime – 'may have been an early sign of the problem. In fact, given its *exuberance* – he gave me a searching look – 'the *intercourse* may have even aggravated the situation somewhat.'

The foetal monitor gave a reproachful little groan of agreement before clicking back into gear. And I could have sworn the old nurse tut-tutted as she gathered up Mia's soiled linen.

The nurse paused with her bundle of sheets and slips, squeezed Mia's shoulder and grunted at her, 'Don't worry, love – it'll all turn out the way it's meant to. You'll see.'

There was something not quite right about her. She brushed past me with a scowl. I was glad she was leaving.

Letting Hill's words sink in, Mia flashed a sideways look at me – and it was not the look of love. She was sitting up. Her face was almost as white as the sheet that she had pulled up to her neck. Hill and I stared at the outline of her abdomen, rising and falling like a bellows.

And the good news kept right on coming. 'The bleeding is most likely attributable, however, to placenta praevia. Scar tissue on the uterine wall that forces the placenta to take up an abnormal position. Probably a result of the *interventions* Mia undertook prior to the birth of your first child.' He looked at me again. 'On top of the other difficulties, the foetus is also currently lying in a breech position.'

Interventions. The two abortions I'd strongly encouraged Mia to have a few years prior to having Callum, our first-born, who had just turned three. My career had been even more important to me in those early days. I often worked till midnight: I didn't have time back then for changing nappies or humming lullabies. I was young, selfish and stupid. And ashamed now because of it.

Mia gave me another look: I suddenly felt as though I was the one being monitored.

'Can you fix it?' I asked stupidly.

'Unfortunately I can't,' Hill replied. 'And neither can Mia. The thing is: the baby needs to be born right now if it is to have any chance of surviving.'

He waited a beat. 'But the problem is we have no idea how the baby has been affected by what's happened.' He waited again. 'And the fact that the baby will be born so early could result in some severe abnormalities.'

Severe abnormalities? In *our* baby?

'What should we do?' Mia's voice sounded disembodied, as if it was coming out of the air conditioning ducts or the washbasin.

Hill held her hand. 'We have to deliver the baby now – for your future health, if nothing else. However—' Hill paused and looked at us both very gravely.

'However what?' I asked.

'However, given the foetus's high risk of abnormality or major health problems, you may choose to terminate it *before* it's born.'

Mia looked to the wall.

'Under state law, you would be perfectly within your rights to request a termination if I, as your doctor, were to assert that not performing the termination would be deleterious to your physical or mental health. In another two days when the pregnancy enters its twenty-fourth week,

8

however, the situation becomes a bit trickier: we would have to move you to a public hospital and the decision would then have to be made not by you or myself but by an ethics committee.'

I walked round to the other side of the bed and tried to catch Mia's eye. But she looked straight through me and turned back to Hill. 'Have you had many other cases like this?'

Hill shrugged his shoulders. 'I've had similar cases but, of course, no two sets of circumstances are ever exactly the same.'

Mia finally met my gaze. 'What did the other women . . . I mean couples . . . decide?'

'Some couples who were childless – or who had strong religious beliefs – chose to proceed with the birth without . . . "intervention". And risked the consequences. The majority of other couples, however – the ones who already had children – chose intervention.'

He gave us a hard little smile. 'You already have a delightful little boy, don't you? I met him with you at my office, Mia, C—'

'Callum,' we said together.

He nodded. 'Callum, that's right. With the blonde hair. And after today's . . . procedure, there's no reason why Mia couldn't become pregnant again some time in the future.' Hill walked toward the door. 'But, as I said, whether you choose intervention or not is completely up to you. I'll leave you two alone now to discuss it.'

'Dr Hill?' Mia was barely audible.

'Yes, Mia?'

'Is it a boy or a girl?'

'It looks like a little girl.'

I didn't know where to look. I certainly couldn't look at Mia.

All I could focus on was the pile of fluffy white towels that the nurse had left on top of the windowsill.

I was woken by a garbage truck air-braking in the dark alley behind the hospital, carting away God-knows-what to God-knows-where. In the cold hour before the dawn, I lay curled on a blue plastic hospital chair, next to my newly empty wife. The chart at the end of her bed read 'Stable'. Whatever the fuck that was supposed to mean.

Mia's arm was dripping into a tube. My nose was dripping onto my shirt.

His and Hers catatonia.

I blearily recalled a pleasant get-together we'd hosted just a few weeks before:

Our wide kitchen window looking out onto shiny green grass and glorious gum trees.

The clink of glasses, the faces of friends.

The exhilaration of anticipation.

Mia was leaning against the sink, crying.

Her oldest friend, Jane, had her arms wrapped around her.

'Oh, I'm such a sook!' Mia laughed, wiping her eyes. 'I've only had half a glass of champers.'

Jane playfully poked Mia's forehead with her finger. 'It's the hormones, you idiot!'

She patted Mia's belly. 'Little Mamma Mia!' Jane assumed an exaggerated Italian accent and refilled her own glass to two-thirds. Then she toasted us both with a big, generous nod.

'To the future!'

Before we'd fled to Cabrini in the cab that night, I'd called Jane frantically and asked her to get over to our place as soon as she could to take care of Callum. The two of them arrived the following afternoon, just as an orderly was wheeling our new dead baby out of the room on a gurney.

After having been given some time by the staff to 'say goodbye' to her, our lifeless little girl had just been left lying there by the wall for half an hour, covered by a thin cotton shroud.

'Bubby' we had nicknamed her during the pregnancy. Our dear departed daughter.

'Daddy!' Callum rushed past the orderly pushing his stillborn sister and into my arms.

Mia had her eyes closed. 'Hello, little man,' I whispered, 'Mummy's just having a rest.' I winked at Jane, who was still standing in the doorway. She smiled back with tears in her eyes, made a coffee-drinking sign and left our family to lick its wounds.

'It's OK,' Mia murmured. 'Come over here, darling.' Callum bounded onto the bed and Mia crushed him to her. 'Oh I've missed you! Were you OK? Were you a good boy for Auntie Jane?'

'Yep. She made me French toast – all the way from Harris!'

'Do you mean Paris, darling?' Mia laughed but then winced. She put a hand to her strangely flat stomach.

It was then Callum noticed the little white crib just outside the bathroom.

He jumped off Mia's bed and ran up to it. He stood on his tippy toes, straining to see over the side.

I couldn't move. I couldn't say anything.

Mia put her hands up to her face.

Callum strained harder to get a peek. He put both hands on the side of the crib and tried to hoist himself up. It tipped, hung suspended in the air for one dreadful moment, then toppled to the floor. The coverlet slid off, forming a soft white puddle next to it.

'Where's Bubby?' he squealed with delight.

'Oh my God!' Mia wailed.

Callum jumped back and screamed.

But, of course, the little white cot was empty.

1

Happy New York

One of the first things you notice about New York is the water towers.

Everywhere you look up in Manhattan, you see rusting, rotting, cone-headed water towers pricking the famous skyline. Big ones, small ones, squat ones – like sage old Chinese gentlemen tipping their hats to each other across the rivers and streams of black and white and grey and yellow far below.

Of course, I'm not Chinese. Nor am I American. I'm Australian.

And I'm still not really all that old.

Although some days I feel 500 years old in here.

In my new office.

It's strange to think back on it all these years later: how I got from 'there' to 'here'.

Was it fated? Predetermined? Decreed by some horrible higher power with a black, brutal sense of justice? Looking back now, I can see how I might have made other choices, taken a different fork.

But I was that man then. That other whiter, brighter version of me in his safe little office with his safe little life.

If only he'd realized how lucky he really was.

But towards the end of the last century, that other me had found his life repetitive, routed, predictable.

His life had become, well, lifeless.

And then there was the thing with Bubby.

He was only halfway through his life, yet he already felt half-dead.

It was a brand-new century, he figured. So why not a brand-new him?

And so he hauled his little family all the way from the cosy familiarity of Melbourne, Australia, to the scabrous streets of New York City.

To #27 West 72nd Street, Manhattan, to be precise.

*

Our new home, the Hotel Olcott, stood proudly in the heart of the Upper West Side.

I'd always been intrigued by atmospheric old buildings and hotels and, according to my Internet research back in Melbourne, the Olcott had an illustrious, if slightly disquieting, history.

The revered character actor Martin Balsam – who famously falls backwards down the staircase in *Psycho* – had been a former resident. Tiny Tim used to tiptoe through the Olcott lobby; Robert De Niro pulls up outside the hotel in *Taxi Driver*, while Mark David Chapman lived there for a short time, before indulging in his own peculiar form of Beatlemania and shooting John Lennon.

In September 1951, Isidore H. Bander, vice-president of a pharmaceutical company, either fell or jumped to his death from the top of the hotel. His body oozed like a marshmallow out of his grey flannel suit all over the 72nd Street sidewalk. He had told his wife he was going out for a stroll but took an elevator straight up to the roof instead.

Yet the Olcott actually went right back to the late 1920s: a fifteen-storey forest of old dark wood, dim yellow lights, claret-coloured carpets, and elevators that worked only when they felt like it. A bit like the porters: who mooched around the lobby, hiding behind newspapers, surreptitiously smoking and sniggering about the guests. When they were there, that is; the lobby was sometimes as deserted as a graveyard, especially once the desk clerk had decamped for the evening.

My friend and fellow Aussie – and new boss-to-be – Anthony Johnson had offered to put us up somewhere swankier, but knowing my fascination for the 'dark and dingy' as he called it, suggested that the Olcott's quaint, Addams Family-ish charm might be more our speed.

We'd managed to avoid any Y2K airplane malfunctions and had cleared customs without a hiccough. And although we'd left Melbourne on a hot and humid New Year's Eve, due to the sixteen-hour time difference it was still 31 December when we arrived in New York. Only now it was cold and dark and snow was whiting-out the windscreen of our first yellow cab.

We slid into Manhattan across the Queensboro Bridge and arrived at the Olcott just after 10 p.m. The Hispanic porter took us and our slew of suitcases up the service elevator and opened up our room.

#901.
Nine is my lucky number. At least it used to be.

First up, there was a tiled entrance hall equipped with three coat pegs, a wall phone and a fire extinguisher. Two steps on, the world's smallest kitchenette. Then a general living area with an ugly round, brown kitchen table, which was obviously too big for the kitchen, and a low-slung three-seater couch facing two chunky armchairs. An art deco lamp flickered ghostly behind the TV, another smaller couch sagged under the window, while a waist-high bookcase bulged with careworn *Readers Digest*s and *New Yorker*s, a musty selection of fat eighties airport novels and old Agatha Christies like *The Murder of Roger Ackroyd* and *The Mirror Crack'd from Side to Side*. Deep-blue faded wallpaper featured flower petal and ivy motifs (or little scowling owl faces, depending on how you looked at them). The bedroom really lived up to its name, jammed with two double beds and not much else.

Callum's favourite bath toys – a one-legged Tarzan and a yellow rubber ducky – would also have to get used to much smaller quarters.

'Welcome to the Waldorf,' I said.

Callum was clinging like a sleeping monkey around my neck.

Mia tried to be upbeat. 'We won't be here long. It'll be fine short-term.' She took in the tiny kitchen, absent-mindedly rubbing her belly and yawning. 'Although don't quote me on that.' She walked two steps into the kitchen and opened the three wooden drawers, one by one. They seemed to be empty except for the very last one, from which she extracted a rusty old fork.

'And we may have to invest in some new cutlery.'

She opened the small metal bin with her toe and ceremoniously dropped the fork into it. I smiled in affirmation.

Moments later, Mia tucked Callum into one of the beds and fell in next to him, still fully clothed.

But I was beyond sleep: it was Friday night, the New Year's Eve of a brand-new century – a brand-new millennium – in New York City. And I didn't have to start work till Monday.

We had a whole weekend to soak up the city and, right now, I felt like a drink. I showered, changed, and rode the elevator back down to the lobby. I asked the desk clerk if there were any decent bars nearby. Sporting a name tag that read 'Michael' and a tie that had Yosemite Sam blazing guns on it, he looked up from his crossword. 'Plenty,' he confirmed in broken-nosed Bronxese. 'But the nearest one is right there,' he pointed with his fountain pen. 'Through that door. My friend, Enriquo, will look after you.'

Like a magic portal through to Texas, you could walk straight through the Olcott's lobby into the Dallas BBQ Restaurant next door. Happy, hungry faces, tantalizing smells and an excessively moustachioed barman – Enriquo, I presumed, handing me my first Corona and lime and a 'Happy New Year, amigo!' – provided the perfect antidote to the day I'd spent in the sky.

I slid onto a stool, but then noticed the jukebox. I craved something suitably 'New York'.

I got up, walked over, dropped my first American quarter into the slot and let Frank Sinatra's 'One for My Baby' float me off into oblivion.

'DADDY!!!!'

My jet lag never had a chance.

Callum had decided that it was time for me to wake up, and dive-bombed me a second time. The sun was just peeping in. I peeked through the curtain: early morning, light snow.

'Aren't you still sleepy, darling?' I whispered hopefully. Unlike Mia and me, Callum had slept most of the way on the LA to New York connecting flight.

'Let's play!' he squealed again.

'Ssssh!' I hissed. 'You'll wake Mummy. Let's go out for a walk and see the snow.'

My son had a mop of blonde hair, which made him look like a little girl when it grew too long. We'd discovered after he was born that his name meant 'dove'. The origin of Callum's angelic locks remained a mystery, but he'd definitely inherited Mia's eyes: dreamy cornflower blue.

I dressed him in the new winter clothes Mamma Giancarlo, Mia's mother, had given him for Christmas and dropped him into his pushchair. Though I soon learned they were called 'strollers' over here – which sounded a lot less like hard work.

'Where are you going?' Mia groaned as I grabbed my gloves out of a drawer.

'To get you your first New York "corfee".'

She pulled the bedclothes back over her head. 'No

thanks. I still haven't got the taste back for it.' She yawned as if from underwater. 'You know, you were babbling in your sleep again last night, Guy.'

'Declaring my undying love for you, no doubt.'

'No,' Mia yawned again and leaned up on her elbow. 'You kept shouting "Stay away! Stay away!" Then you started mumbling something else, though I couldn't understand what you were saying. You were quite agitated. At one point you grabbed hold of one of my fingers and started pulling it, really hard. I had to thump you to make you stop!' She smirked at me.

I found Callum's blue woollen hat and put it on his head. 'See ya later. I'll bring back the papers.'

Mia rolled over again. 'Hey – can you also get me some more sleeping tablets from a pharmacy? Dr Hill gave me a script that I can use over here. It's over there in my handbag.'

'*Dis bag here, lady?*' I said, in my best New York cop accent.

She folded back the bedclothes and nodded. Mia slept a lot these days, except on planes. Her eyes were red and puffy. I had a vague memory of her crying in the middle of the night through my beer-soaked dreams.

'You OK, honey?'

'Just a bit jet-lagged, I think.' She popped two blue pills out of the blister pack by the bed and reached for her water. 'I'll try to grab another hour now.'

Light was spilling like honey over the frosted hemline of Central Park.

I pushed Callum's stroller down to two-wheel drive to make it easier to plough through the snow on the pavement, his little legs kicking excitedly in the snap-frozen air.

After one hundred mushy metres, we finally made it to the corner. I got a shock when I looked up, even though I already knew from my Melbourne research what I would find here at the corner of 72nd and Central Park West.

There it stood in all its dark, gothic glory: 1W72 – the Dakota.

Looking every bit as ominous as its haunted-house reputation, the filigreed wrought-iron gate and carved reliefs were straight out of Poe – or Transylvania itself. So too were the high gables, pitched roofs and wide porte-cochère entrance for horse-drawn carriages of yesteryear. Gargoyles glared from the stone block walls, low enough for Callum to reach out and touch – although he quickly changed his mind once he got up closer to them. A glowering Indian warrior kept lookout atop the central gable.

A charnel house in popular culture, up close and in real life the Dakota seemed equally foreboding.

I shivered.

We pulled up outside the guardhouse. Right there, just a few feet back under the archway, was the exact spot where John Lennon had been shot. I recalled that famous photo that Annie Leibovitz had taken of John just hours before he died: he was curled up naked in the foetal position with his arms around his beloved Yoko – or 'Mother' as he used to call her.

Inside the wooden sentry box, a fat face under a blue cap was scanning the *New York Post* and chewing a pencil.

ALL VISITORS MUST BE ACCOMPANIED read the sign on the low chain slung across the entrance. I also remembered reading somewhere that Mark David Chapman, Lennon's chubby assassin, had actually patted five-year-old Sean Lennon's head and told him not to catch cold just a few hours before he murdered his father.

A Japanese tourist wearing a ridiculous golf hat and a serious-looking camera snapped a photo of Callum and me in front of the box, just before an evil-smelling bag lady with big dark glasses cursed at me as she almost ran her home over my foot. We were already being introduced to the city's manifold charms.

My stomach was no longer jet-lagged, so we squelched into a gleaming new Starbucks on the corner of Columbus and 73rd. I ordered a medium latte, a chocolate chip cookie for Callum, and waded into the first *New York Times* of the new millennium.

Callum, meanwhile, drew a little smiley face with his floury forefinger on the window pane.

'Look, Daddy,' he smiled. 'I drawed Bubby!'

The rest of the weekend was as special and as memorable as any first weekend in New York could possibly be, ticking off virtually every tourist cliché. We clip-clopped round the Park behind a fairy-tale white horse, checked out the park's little zoo and carousel, and sat Callum astride the burnished back of Balto, hero husky to the sick children of Alaska. Mia ogled the art at the Met while Callum and I threw snowballs on the steps outside. We visited the Warner Brothers Movie Store where a giant talking Tweety told Callum that he had indeed just seen a 'puddy tat'.

At Anthony's insistence, I took a chopper flight over the city, scooting between the skyscrapers then swooping low over the park and the East River like a hornet headed for the Hamptons. The people below looked like tiny figurines in an elaborate toy kingdom.

We rode the Staten Island Ferry and marvelled at the 'Big Green Lady' of Liberty standing on top of the water. We bought me some new 5th Avenue winter clothes and shoes. We feasted on pastries at the famous Muffins Cafe on Columbus, Callum rebranding their mouth-watering wares as 'nuffins'. Callum and I rode up and down the Olcott elevator, and he delighted in yelling out 'L for Lobby!' every time we reached the ground floor.

I snapped two whole rolls of film. And we walked – God did we walk, block after block after block.

It was good to start leaving our miserable Melbourne selves behind.

'So waddya think?' I asked Mia on the Sunday night. Callum had already fallen asleep in front of *Scooby Doo*.

My wife was beautiful. Not beautiful like a magazine model, but in a natural, soulful way. Her southern Italian features were more deliberate than delicate. She had a cute snub nose and thick black eyebrows that she plucked loudly and religiously. Her lips were full and heart-shaped and her teeth were soap opera white. She had a killer smile. But it was those eyes that I'd really fallen for. The lashes were unnaturally long and her irises were the most heartbreaking hue of blue, dramatically offset by her luminous olive skin.

I adored her with all my heart.

'It's way too early to tell.' She sipped her Galliano white. 'We've only had a tourist weekend, not a real weekend.'

She was right. Living in a hotel and seeing the sights was far removed from the day-to-day challenges of 'normal' New York life – whatever that was going to mean. We'd have to wait a few weeks before our new reality set in.

'But we had fun, didn't we, Bucko?' She kissed her finger and touched my cheek. She seemed happier than she had for a while. But her happiness was like a veil. I knew that she still carried a world of hurt underneath.

'Now get some sleep. The Big New Job starts tomorrow.' She made for the bedroom.

'Yikes!' I cried, like Shaggy running scared in *Scooby Doo*.

But I was still way too wired to sleep.

So after Mia went to bed, I sank into one of the spongy old armchairs with a dog-eared *New Yorker* I'd picked from the shelf.

I started to read an article about Jackson Pollock's Herculean artistic and alcoholic adventures out in the Hamptons during the forties and fifties.

It reminded me of the first time I'd met Mia, fifteen years before.

I'd hosted one of my legendary weekend 'Barbie-Benders'. These explosive bacchanalian festivals usually kicked off mid-Saturday afternoon at the house I shared with a

PhD philosophy student and a primary school teacher, and often didn't finish until thirty-six hours later. Grass, hash, speed, coke, microdots, magic mushrooms, MDMA: whatever anyone threw into the ring, we had it. All washed down with gallons of beer, scotch, brandy, white wine and anything else we could pile into our dirty bathtub.

We were a grungy, nihilistic, pleasure-seeking collective of dissolute advertising creatives, talentless musicians, tyro academics, loud left-wing teachers and out-of-work actors. Looking back, the only thing we really had in common was our youth and our obsessive and sometimes dangerous love of partying. Anthony was never part of that crowd and never would have been: he was already over at business school in America by then, making himself even smarter.

Anyway, that Sunday morning saw the bitter end of a particularly indulgent bender. My mate, Smithy the geography teacher, had mailed some peyote back to himself from Mexico, and I'd made the mistake of sipping the rancid tea you make with it. Soon I was solemnly declaring to anyone who was still awake that I wanted to see God at dawn.

Predictably, God never appeared. But as I staggered like a madman across the football ground behind our house, I saw Satan's face laughing with delight in the clouds as angry trees tried to reach down and stab me with their branches.

Mia found me shuddering like a scared little kid at the feet of a terrifying green giant disguised as a bush. My arms were straitjacketed around my knees.

'Well look at you, Bucko ...' She dropped to her haunches with a wry smile as her Labrador's slobbery tongue started to unroll across the grass like a long red carpet. 'Who's been a silly boy then?'

She lived in our street. We used to wolf-whistle at her from our front balcony as she lifted heavy prints and paintings in and out of the back of a grey minivan that had the name PICTURE PERFECT adorning both sides. I later learned she had her own successful niche business working as an art broker to companies and high-end individuals, often storing the works in her hallway before delivering them to prospective clients to hang in their foyers, boardrooms or bedrooms at a later date.

A couple of weeks before the party, the two of us had been vying for the same parking spot. I'd unchivalrously beaten her to it, but then let her have it anyway, and even helped her carry a couple of heavy, gilded frames to her doorstep.

I'd always fancied her smile. And those beautiful eyes.

God knows what she saw in me – except perhaps the challenge of major rehabilitation.

Anyway, Mia took me back to her place, gave me some charcoal to offset the effects of the drugs – she'd been a nurse before deciding she was really much more interested in art – cleaned me up, and put me to bed. And that was it: I never really moved back to my own place after that.

But we didn't really come together until her dog Sky died.

It happened about three months after I'd moved in

with her: a P-plate driver; an old dog's wonky eyesight; a foot slamming on the brake pedal just a fraction too late . . .

Sky had been Mia's faithful companion since she was seven. The old Lab had been by her side through countless boyfriends, a hundred haircuts, a handful of addresses and the thousand ups and downs that attend the flowering of a girl into a young woman. In the short time that I'd known her, I'd never seen her so upset.

I buried Sky for her in the park where we'd first met – near the now strangely benign green bush. Before I covered the grave, Mia threw in a new bone and an old *Sesame Street* doll that he'd liked to chew, and then motioned me out of earshot so she could say a few final private words to her beloved friend.

Such was her grief, she could barely walk home.

So I picked her up in my arms and carried her back down the drowsy, dappled street to her bed.

As the blood-red sun sank below the horizon, I lowered Mia's head to the pillow and kissed her hair. Then her furrowed brow. Then, through her tears, I kissed her eyelids. Then I kissed her cheeks and her cute little nose and her lips. She couldn't stop crying. I couldn't stop kissing her.

I wanted to kiss her better.

It took her a week to get out of bed after her dog died.

A true Italian, I discovered that Mia could be highly emotional and took some things very hard.

But when she wasn't crumbling herself, Mia was a rock.

I'd lost my way after my mother died and Mia became my compass.

But in recent months, my darling wife had run a little off-course herself.

And I was still trying to work out how to bring her safely back home.

*

The Big New Job was at 1160 Avenue of the Americas: Suite 1999.

Brave Face Public Relations was a company that had been established in the UK in 1988, before rapidly expanding its operations into Europe, Scandinavia, Asia and, more recently, North America.

The office was located halfway between 46th and 47th Streets, in the middle of Midtown. A stone's throw from Times Square.

My subway commute on the B line from W72nd to Rockefeller Center was only ten minutes. That didn't really give me much time to reconsider how I was going to make this whole crazy thing work. I had spent many hours back in Melbourne dreaming and scheming about how my little one-man agency was going to grow, under Brave Face's auspices, into a global communications conglomerate of Saatchi & Saatchi proportions. But now, as I was riding up the elevator for Day 1, I wondered if I hadn't made some catastrophic mistake.

Back in Melbourne, I had at least been somebody: writer and creative director on a number of high-profile automotive accounts; a Cannes Gold Lion for a skin cancer public service TV ad; author of the well-loved tagline 'Go to zzzleep' for an international bed manufacturer.

But now, here in New York, I was suddenly the newest kid on the world's biggest block.

Anthony Johnson was the man I held largely responsible for my temporary insanity.

'Hello, mate!' I extended my hand.

My old friend bear-hugged me. 'Maaaate – you made it! Without getting mugged? Over your jet lag yet? What have you seen? How's Mia?' Running a manicured hand through his impressive thatch of blonde-white hair, he was the epitome of the successful PR man.

Anthony had been one of my best mates at uni. He'd been in my Modern English Literature tutorial in second year, but I didn't really get to know him until I fell into the notorious 'Booze Brothers' drinking club, which met irregularly at a variety of ignominious venues both on and off-campus.

Anthony had then graduated with a law degree combined with a masters in marketing and economics and moved to the States to further hone his nascent business skills. After that, he spent some time in London learning the PR ropes at Burson-Marsteller. But he'd returned to Melbourne quite a few times over the years and we'd always caught up, had a few beers – although he'd curbed his prodigious university intake considerably by then – and discussed our respective careers.

Anthony Johnson had a rapid-fire laugh, but his mind was even quicker.

He gave me the grand tour. Brave Face occupied half the tenth floor, had nineteen efficient-looking employees, eleven offices and an L-shaped boardroom that boasted a heart-stopping view of the Chrysler Building. The other half of the floor was let to a dotcom company called v-deliver: an online service that delivered videos directly to your home – like pizza – saving you a trip to the store.

'Good idea, but probably five years ahead of its time,' Anthony said.

Unlike the gauche fit-outs of many communications agencies, Brave Face's decor was stylish yet understated. Cool green and soft off-white walls were enlivened by big, classy contemporary prints and a long row of framed PR awards. The effect was pleasing: Anthony had always exuded impeccable taste as well as enviable chutzpah – qualities immediately evident from his *GQ* wardrobe of handmade Savile Row and Milanese suits.

'I'll show you to your office. It's not huge but it should at least accommodate your colossal ego,' he said.

'Thanks, mate. It's half the size of yours then, eh?'

He was right. The office itself was nothing to write home about: a shiny new ruby iMac, a desk, a bookcase, a coat stand. But the view was a New York postcard. Like the boardroom, my window also looked directly out towards the Chrysler Building. I whistled softly.

'Thought that might inspire you. Come on – let's go

meet the team. They're all very excited to meet the new creative director.'

The rest of the day was a brain-blitzing blur of faces, names and titles. Almost everybody seemed to be a vice-president of something or other, even if they were still in their early twenties. And as I was being introduced around, my obvious ignorance of American business jargon was cause for some good-natured ribbing from Anthony and my other new colleagues: 'heads up', 'gap analysis', 'bandwidth' and 'knock-on effect' were all a foreign language to me.

'How was it?' Mia called out when I walked in the door at seven. I kicked the last vestiges of snow off my new Kenneth Cole brogues and shook some more out of my new Barneys scarf. 'It was *awesome*,' I replied in mock-Americanese. 'Actually it was good. Anthony looked after me and everyone was super-friendly in that super-friendly Yank way.'

She was searching for something in the cupboard-sized kitchen.

I hung up my new Zegna pea coat. 'What are we eating? Should we get takeaway or what?'

'It's called "take-out" here, Michael, that funny desk clerk told me. No, I'll cook with one foot out in the hallway because I got us a couple of prime New York sirloins in honour of your first day in the Manhattan work force. I finally managed to pick up some decent cutlery today, too.'

Without turning around, she held up a brand-new, black-handled, two-pronged carving fork.

Just then the phone rang on the hall wall behind me. 'I'll get it,' Mia brushed past me with the fork still in her hand. 'That'll be Michael with exciting news on getting some extra sheets and pillows up here as well.'

As she scooped the handset from the cradle, a subterranean memory from long ago rose up in me.

I'd been reading a Mad *magazine when the phone rang.*

'May I speak to your mother, please?' the important-sounding lady at the end of the line had asked.

'Who should I say is calling, please?' I almost added 'ma'am' as she sounded so officious.

'Er, can you please just put your mother on, young man? I'll explain it all to her.'

I dropped my magazine and covered the mouthpiece.

'Mu-um! Phone. Sounds important.'

I could hear my mother spluttering and cursing in the bathroom — she hated having her bath interrupted.

She padded out in a ratty, threadbare towel, leaving watery footprints behind her, and snatched the phone from me.

'What are you looking at, boy? Give that here. Hello . . . ?'

And as I watched the expression on my mother's face dissolve from anger to agony, I knew that something had just been broken that could never be fixed again.

I shivered as Mia hung up the phone and playfully poked the fork towards my abdomen. 'Hmm put that thing down, will ya? You look dangerous,' I said.

I followed her back into the kitchen as she dropped the new fork back in the drawer. I tried to cuddle her from behind, but she suddenly froze. It was a distressing new habit she'd developed over the past month or two. 'Where's our little space ranger?' I asked, trying to restore the initially jovial atmosphere.

'Bouncing on the beds like Austin Powers.'

I held up the cute white shirt with the tomahawk emblem. 'Anthony gave me a little Braves top for him.'

*

'. . . And so the big old giant never bothered the people of that town ever again. *The end.*'

'Hmm.'

'Did you like that story?'

'Yeah. But it was a little bit scary.'

'But they got rid of the giant in the end. Then all the people were happy.'

Callum considered this and then had a thought. 'Daddy, would I be like a giant to Bubby?'

'Yes, you would have. But Bubby's gone away now, remember?' I kissed his head. 'OK, darling, ni ni.'

'Daddy?'

'Yes?'

'Where did Bubby go?'

I hesitated. 'I don't know. Maybe she didn't want to come to America so she hid somewhere back home.' I had had no idea how to answer that question, and was so unprepared for it that I said the first inane thing that came into my head.

'Oh,' he sounded unconvinced. 'I still miss her.'

'We all do. Now cuddle Buzz and go to sleep.'

I really didn't want to be reminded of Bubby. Bubby's sad, short life had had a terrible impact on all of us, but particularly Mia.

As I switched off his Noddy lamp, Mia was standing in the doorway. I smiled but she didn't smile back. She stared at me through the half-light like one of the Dakota gargoyles. It was as though she could read my mind. Mia didn't want to forget Bubby any more than Callum did. She couldn't forget. How could she? I was the monster trying to erase her pitiful little memory from the family archives. Mia brushed past me, kissed Callum on the forehead and climbed silently into the other bed, fully clothed.

I went to bed myself soon after. Even though I hadn't done any actual work yet, the first day on the job had been as enervating as it was exciting. Mia was already exhaling deeply beside me as I dozed off into a recent happy memory.

The three of us – four including the baby – were lying on our bed back home in Melbourne as Sunday afternoon rain serenaded us through the window. Callum had drawn a big smiley face on Mia's bare bulging belly with a black Texta colour. As we succumbed to the natural lullaby outside, I had the feeling that we were on a lovely soft raft. Drifting together on a huge, gentle and kindly ocean.

*

Part of Brave Face's new business-building strategy was to offer advertising as well as their usual PR staple to the ever-expanding roster of FMCGs, utilities, government departments and dotcoms they wanted to snare. And that's what I did: advertising; peddling powders to the great unwashed; feeding the piranhas.

After studying Anthony's 'Clients We'd Love to Work With' list, I surmised there were about eight companies that could benefit immediately from running targeted B2B or consumer campaigns – mostly dotcoms based in the giddy gold rush of Silicon Valley, as well as a couple in New York's own 'Silicon Alley'. One of the reasons Anthony had hired me over a local recruit was because he suspected a direct, no-bullshit Aussie approach might be enthusiastically received, especially by the fast-moving new Internet companies he now wanted to target. (The other reason, of course, was that he was a good guy who wanted to help give a buddy a fresh start.)

I ran the names by him. Based on his broad knowledge of the dotcom sphere, he scratched out a couple of my suggestions and added three new ones that hadn't made his master list yet.

'There you go, Girly,' he said one evening in my office as the sun kissed the Chrysler Building goodnight. 'Nine companies, nine new business pitches. That should keep you out of trouble for, what, how long?'

Anthony often called me Girly – as in 'Guy/Girl'.

'Just strategic and creative first thoughts? Or fleshed-out spec campaigns?'

'Say spec campaigns for the most promising half and strategic outlines for the rest – I'll tell you which ones.'

'Give me a week to organize an art director. After that, maybe a presentation every fortnight?'

'Good – you're busy for the rest of the year, then,' he grinned. 'So I reckon you'll be looking forward to a summer break with us out at North Fuck in July?'

'North what?'

'Sorry,' Anthony laughed. 'That's what Susanna and I call our holiday shack out on North Fork, Long Island. Getting away from the Big Bad Apple can do wonders for your sex life.'

'Really? What about *Sex in the City*?'

'Nah, that's just a TV show for women who orgasm over their shoes.'

North Fuck in July: it sounded good somehow.

'You're on. I'll bring the massage oil and the Barry White CDs.'

I soon developed a productive and enjoyable routine: in the mornings, I researched the clients we were planning to pitch to; in the afternoons, I interviewed art directors. At lunchtimes, I tried to get out of the office and explore the neighbourhood. After all, with Times Square just a block behind us, I was virtually at the centre of the universe as we know it. Sometimes I'd check out the CDs at the Virgin Megastore. Or wander down and see what films were playing at Loews.

Mia, meanwhile, busied herself with apartment hunting. Anthony had agreed that Brave Face would cover our hotel bill for the first six weeks – after that we were on our own. Fortunately Susanna Johnson had kindly offered to help Mia get her real estate bearings. Susanna's first-hand knowledge of the local market – she and Anthony had survived three Manhattan address changes in eight years – as well as her landlord-lacerating tongue, were sure to save us a lot of time and money.

As well as organising a splendid welcome dinner for us at the Four Seasons, Susanna also introduced us to a nanny for Callum called Esmeralda. A doe-eyed Mexican woman in her early thirties, Esmeralda had previously been nanny to Anthony and Susanna's seven-year-old daughter, Courtney, for a short time before Courtney had gone to school.

Until we could get Callum booked into a suitable day-care centre, Esmeralda would be an excellent, if expensive, solution.

Things were starting to look up – we were slowly becoming happy again.

Lay not that flattering unction

'Are you interested in taking the kids out to Coney Island tomorrow?' Mia asked, with one of her 'this is more of an instruction than a request' looks. After only three weeks at Brave Face, I was already falling behind in my familial duties.

'You haven't seen much of Callum lately – and I know it's because you've been so busy at work – but I told him there was a beach there that had lots of merry-go-rounds and ice creams and stuff, so he's obviously pretty keen.'

I sipped my Folgers. 'Kid-*s*?' I emphasized the plural.

'Susanna had organized a play-date for Courtney and Callum tomorrow anyway, so I thought maybe she'd like to go, too.'

'While you and her mother go and play in Park Avenue?'

'That's the evil plan, Bucko.'

I nodded and took her hand. I was glad that Mia had a new girlfriend to hang out with. It would do her good to get out and have a coffee or a drink and a few laughs. With someone who wasn't me.

*

The clickety-clack soundtrack out to the Atlantic dropped me into a meditative mood: the decrepit warehouses and graffitied bridges flickering by like a visual Valium.

Courtney had Callum in stitches with her repertoire of face-pulling, off-colour jokes and Little Miss Madonna dance routines. She was a born performer, that girl: a formidable combination of Susanna's street smarts and Anthony's endless reserves of energy. I had no doubt she'd be lacerating landlords of her own one day.

'My dad's a rider at your dad's work — so he can ride on the go-merry-round, too!' Callum cried as he jumped across the aisle into my arms.

'What's a "go-merry-round"?' Courtney asked, pulling a 'that does not compute' face.

'A carousel,' I explained. 'You know, with horses and music and stuff.'

'Oh. Anyway, your dad's a *writer* not a rider, Dumbo — isn't that right, Guy?'

'Yes that's true, Courtney. But please don't call Callum "Dumbo" — he's only three, remember. And yes, I would like a ride on the "go-merry-round" with you two.'

The crisp bite of the ocean air and cement sky meant the fun parks were virtually empty. That didn't seem to bother the kids though — it meant they had the run of all the rides and didn't have to line up.

Hiding behind pink bouquets of cotton candy, they looked up at a scary-looking ghost train ride called Dante's Inferno. Purple cerberuses snarled down at us from opposing towers as a werewolf mugged out of one window and skeleton warriors rattled chains in another. The centrepiece was a large, grotesque devil holding down a terrified human victim whose head merged with the huge lolling tongue of a bug-eyed, upside-down African witch doctor.

Dante's ride was no merry-go-round. But I let Court-ney go on the skyscraping Wonder Wheel and the slightly less scary-looking Spook-a-rama while I hugged Callum close to me on the Roger Rocket and the Mini Train.

For lunch, we hit the Boardwalk. The kids devoured hot dogs and slurped ice creams — *was the island named after ice cream cones?* Courtney wondered — while I went local with a plate of Atlantic clams washed down with Brook-lyn Lager.

We picked up the leftover shells and took turns frisbee-ing them out to the gulls. Further out, a long, skeletal black bird perched on a blue buoy, watching our game like a crabby old school ma'am.

'Dad, can we rewind the world?' Callum asked on the train ride home.

He'd come up with his 'rewind the world' concept one day back in Melbourne after rewinding his *Toy Story* video back to his favourite scene. He'd wanted to know: if you can rewind a video, why not life itself?

'Why do you want to?' I asked.

'Cos this is one of the best days ever, isn't it?' he beamed through his ice cream beard.

'Why is that, Son?'

'Cos it's just you and me!' He turned to Courtney as an afterthought. 'And her, too!'

'Gee thanks, Callum,' Courtney deadpanned. 'You're like my best friend, as well — not!'

He pushed the concept further. 'And if we could rewind

the world then Bubby could come back and then Mummy would be happy again, wouldn't she?'

'Who's Bubby?' Courtney smirked. 'Your imaginary friend?'

'That's enough, Courtney.' My voice suddenly had an edge to it so Courtney looked out the window and started whistling. Callum had started mentioning Bubby a bit more frequently over the last couple of weeks and I was starting to find this somewhat disquieting.

I put my arm round him. 'Unfortunately we can't rewind the world, Son. But don't worry: I'm sure Mummy will start feeling happy again soon. Especially now we've come to such an exciting new place to live.'

But it was indeed good to be spending some quality father/son time together. 'Maybe we could just "pause" the world instead,' I suggested. 'And stay on this day for ever.'

*

It was the Monday morning of my fourth week in the saddle.

I'd already seen two or three art directors, but I was enjoying this interview much more than the previous ones. Maybe it was the cheeky twinkle in this guy's eye as much as the work itself.

'So, where have you been working lately?'

He scratched his dark, shiny head. 'Ahhhh lemme see . . . BBDO – where I did some nice stuff on Snickers and M&Ms . . . Y&R, Kirshenbaum & Bond . . . And a few of my own small but handy clients, heh heh heh.'

His credentials were impressive. His folio was kick-arse. His name was Bill West.

I closed the last page: a Clio Award-winning magazine ad for Folgers Coffee. 'Look, here's the deal,' I said, outlining the arrangement that Anthony and I had cooked up. '650 bucks a day. And then if we win some business – and you and I get on OK – you can join us full time as the business grows. Interested?'

'Sure,' Bill zipped up his big black bag and handed me his business card. It featured a small cartoon of himself wearing a ten-gallon hat, holding a marker like a six-shooter with the words WILD BILL WEST. SMOKIN' ART DIRECTION underneath.

'When can you start?'

'How about right now?'

We would spend the rest of the week road-testing each other's brains. My already smallish office became even smaller after Bill moved in and started spreading all his photography books, layout pads, marker sets, and what I would come to call his general 'Billshit', over every possible surface.

One of the most likely prospects on Anthony's list was a hot new webcam company called coolcams.com. And so he had assigned a gung-ho young account supervisor (although her business card said 'Vice President Client Services') to work on the project with Bill and me.

At her last agency, Lucy Tate had worked on the highcams.com account – a leader in the fast-emerging webcam category. A blonde, hazel-eyed, early-thirties go-getter from Preston Hollow, Texas, Lucy answered all of our stupid and ignorant questions with alacrity, insight and imagination. In fact, she quickly demonstrated considerably more intellectual depth than many of the 'suits' I'd worked with in the past, having graduated summa cum laude in International Affairs at Georgetown University. Her mentor there had obviously inspired her: after a solid grounding in PR and marketing, Lucy told me she was planning on entering the diplomatic corps.

And though she wasn't attractive in that prissy, thoroughbred Upper East Side way like some of the other women in the office, her impressive intellect and southern sassiness gave her a unique appeal; while the freckles on her nose and plump, dimpled cheeks added the earthy allure of a naughty farmer's daughter.

She ran on Diet Coke and adrenalin. And the rumour round the office, though surely it couldn't have been true, was that she'd been dating JFK Junior just before his plane went down the year before.

It was the end of the week, and Lucy – and Anthony – loved the work.

In just a few short days, Bill and I had developed a complete, integrated campaign for coolcams: print ads, posters, direct marketing, internet and guerrilla (or 'under the radar') ideas. We even threw in a TV concept which we knew the client's limited budget probably wouldn't stretch to but, hey, we were out to impress.

'I think those drugs you boys have been taking have

really kicked in.' Lucy laid her soft hand gently on my back and thrummed her fingers.

Her lingering digits made my balls tingle. Then she rubbed Bill's smooth pate, making him moan with exaggerated orgasmic pleasure.

'Just keep those time sheets up to date, Billy Boy, and I'll rub your head whenever you want.'

*

To celebrate the positive in-house reaction to our cool-cams work, I junked my usual lap of Times Square and invited Mia to have Friday lunch with me instead.

Esmeralda had asked for the morning off, so Mia had booked Callum into a local playgroup on Broadway for a couple of hours; proper childcare would have to wait till we knew where we were going to be living after the Olcott.

It was a sunny day, so we arranged to meet at Bryant Park. A Harlem gospel choir was up on a makeshift stage, keen to remind us that *Jesus was a working man, too*.

Mia handed me my brown bag and we sat and ate and listened to the angelic voices.

'How was Callum when you dropped him off?' I finally asked, tossing the crust of my sandwich to a pigeon that cooed politely for it.

Mia wiped her mouth with a napkin. 'A bit clingy initially. But when he saw the big slide and all the other kids up to their elbows in Play-Doh, he was fine. The woman running the place just scooped him up and sat him down at a table with some Puerto Rican boys. He was as happy as Larry.'

A young mother with a ponytail, track pants and a Kathmandu coat was wheeling a pram towards us. She was looking down into it, making the usual silly Mummy faces and gurgling noises.

Mia frowned at her a little.

The woman parked at our bench and lifted out her heavily swaddled, pink-cheeked baby. 'Do you mind if I feed her?' she smiled.

'Not at all,' I replied.

Mia said nothing.

The mother unzipped her jacket, unbuttoned her shirt and the cup of her bra and pushed the hungry baby's mouth to her fat red nipple. Then she turned to watch the stage.

The Lord saves us all, the choir promised.

The pigeon fluttered up onto the table and pecked at my bag.

Mia looked at me.

Her eyes were wet, and it wasn't just because the sun was shining into them.

Towards the end of the day, I learned that Anthony had set up a presentation for us for the following week in San Francisco, where coolcams were based.

'I reckon we're on our way,' he said, handing me a dirty cup to rinse as the fresh coffee started to *blop blop blop* through the machine. 'You've done well in your first month, Girly. And Bill's a fucking crack-up, isn't he?'

'Yeah. He's been great.' I turned on the tap and started to rinse a cup out for me, too. 'We work well together.'

The tap gurgled like an ogre clearing his throat. Brave Face's decor may have been cutting-edge, but its plumbing was positively prehistoric.

'I reckon we all do, mate. Cos at Brave Face, we're all self-starters – Lucy's a gun, too. You know the old saying *If it's to be, it's up to me.* I live by that and I reckon you do, too.'

I nodded in recognition – I certainly did know the saying but I hadn't thought of it for a very long time.

I leaned forward on the edge of the sink on my palms. I suddenly felt a little unsteady. It almost felt like the water was filling up my head, flooding my brain with something harsh and poisonous.

How I hate that voice.

That cunty, carping, wheedling, needling, emasculating, enervating, never-ending voice.

The voice that drove my father away.

The voice that exists only to hear itself.

I arrive home from school, hot and bothered.

I'm in the second-last month of my final year.

I know exactly where she'll be: sitting in the front room listening to Roy Orbison or Shirley Bassey with an ashtray almost full and a bottle of Cinzano Bianco almost empty on the crooked little table beside her.

Or in the bath, trying to wash away her myriad sins.

I hear taps rumbling and a splash from the bathroom.

And then the voice starts up like it always does.

'Is that you home, boy?

'Bout bloody time.

You been spending all my money on them bloody useless books of yours again?

If it wasn't for you, I'd be much better off.

You're half the man your father was and he was a bloody nobody.'

She's a demented Judy puppet from a relentless, never-ending pantomime.

I unsling my schoolbag and drop it on our grubby kitchen table. My thrift-shop copy of Hamlet *is sticking out of the top of my bag: I have a test on the death of Polonius tomorrow.*

The other boys my age in the neighbourhood are all doing trade apprenticeships by now.

Or their first stint in jail – like my old mate, Timmy.

So I study like a demon.

Over and over, I repeat a phrase I once heard a football coach say on TV:

If it's to be, it's up to me.

You there, boy? she calls in that unbearable voice.

My mother and I have lived in this shitbox just the two of us for the last six years.

We circle each other like tigers.

But not for much longer if I can help it.

If it's to be, it's up to me.

If it's to be, it's up to me.

Guy! She screams out from the bathroom now.

Guuu-yyyy!

'Uh, Guy,' Anthony had placed one hand on my slightly trembling shoulder while he turned off the tap with the other. 'I think the cups are well and truly clean now, mate.'

*

'Hi, Esmeralda.'

'Hello, Guy.'

'Daddyyyyyyy!' Callum came barrelling out of his hiding place behind the end of the couch and crash-tackled my knees.

'Jesus – you little devil! I'm going to have to get you a grid-iron helmet.'

Esmeralda was standing on the arm of the couch, fiddling with the cord to the curtain, cocooning us in for the cold night ahead.

The sight of it unsettled me.

'That looks dangerous – you might fall,' I said to our new nanny. 'Where's Mia?'

Esmeralda stepped down lightly. 'It's hokay – I'm used to it! Mia still don't come back from the realtor yet. He found some more places for her maybe.'

'So what have you two been up to today?'

Callum's words burst out like a geyser. 'We goed to da park an' I played on the swing an' dere were lots of peoples there an' I had an ice cream and there was a clown who didn't talk cos he was too scary so we comed back home and watched TV—'

'A scary clown?'

'Oh, he was one a those . . . waddya call them? . . . mime artistes.' Esmeralda said, freezing her arms to demonstrate.

'He was just like standing there and not moving for like fifteen minutes.'

'. . . An he had a white face and really really really scary eyes,' Callum's own little eyes bulged at the memory.

'Yes, he was a leedle scary for the children,' Esmeralda picked up her bag. 'Even maybe for the grown-ups, too. My second cousin, Estella – you know, Anthony and Susanna's maid? – she was with us and she was freaked out, man! His face looked like a death mask where I come from. Like a copse.'

'Corpse.' I gave her back the 'r'. 'Well, apart from Mr Scary, it sounds like you two had quite a good time. Callum, Esmeralda's going now – say bye bye.'

'Bye, Melda.'

'Bye, leedle man. See you tomorrow.'

I saw that Esmeralda and Callum had documented their outing together on Callum's blackboard. There were some trees, a swing set, two larger stick figures, *Estella* and *Esmeralda,* a smaller one with an ice cream holding Esmeralda's hand, *Callum,* and a white unnamed blob at the extreme right.

Mia was tired. And seemed depressed.

The apartments had all been a waste of time.

I poured myself another glass of red. Mia had refused a third glass, though she seemed to have rediscovered her taste for wine if not coffee.

'You look weary,' I said. She'd recently cut her hair into a short, sixties bob with a hard, horizontal fringe. I thought it made her look a little severe.

'I didn't sleep well last night. I had a very strange dream about Callum.'

I nodded as I put her plate on mine.

'He was flying through the air with his arms out-stretched—'

'Was he wearing a cape?'

'Ha, ha, Guy. No. But he was really scared. Terrified. Like he was falling rather than flying. And he couldn't stop himself.'

'Paging Dr Freud! You're probably just worried about how he'll adjust to living out here.' I put my hand over hers. 'The change will be good. For all of us, I reckon. Kids are very adaptable.'

'Mmmm.' She seemed unconvinced. 'But it was *so* vivid. And he was flying through the dark! Poor little baby.'

Since we'd lost the baby in September, Mia's moods had been erratic. She seemed to be fighting an internal battle of attrition.

'Why don't you take it easy for the rest of the week?' I suggested. 'We've still got a couple more weeks after that to find somewhere to live before Brave Face stop footing the bill. Do some shopping. See some galleries.' Mia had had vague plans to resurrect her art-brokering business once we'd found Callum some reliable day care.

She held up a little brochure with the words Polonius Realty and a robotically happy couple about to open a stylish-looking front door on the cover. 'But Susanna's already made three appointments for us tomorrow. She's been so helpful. Today she told this sleazy little landlord he was the "scuzzball of all scuzzballs". She looked like she was gonna start beating him with her handbag!' Mia yawned and headed for the bedroom.

'Really?' I stood up with the plates. 'Well, see how you feel tomorrow. Just don't overdo it. OK?'

'OK.'

After she'd gone to bed, I planned on going through Mia's handbag and grabbing one of the names off the 'Shrink List' that Susanna had also kindly provided in case Mia felt like talking 'to someone professional'.

I stepped into the kitchen and turned on the taps.

The same awful memory I'd tried to submerge in the Brave Face kitchen rose back up again to the surface like soap scum:

How I hate that voice.

That cunty, carping, wheedling, needling, emasculating, enervating, never-ending voice.

'Guuu-yyyy!' she screams.

'Guy! Bring me my towel will ya, you little shit!'

She often forgets to take her towel with her into the bathroom when she's been drinking. Which isn't uncommon.

'It's hanging on the chair in the yard!' she calls.

On the way home from school, I've actually been thinking about Hamlet's mother:

Mother, for love of grace,

Lay not that flattering unction to your soul . . .

'I'm not mad, it's you that's bad,' I've written in the margin of my book.

I like Shakespeare; I like the sound of the words, even when I don't know exactly what they mean.

But I always make notes and find out later.

And I'm still debating whether Polonius was stupid, unlucky or both.

I wonder the same about my mother now as I retrieve her towel from the back yard and re-enter the house.

I hear water beginning to gurgle down our often-blocked drain.

I walk into the bathroom and try not to look at her as she stands up in the bath.

'What have you been doin' out there?

'You're a disgrace.

'You'll never be anything.

'You're useless.

'I can't stand you.'

But today Mr Punch has a surprise: I step right up close, holding her towel out to her with a great big smile.

And for once Judy is lost for words.

The little bed on the wheels

Leave Monday afternoon, back Tuesday afternoon: Anthony was right – San Francisco was a blitz.

A long wagon train of clouds plodded past my little oval window. A yellow tear across one of them made me feel anxious, as though something ungodly was oozing from the heavens.

I flicked distractedly through the *Red Herring*, *Industry Standard* and *Wired* magazines I'd bought at the airport newsstand. I was nervous. This was my first test at Brave Face. I wanted to repay Anthony's faith and investment in me. I also wanted some sort of divine affirmation that making the trip to the States had been the right decision, not just some crazy whim. Winning a new piece of business within just a few weeks of arriving would be a very reassuring pat on the head from above.

Anthony, by contrast, was the epitome of confidence. He made phone calls and wrote strategies for other forthcoming pitches. And he drank endless cups of the dreadful black aircraft oil that masqueraded as coffee.

By the time we checked into the Hotel Powell in downtown San Fran, it was already 7.30 p.m. – so 10.30 p.m. back in New York.

I phoned home. 'Were you asleep?'

'Not yet,' Mia yawned. 'Just checking out some more apartments on the net.'

'How's my boy?'

'He's good. We just watched a great doco on Discovery Channel about panthers and pumas – did you know they're actually the same animal? And today Esmeralda took him to the Natural History Museum and he really got off on the dinosaurs. I thought he might have been scared, but he loved them. He misses you.'

'At least someone does.'

There was a long pause before she yawned again.

'Anyway, I'm just exhausted. Good night. And good luck tomorrow.'

Polite. Perfunctory. Not at all like the old Mia I knew and loved.

'I'll call you afterwards,' I told the cold-sounding woman now impersonating my wife.

Before I left for Frisco, I'd made Mia agree to see a counsellor with me. Our move to New York hadn't had the resuscitative effect on her mental state that I'd hoped it would. Maybe this counsellor, who I'd booked us in to see Wednesday lunchtime, could help thaw her out a little.

*

'So that's how we're going to make the world appear more interesting, more exciting – and, of course, more profitable – through coolcams.com.'

Anthony smiled and rubbed his hands together, like a

surgeon scrubbing down after a successful operation. The room was silent. 'Any questions, guys?' His face was still set on 'trust me'.

The three kids who'd started the company broke into loose spontaneous applause and let out a couple of enthusiastic 'whoa's. Even the forty-five-year-old suits found it hard to disguise their excitement: they too grinned like love-struck teenagers.

The larger of the two VCs tried to rein in the excitement a little. He'd seen a pitch or two in his time and knew that first impressions didn't always count, despite the obvious chemistry between our two companies.

'Thank you very much, Anthony and Guy – and the other members of your team who put such a lot of work into today's presentation. Your efforts have obviously struck a chord with some of us here today. But, as you know, there are three other agencies in the race and we still have one more to meet with.'

'Thanks for giving us the opportunity, Bob,' Anthony responded, now in full statesman mode. He straightened his tie and ran a Rolexed hand through his wheatfield hair. 'We've really enjoyed working with you on this project and hope that – if we're fortunate enough to win your business – we can work together to make coolcams something really, really special.'

We packed up our boards and Anthony's Dell laptop and shook a warm circle of hands. My boss couldn't resist a final little plug. 'And remember, even if you choose *not* to use Brave Face as your ad agency, we can still help you out with your PR – if we're still talking to you, that is!' The coolcams crew laughed. It's a good closer.

'They'll probably want to make a decision relatively soon,' Anthony smiled. We were approaching the airport car park.

'When do you think we might hear?' I asked.

'It seems like they want everything yesterday.' Anthony swung the hire car into the Hertz check-out lane. 'Not surprising when you're smart-ass kids with big ideas and egos to match.' We parked, got out, and started trotting towards Departures.

'I reckon they'll get back to us by the end of the week. At the latest.'

'Olcott Races, Callum's Day, doo dah, doo dah . . . Olcott Races, Callum's Day, oh–the-doo-dah-day . . .'

Even though I'd only been gone a day, I'd really missed my boy. 'Go!' I yelled. We raced each other down the long ninth-floor corridor.

I usually let Callum win. But every now and again, I sprinted at full tilt – just to freak him out.

'Wow, Daddy!' he panted as we trotted back and round the dogleg to room 901. 'You're even faster than a . . . really fast rocket!'

He paused and pointed to an electrical socket on the corridor wall between our room and 902. 'Hey, "rocket" – that sounds the same as "socket", doesn't it, Daddy?'

I nodded. I didn't even know he knew the word

'socket' – it was quite advanced, even for an especially curious three year old.

'Stay away from the sockets, Daddy!' he cried gaily as he pushed our door open and bounded down the hallway.

A sudden chill passed through me. I felt a little faint.

Mia frowned at me from the kitchenette with a ladle dripping passata sauce in her hand.

'What's wrong, Guy?' You look like you've just seen a ghost?'

She was right: in a way I had.

*

'And what brings you good people here today?'

Our counsellor was wearing an open-necked Ralph Lauren check shirt while a heavy gold chain encircled his fat bull neck.

Dr David Kane looked a little like Henry Kissinger. I hoped he shared some of the former's diplomatic expertize. On his side table, there was a green Post-it pad with *Freudian Slips* printed across the top.

Mia hadn't wanted to come. She'd spent the first seven minutes crying. I knew it was seven minutes because Dr Kane also had his alarm clock set up on the table beside him.

Dr Kane and I either looked at each other or out of the window. He sucked on his teeth, then handed Mia a box of tissues and folded his hands over his ample belly.

Mia blew her nose and finally gathered herself.

'I . . . I . . . I lost a baby last September. Back in Australia.'

'Go on, Mia,' Dr Kane smiled benevolently. 'Take your time.'

Mia started weeping again. I reached for her hand, but she left it dangling over the arm of her chair like a dead eel. And then she turned to me. 'We lost a baby . . .'

We. At least now she was including me in the terrible equation. ' . . . but despite what the doctor there told us at the time, I'm just not sure we did everything we could to save her.'

She continued to stare at me. I realized that I'd been holding my breath for quite a while, and let it out like a punctured tyre. Was it a question or an accusation? I looked at Dr Kane again for some support.

I can see what you're dealing with here, his expression seemed to say. He checked his clock and opened his hands out to both of us. 'Well, why don't we talk about it?'

Mia pointed angrily at Dr Kane and turned back to me. 'But *he* wasn't there! He doesn't know!' She dropped her head and sobbed. '*How* can *he* help us?'

Kane looked bemused. 'Mia . . . I can't help you, unless—'

Mia sprang up and ran out of the room, taking the tissue box with her.

I jolted awake in the wee small hours: Callum had been crying in his sleep. Really bawling.

'What is it, darling?' I asked him.

He snorted then choked: 'T-t-there was a scary 'lectric

skeleton and it was chasing me and Mum so we ran up on the roof!' He started to wail again. 'Our old roof house. In Stray-ya.'

I tried to stroke the fear out of him. 'Yes? And what else did he do, this scary skeleton?'

His little face turned to me in the glow coming from under the bathroom door. 'H-he hided under your desk and he plugged hisself into the wall. Into the socket.'

Socket.

There was that word again.

I shivered.

'Then he was all red on the inside. And bright, too, like a fire!'

'Then what happened?'

'I sneaked down and pulled out his plug . . .' He stopped sniffing for a moment, surprised at the thought of it. 'But then he plugged it back into hisself and started chasing me again!'

I got up and switched the main bedroom light on and unplugged Callum's beloved Noddy lamp and the voltage converter. I pointed at the harmless empty sockets.

'Well look,' I said brushing the tears from his cheeks. 'There's no scary skeleton in this room now – just your good old Noddy lamp.'

Callum nodded uncertainly. He wasn't convinced.

Before I reinserted the lamp plug, I looked twice at the socket myself: for a moment, I could have sworn it was grinning malevolently at me.

I eventually managed to rock the both of us back to

sleep, my last thought being that Mia had been in the bathroom a long while. Maybe she'd fallen asleep in there.

*

Anthony was right: we heard late Thursday.

Bill and I had decided to visit the Museum of Modern Art. Research for our next pitch: an online art exhibition site for a major phone manufacturer. There was a huge floor-to-ceiling hanging banner in the foyer showing a little boy crying and a headline that said: I WANT MY MoMA!

'Commerce usurping art once again,' Bill sighed, pulling his coffee-stained brief out of his moleskin bag. 'Enough to make one puke, hey, bro?'

My mobile phone rang. I still couldn't get used to calling it a 'cell' – it sounded like something you'd use in prison.

'Hey, Girly, get straight home and put your bloody drinking shoes on!' It was Anthony. 'And tell that cheeky bald-headed bastard to do the same!'

'What? We won?' I asked. My heart began ricocheting round my rib cage.

'Not only did we fucking win, you bloody creative wanker!' Anthony paused to prolong the suspense. I thought I could already hear liquid sloshing in a glass at the other end. 'Those snotty-nosed coolcams kids got second-round funding this morning and are going to double both the ad—' another delicious pause '—and the PR budget!'

'What's he saying?' Bill mouthed silently, his smile widening.

'He's saying that we have official permission from the boss to go out and get completely legless!'

To celebrate, Anthony had booked the tiny circular bar at the Royalton. It was the perfect place to down a few martinis. There seemed no point now in either going home or back to work; my Nikes would have to double as drinking shoes. Anthony said he'd meet us at the bar in half an hour – along with Lucy.

I rang the Olcott.

'That's fantastic,' Mia said. 'Well done.'

But she sounded a little flat. 'How was your day?' I asked.

'We didn't get it,' she said glumly. 'The apartment, I mean.'

A two-bedroom with lots of natural light up near Carl Schurz Park on the Upper East. She'd had her heart set on it.

'Don't worry, I'm sure you'll find something soon.'

She sounded really forlorn now. 'I hope so – we have to start paying the Olcott bill ourselves after next week, remember? Now I know how Bubby must have felt: nowhere safe or happy to live.'

Now Mia was bringing up Bubby as well. I didn't know what to say, so I changed the subject. 'Is Callum there?'

'No, Esmeralda hasn't brought him back from playing with Courtney yet.'

'Well say goodnight to him from me. I'll be home—'

'Late,' Mia knew. 'Enjoy yourself.'

But she didn't sound like she meant it.

*

'I've had enush.' After six hours on the grog, Anthony could no longer keep up with us.

'Hey, mate,' I toasted him. 'I'm going to let the old Booze Brothers boys know about your piss-weak performance here tonight and you'll be thrown out of the club!'

He frowned at his gabardine Canali coat as if it was some unsolvable cosmic conundrum, inserted his arm into the wrong sleeve, shrugged and decided to wear it like a poncho instead. 'Don't be rude to your boss or . . . ' He tried to think of a parting rejoinder, but at this stage of the game decided a gentle pat on my shoulder was easier. 'Say goodbye to the bald bastard.'

Bill was at the bar, getting us another round and some cigars.

Anthony saluted Lucy, threw his scarf flamboyantly over his shoulder like Warren Beatty on a yacht and weaved unsteadily towards the Royalton's exit.

'So, Guy,' Lucy leaned forward, 'how are you and the family settling in?' Her hazel eyes were kind and genuine. It'd been all work talk, office gossip and silly anecdotes up till this point. But the crowd was thinning a little now and the mood was becoming more intimate.

'Well, you know. Mia's hunting for apartments like a madwoman. Callum, my little boy, seems to be enjoying himself. But I guess moving from one city to another is always going to be tougher than you think.'

Lucy nodded. 'Took me at least six months to get the measure of this town – even though I'd already lived in Washington and Chicago and LA.'

'LA?'

'Record company assistant. Sweet Jesus, the things they expected me to do!' Her deep, throaty, smoker's laugh was very pleasant on the ear. 'Those guys make advertising seem like the priesthood. It's so true what Hunter S. Thompson said about the music business being a long, plastic hallway where thieves and pimps run free.'

I wondered what things they'd 'expected' young Lucy to do exactly.

Her low-cut boho blouse and thigh-high snakeskin boots had already given me a few ideas of my own – and not ones appropriate for a married man.

One of Lucy's shapely knees brushed mine as she leaned in closer. 'Guy, I hope you don't mind me saying, but Anthony told me about what happened with you guys last year back in Australia.'

I couldn't bring myself to look her in the face. I sipped my Jack Daniels instead. I'd lost count of how many I'd had.

She put her cool, bangled hand on mine. 'That must have been just awful.'

'Yeah, it was no fun park,' I conceded, enjoying the soft warmth of her hand. The *Dante's Inferno* ghost ride flashed through my mind. 'For any of us.'

Lucy's gaze was level and direct. She really did have the most enchanting eyes.

'Well if you ever want to talk to someone, I'm just across the hall.'

Then Bill was back. Leaning across Lucy's lap and batting his eyebrows like Groucho Marx, he fanned out the Monte Cristos like he'd just won an Oscar or something.

'Do you know what Freud said about cigars?' he hiccoughed.

'Yes.' I unwrapped one and handed it to him. 'Freud said, "Sometimes a cigar is just a cigar."'

Lucy lit mine as I was still swimming in her eyes.

After falling in the snow twice on 72nd Street, I rolled into the Olcott sometime after midnight with half a Gray's Papaya hot dog hanging out of my jacket pocket.

The same Hispanic porter who had carried our suitcases up that first night now had to almost carry me through the mysterious wind tunnel that had suddenly sprung up in the lobby. He propelled me into the service elevator and pressed 9. At first, I tried to fight him off. But he finally managed to convince me that he wasn't trying to steal my precious hot dog.

I squinted at myself in the narrow strip of mirror in the corner of the elevator: a Mr Hyde with wild hair, yellow eyes and a mouthful of knives grinned back at me. The doors slid open at my floor and I bounced off walls down the deserted corridor. By some miracle, my key opened the door. I zigzagged down the hall before carefully placing my hot dog on top of the bookcase.

Callum was snoring in the bedroom, lying on his back in a nappy like Cupid in the lamplight. The Olcott was heated to a constant tropical temperature so we never wore much inside. Mia was on her left side in blue panties, whistling through her nose.

Lucy had lit a fire in me: I slid in behind Mia, horny as a rhino's face. I cupped her buttocks and swallowed her ear. She stirred, groaned and then spoke with the brutal honesty of the half-asleep. 'No. Not now. Not again.'

Then she stumbled across to the other bed and crawled in next to Callum.

The rejection stung. I turned and exited the bedroom, flopped down on the couch and burped painfully. But I supposed I couldn't blame Mia really. The last time we'd had sex all those months ago back in Australia had possibly contributed to the thing with the baby.

We'd been out celebrating a new insurance account win at a bar near the agency. Then there'd been Pinocchio's Pizza and red wine and then more drinking at another bar. And then somehow I was home.

Stupid with lust and bourbon, I pulled her panties down to midthigh. I stuck two fingers deep inside her.

Her vagina was already slightly moist. I tasted my fingers – I'd always loved the salty/sweet taste of her. I slid my cock into her. She was awake now but still half-dreaming. She moaned irritably, annoyed that her own sexual instincts were disturbing her sleep.

I moved my right hand around to her breast and let it fill my hand as I sunk deeper into her. She lifted her right leg a little to increase the opening. She knew that if I was drunk, it would take me longer to come – so the more she helped, the sooner she'd be able to go back to sleep. I also stuck my little finger into her arsehole. She sometimes liked that.

'Fuck me!' she whispered urgently. 'Fuck me, fuck me!'

I pushed faster but really wanted to prolong the enjoyment. Because Mia's pregnancy had been making her feel queasy, it was the first sex we'd had in a few weeks.

'Fuck me!' she said more loudly. I thrust as hard as I could.

'*Fuck . . . Ow!*' *she suddenly groaned.*

'*What's wrong?*' *I whispered loudly. But I kept right on fucking her. It was like I had a wild animal inside me or something.*

*She pushed me out of her and away. '*That really hurt!*' She rolled away.*

'*Have you forgotten I'm pregnant, Guy? It felt like you were stabbing the baby.*'

'*Sorry.*' *But my still-pulsing cock wasn't sorry. '*I suppose a blow-job's out of the question?*'

'*Go to sleep. You're drunk,*' *she sounded really annoyed now.*

'*But—*'

'*Go fuck yourself instead.*'

There were some small spots of blood on the sheets the next morning.

'*What's this?*' *I was still trying to open my other eye. It felt like someone had stitched the lids together overnight.*

'*It's just spotting,*' *Mia said without emotion. '*It's happened before.*'

'*I'm sorry. I—*' *I tried to touch her.*

'*Forget it,*' *she moved away to strip the bed. '*I'll call Dr Hill. It'll be OK.*'

'*Here, let me do that.*'

*But she yanked the spattered sheet away from me like a matador feinting for the kill. '*Why don't you clean up the bathroom instead,*' she growled. '*You completely missed the toilet. There are even flies buzzing around in there.*'

That unsavoury recollection brought the bile back to my throat: I took the half a hot dog off the bookcase and tossed it in the kitchen bin. I sat back on the sofa, turned on the TV, and flicked on the soothing soft porn of Channel 35.

*

Early the following afternoon, Rosemary, the Brave Face receptionist, called through to the boardroom phone. My hangover was still hurting and the bleat of the phone was like a drill to my skull. Bill passed me the handset.

'Sorry, Guy, but your nanny's on the line and she sounds quite upset.'

'Esmeralda?'

'Oh, Guy!' She *was* upset. 'Sorry to bodder you at work but Mia has goned to the hospital. Mount Sinai actually.' She gave a little cry.

'Jesus Christ! Why? Has she had an accident? Is she OK?'

Bill bit his lip.

'Yeah – she's OK and it wasn't an accident hexactly.' She sniffed, trying to keep herself together. 'Um ... I dropped by to pick up my money for the week – usually Mia give it to me on Mondays, but Estella and me was going to Delaware this weekend to visit a friend and I needed some extra money so I dropped in today instead – and you know how I have my own key, Guy?'

'Yeah?' I didn't really – Mia handled all that stuff.

'Well I didn't know whether Mia was even home today so I went inside and—'

'Go on,' I said to her. 'It's OK.'

'Well I goed inside and there was a rolled-up wet towel near the door and I could smell gas. A lot of gas, Guy.'

I could almost smell it myself. I was starting to feel a little woozy.

'Was the oven leaking?'

Long pause. 'No, it wasn't leaking.' She went quiet for a minute.

'Well what was it?'

'Um, well I could see that there was an empty bottle of wine on the table . . . ' She paused again. 'And then I slided open the door to the kitchen and there was another wet towel on the ground to stop all the gas getting out.'

'And where was Mia?'

Long pause.

'She was lying there on the ground in the kitchen. She had passed out.'

Jesus. 'And where was Callum?'

She gave a loud, sad snort. 'Oh don't worry – he's OK. Mia took him to Susanna's house this morning. He's still there.'

'How did you know that?'

'Oh, well cos I threw some water on Mia's face and I slapped her to make sure she was still breathing. And I turned the gas off, of course, and I dragged her out to the hallway and into the lounge room and opened the window. And then I called Michael downstairs and he called the ambulance but by the time the men come to get her, Mia had already waked up. She was sitting up and crying so I make her some tea. But then she was sick.'

'Oh.'

'She said she was very sorry for me to find her that way and that Callum was with Susanna and that I should call you at work. So after they take her away on the . . . little bed on the wheels?'

'The stretcher.'

'Yeah, the stretcher, I ask Michael and he give me your number.'

'Oh.' I should have been rushing off to Mount Sinai, but instead kept spouting banalities. Maybe I was in shock. 'Did Mia give you your money?'

Bill could tell by my tone that no one had actually died. He gave me a hopeful little wave and closed the door on his way out.

'Oh yes,' Esmeralda almost sounded normal again.

'She leaved it under the vase on the table for me.'

I just kept sitting there in the boardroom. I knew I should leap into action and rush over to the hospital but I'd fallen into a kind of turbid, morbid trance.

It wasn't the first time. Mia had actually made a half-hearted suicide attempt in her youth: there'd been a broken romance on top of her father's death. A packet full of pills seemed like the only logical salve to her teen-age angst.

She'd told me she 'felt like dying' after her dog Sky had died, too.

But this time, Mia had experienced what I supposed the doctors were going to tell us was a 'severe, delayed post-natal reaction' to Bubby's death.

Eventually I buzzed Anthony and briefly explained what had happened and that I had to get over to Mount Sinai immediately. I ducked into our office to grab my keys and briefcase.

Bill was inserting a Joy Division CD. 'Everything OK?'

'Not really,' I said. 'Mia's in hospital. She's . . . not feeling well.'

'Oh.' He could tell that I didn't want to give any more away. 'Anything I can do?' He followed me back down the hall towards reception, holding a sheet of paper in his hand.

'No. But thanks for asking.'

I paused outside the boardroom and indicated the layouts on the table we'd been working on. 'Let's go through those when I get back. I'm not sure when that will be.'

'OK, Bro.'

Out of habit, I flicked up the edge of the paper he was holding to see what he'd been working on. On it he'd scrawled an evolving positioning statement for our new client:

> coolcams: just do it
>
> coolcams: just see it
>
> coolcams: see it
>
> coolcams: you'll see it
>
> coolcams: you'll see

The last line had been circled for consideration.

'Waddya think?' Bill twirled his marker through his fingers like a drum majorette.

I sighed. *You'll see.* The phrase was indeed perfect for our new client, both literally and metaphorically. And yet there was something about it that tied another nasty knot in my gut.

North Fucked

'You are *not* working this week.' Anthony handed me my second Bud. 'We'll call it "Compassionate Leave" or some such shit so you won't lose any of your vacation time. Fair enough, Girly?'

They'd let Mia out of the hospital Saturday evening. It was now 11.30 Tuesday morning. We were in some dank, dark dive on 8th Avenue whose only virtue was that it was open at that hour. It was hardly Anthony's typical milieu, but he had a meeting nearby at 12 in the Garment District. There were tawdry peep show joints either side of the bar, which were also already open – or maybe they never closed.

I heard a cough and looked up at the owner: fat, blotchy-faced and wheezing on his cigarette as he spit-polished glasses with a dirty towel. He looked just like I felt.

'What about coolcams?' I asked. Though work, advertising and coolcams were in reality the furthest things from my mind.

'Fuck fucking coolcams,' Anthony growled. 'Bill knows every fucking creative in New York. We can get someone to fill in for you for the rest of this week. And next week too – if you need it. Or however long you and Mia need.'

'Thanks, mate.' The beer tasted like sludge. I slugged it back anyway.

Anthony handed me a set of keys.

'What's this?'

'North Fuck. The shack. Go up there for a week. It'll do ya good.'

'I don't know what to say, mate. You've been too good—'

'Enough,' Anthony held up his palm. 'The keys to the Passport are on there as well. Just take care of yourself and your family and we'll worry about work later.'

He handed me a piece of layout paper, folded over. 'Oh, and this is from Bill.'

On it, my art director had drawn a cartoon version of me lying on a sun lounger in bathing trunks, sipping a cocktail under a red-and-white striped Bacardi beach umbrella. On the other side of the page, he'd drawn himself sweating buckets at his desk under a speech bubble that said *Hang loose, Bro – I'll take care of everything here.*

Tears stung my eyes.

'Oh, and this,' Anthony reached into his suit jacket, 'is from Lucy.' He gave me a slightly searching look. It was a beautiful and obviously very expensive condolence card. She'd signed it *Love Lucille*.

Anthony burped uncomfortably – he really wasn't much of a drinker these days. 'Well, I better get myself a packet of mints and get going. Give Susanna a call and she'll give you the gen on the holiday shack. Call me if you need anything else or if you just want to talk.'

For the first time in years, I bought a pack of Stuyvesants.

Mia wasn't talking much. Not to me anyhow.

But once she returned to the Olcott, she had long, tearful phone conversations with her mother. And with Jane. And a series of longer conversations with Susanna. Both her mother and Jane offered to fly out to be with her. But Mia's mum was really too old to fly and Jane had two teenage kids of her own. So they were more gestures than serious offers. In any case, I hoped that they – and the anti-depressants – were able to help Mia in some way. Because I sure as hell couldn't at the moment.

As if he shared Mia's crushing despair, Callum had also grown disconcertingly quiet. Although the night that Mia came home from the hospital, he'd looked up from his *Balto* video with the saddest little face I'd ever seen and declared apropos of nothing, 'Maybe Balto could have saved Bubby?'

But Balto was a one-off: when I thought about it, Callum hadn't really been very interested in his movies or stories for the past couple of weeks. And he didn't want to go to the park. He'd just sit quietly on his bed or on the sofa holding his Buzz. Or play quiet, emotionless games of Uno with Esmeralda.

And like Mia, he was now sleeping a lot.

If we weren't so fucked-up ourselves, I'm sure we would both have been a lot more worried about him.

Anthony kept the Honda Passport in a parking garage down near Union Square. By the time I got back early afternoon, Mia had miraculously managed to become her practical old self for half an hour and had packed all our clothes for the trip. She and Callum were sitting quietly at the end of our bed like two frozen models from the Gap winter catalogue.

And then it was time to go. Suitcase in hand, she looked across at Susanna's beautiful bouquet of pale-pink tulips on the table.

But neither of us could bring ourselves to throw them out.

We left them wrinkling in the vase.

*

I read the opening blurb of the visitors' book on the cold kitchen bench top.

> 'Manhattan' – in the Algonquin language – meant 'the High Hills Island'. It was the summer home of the Carnasie people. But in the winter, they always returned to the place they called 'Metoaca' or 'the Long Island'.

The Johnsons' holiday home was only two hours' drive – although once we got there, it could have been a million miles away.

Halfway between Kingsville and Cutchogue on the northern tine of the Long Island fork, the area was known locally as Arcadia, after the name of the high-end building firm that had created the exclusive ten-title development in the late eighties. The properties were separated by lines of adolescent white oaks half a kilometre apart, while majestic frontages unfurled right down to the water's edge of the Great Peconic Bay.

'Shack' didn't really do it justice. Two storeys, six bedrooms, three bathrooms, an office, and a balcony that looked straight out onto the choppy grey waves and deep-blue sky. In fact, its only concession to 'shackiness' were the magnificent American oak beams – salvaged from old local barns – that had been used in its construction. Although the house was only about ten years old, the redwood had already weathered beautifully, giving the exterior a distressed frontier cabin look – classic Americana.

Inside, the high ceilings and exposed beams and rafters created a cosy ski-lodge ambience. Susanna had decorated the walls with hand-made Navajo blankets and wall hangings, Mexican carnival masks (according to Esmeralda), and Civil War muskets, muzzle-loaders and cannon balls in wrought-iron brackets. Central to the expansive kitchen/living area was a huge old pot-bellied stove that Susanna had had shipped from her grandmother's house in Tennessee.

We'd brought Esmeralda with us. Looking back, it perhaps seems strange that we invited a relative stranger to come with us so soon after what had happened. But neither Mia nor I were thinking straight. So, from a purely practical point of view, Esmeralda's presence made sense.

Besides, Callum liked her. Perhaps she could cajole him out of his very un-Callum-like inertia.

After we'd unpacked, Esmeralda checked out the well-stocked pantry and Mia went for a lie down upstairs while

Callum and I did a quick, cold lap of the grounds before scurrying back to the crackling warmth of the stove.

I challenged Callum to a race around the outside of the house, but he claimed he needed a 'cowwidoor' like we had at the Olcott.

Esmeralda made us all some Mexican eggs for dinner while I chugged down one of the Budweisers Anthony had kindly left in the gleaming Miele fridge. I silently toasted my ever-thoughtful friend and boss as I reached for my second.

*

A strange new physical thing happened to me at Arcadia almost as soon as we arrived: I found that I couldn't bear to look at the little white electrical sockets along the walls or in the bathrooms, or behind the toaster or the coffee maker in the long galley kitchen.

Back in Australia, sockets featured three narrow slits to house their plugs. But here in America, the three socket holes were round, which made them look like two eyes and a mouth.

So now I tried to avoid looking at them at every turn: because to me, every little white socket looked like a little white face screaming.

I spoke to Esmeralda from behind the broad marble benchtop. 'Mmm, that smells good.'

Esmeralda had also cut her hair into a short round bob: she looked like Mia's little sister. It was late on our second day at Arcadia and she was stirring up some magic in a big beige Le Creuset pot. The chopping boards were a delicious patchwork of white onions, bright-red chillies, taxi-yellow corncobs, limes, and blood-red pork skin.

'Is called *pozole rojo*,' Esmeralda replied. 'My grandmuddah, Ana Claudia, used to make this when we was children. So my seesters and me call it "Ana-Claudia's medicine". Is very good for the cold wedder.'

'Well, we certainly have that here,' I said, nodding at the sheet of snow billowing towards us from across the bay. 'You must really hate the cold, eh, coming from Mexico?'

'Well, when next summer comes, Guy, you will soon see that New York City can get as hot as San Juan del Rio – where I come from. But the New York winters . . . ' she gestured at the white world outside with her ladle '. . . brrrr – it's crazy cold for me, man.' She kept stirring. 'This soup will be a leedle hot for Callum with the chillies and so I haf maked him another bowl without chillies for hisself.'

It struck me that both Esmeralda and Callum enjoyed experimenting with tenses, pronouns and verb agreements.

'How's Daddy's boy?'

I plonked myself down next to him on a soft wide couch in the cavernous living area adjacent to the kitchen. Callum didn't respond. He was watching TV for the first time in days. Mia was upstairs, still sleeping or reading.

Or crying perhaps.

'What are you watching?' I tried again.

'I don't know,' Callum said in a small voice.

I looked at the screen myself. Up until a second ago, I could have sworn that he had been watching *Toy Story* for the thousandth time. But now the screen was all fuzzy and dark with rough, broken white lines strobing rhythmically through it.

'Is *Toy Story* finished?'

He didn't answer. He was staring dead ahead as if concentrating very hard on something. There was no sound coming from the TV now either. Just little *chop chop chops* from Esmeralda behind us.

Something was now happening on the screen. The white lines slowly became more cohesive, forming themselves into one continuous, moving line.

Like the silhouette of something alive.

I gasped. It was a shape I'd seen a number of times last year. It looked half human, half frog; an amphibian caught in amber. The abnormally large, bulbous head tilted up and down at rapid speed while the little limbs looked as though they were frantically scratching or clawing at something. It was as if the TV was an aquarium and the thing really was just there behind the glass – a little prehistoric monster from the deep.

It was the outline of a baby in utero.

Floating from profile to front-on, the little creature was now staring straight at us with its wide, black fish eyes. Its round, rubbery mouth gaped horribly, as if venting a long, silent scream.

I'd never noticed before how much the face of an unformed baby resembles that of a very old person – with their taut, skeletal features sputtered and blotched with detritus. For one long, monstrous moment, the little fishy face transmuted into the visage of an old woman.

Then, with its webbed hands pressed against the inside of the screen, it angrily began beating its tiny fists: little *rap rap raps* syncopating with Esmeralda's expert knife work behind us.

Callum stuttered. 'Bu . . . Bu . . .' He couldn't complete the word for some reason.

Bubby?

I snapped my head around. 'Esmeralda – look!'

She stopped cutting and looked up. 'Look at what, Guy?'

I turned back to the TV. There was no foetus there now – just that silly Space Ranger, Buzz Lightyear, showing off to Mr Potato Head by executing an elaborate loop-the-loop.

Callum's eyes were a little glazed, as if he'd just woken up. 'What did you say before, Son?' I asked. I suddenly realized I was sweating and wiped my brow.

'Bu-zzzz! See, Daddy – I told you!'

He pointed at the screen and then gave me a twisted little grin as if I was the one who was acting strangely. Buzz was back, and he, Callum, was now fine and dandy.

He yawned and sat his own Buzz doll back on his lap as he settled in for the rest of the movie.

Esmeralda shook her head slightly and resumed her chopping: Mr Russell had apparently gone a little gaga.

Maybe what I thought I'd seen had just been a kink in the tape – or a temporary fault in the TV?

I shook my head in an attempt to clear it.

A dead baby, a stressful new job in a brand-new country, a suicidal wife. It was no wonder I was seeing things.

Maybe I just needed some fresh air?

I mussed Callum's hair and disappeared out into the squall with my cigarettes.

*

The next morning, I decided that I needed someone to reconnect me with good old-fashioned reality. So I rang Bill.

'Hey, Crayon Brain – haven't they fired you yet?'

'Is that any way to speak to your respected co-worker and undeniable superior in virtually every department?'

'Wassup?'

'Wassup with you, slacking off up there in the boss's tax dodge?' His humour sounded forced. Given the unfortunate circumstances that had taken me out of the office, it was difficult for Bill to be his normal shit-shooting self. But I wished he would.

'Well, we've tried to get by in your regrettable absence, Kangaroo Boy,' – Bill frequently goaded me with this nickname, along with references to *The Crocodile Hunter*, as he knew how I felt about clichéd Australian stereotypes – 'and I admit it's been difficult. I've got a writing friend in here – Jay Spiller, ex-DDB – but unlike you, he's actually quite good at his job so we finish all our work by noon.'

'Really?'

'Really. Oh and he doesn't insist on repeat-playing maudlin pukey Aussie yodellers over and oooover again, so the quality of in-office music has improved one hundredfold.'

Bill had a great antipathy for Stephen Cummings, my

favourite Australian singer-songwriter. He called him 'Mr Sob Stories'.

'Really?'

'Yeah – Jay's been a blast, actually. Much more fun than you. Which wouldn't be hard. Hey, do you even have to come back? I might have to have a quiet word to Anthony about that.'

I laughed. It was a sensation I'd missed lately.

Bill then filled me in on all the latest office gossip, starting with the fact that his beloved coffee machine in the Brave Face kitchen had broken down so he'd had to schlep over the road to Café Europa four times a day for his hits of 'black heroin', as well as the slow but steady progress on the coolcams campaign.

Apparently the client had now rejected the initial TV concept we'd pitched – a kind of contemporary *Candid Camera* with people being caught doing crazy or embarrassing things through a webcam – as 'not slick enough'. Since they'd got second-round funding, the kids were hyped-up, cashed-up and demanding we came up with something 'super-cool'.

One of the new concepts Bill and Jay had been tossing around involved editing some pre-existing footage from Hitchcock's *Rear Window* and then cutting in some new scenes featuring a coolcam.

Their idea was that Jimmy Stewart's character – the wheelchair-bound Jeff Jeffries – has a coolcam installed in his apartment. He trains his camera on the apartment across the courtyard and witnesses the bad guy snuff out his wife via his computer screen, rather than through binoculars as per the original film.

But that was really as far as the boys had got. The idea needed a nice ironic twist that made the coolcam more of a hero but in a more subtle way. And maybe *Rear Window* was simply too dated to appeal to today's ubersophisticated Generation Tech? Plus, what seven-figure sum would it cost to buy the rights from the copyright holder?

'Yadda, yadda, yadda,' Bill said after I'd voiced my concerns. 'We already know all that. And we agree. We just wanted to prove we've been working on something since you've been away. Plus, we've got some other stuff and it's not all puke. So don't worry your pretty little head about it. Anyway your friend and mine, Terry the Terrible (a Brave Face account man we didn't like), is pacing the halls, threatening us with another fortune cookie masquerading as a brief – I gotta go.' He hung up.

The work discussion about *Rear Window* had whetted my appetite for a good holiday movie to watch that night.

There was an interesting collection of old film noir videos neatly racked up in the shelves above the TV: *Kiss Me Deadly*; *Out of the Past*; *Criss Cross*; *Double Indemnity*; *The Lost Weekend*; *Night of the Hunter*.

I really wanted to see *Hunter* again. I pulled the box down. There was Robert Mitchum, insanely menacing in his black-rimmed hat with the word 'love' ironically tattooed onto the finger joints of his right hand. (Ironic because we know he also has 'hate' tattooed on the left hand we can't see.)

I took the video out of its case and went to load it into the slot.

But I suddenly discovered I couldn't.

My hand started to shake. I looked over towards the darkened kitchen: Esmeralda had taken Callum upstairs an hour ago and hadn't come back down. Mia hadn't surfaced all day.

The thing was – I was now simply too fucking frightened to watch the TV by myself.

Bill had told me not to worry my pretty little head. But with what I'd seen – or thought I'd seen – on the screen yesterday with Callum, that was easier said than done.

I put the video back in the rack. The room suddenly felt very cold, despite the low hum and crackle of the stove. I walked over to the back door and pulled Anthony's big greatcoat off the hook and wrapped it round me. Then I went back to my new favourite chair next to the bookcase and introduced Jack London to Jack Daniels.

*

Anthony didn't just collect old noir videos – he had also amassed an impressive rack of local wines, collected from the many boutique wineries on the North Fork. Just before dinner on Friday night, I pulled out a '96 Pindar Cab Franc and hunted for a corkscrew.

'Chicken *mole*,' Esmeralda nodded to herself, licking the wooden spoon. 'Maybe not as good as *pozole*, but still pretty yummy.'

'Smells like it,' I said. I felt a bit calmer tonight.

'Is Mia eating with us?' she asked.

Mia had spent most of the day in her room again. Callum had gone in briefly and she'd read him a story. But I'd been reading more Jack London and hadn't seen her all day so I really didn't know her dinner plans. 'I'll go and find out,' I told our cook and nanny.

I tapped lightly on the bedroom door. 'Room service.'

Mia looked up groggily. 'Hi,' she murmured. She was still in her pyjamas. Her bedside lamp was on. Her book lay across her chest. *No Logo* by Naomi Klein. A *Vanity Fair*, with Madonna cuddling Rupert Everett on the cover, was also keeping her company on the side table.

'Hi. You hungry?'

'No. Esmeralda brought me a snack at lunchtime. I think the medication has killed my appetite.'

'You OK?'

'I don't know,' she sniffed, 'I really don't know, Guy. I just want to sleep for ever and then wake up and find that it's all just been a horrible dream.'

The doctor who'd examined her at Mount Sinai had warned me that she wouldn't be herself for a while. He told me that the only thing I could do – that anyone could do – was to 'be there' for her. Whatever that meant.

'Sleeping's good.' I said. Actually, I knew that excessive sleeping wasn't good at all – it was a sign of depression. But it had only been a few days since Mia had tried to put herself to sleep permanently, so I decided to cut her some slack. Let her get it out of her system.

'Sleeping may be good but nightmares aren't.' She rubbed her eyes. 'I had that awful dream about Callum falling again.'

'Well, don't worry. He's downstairs right now eating Esmeralda's Mexican chicken.' I sat on the edge of the bed, almost on Ms Klein.

'And I haven't told you yet . . . but the night before I—'

Turned the gas on. I knew what she meant so I just nodded.

'I had *another* dream, a much worse one. And that morning, when I woke up, I just couldn't stop thinking about it.'

I nodded.

'It was unbearable because it had felt so real. I couldn't concentrate on anything – I thought I was going crazy. So I shipped Callum off to Susanna's – left him with Estella – and bought a bottle of wine from Fairway.'

I wasn't sure I wanted to hear what was coming next, but I nodded again anyway.

Mia's pupils dilated with the retelling. 'I dreamed I was in labour and it was painful beyond belief. It was so bad, it made normal labour feel like a nice massage.

'There was no doctor there or anything, but Callum was asleep on a chair in the corner, which was strange given the amount of noise I was making. Anyway, I had to keep pushing and pushing for days and days and days and I was screaming in agony and then finally this horrible adult-sized old woman slid out of me, all covered in blood and slime. It was just awful!'

Her eyes were wide and frantic.

'The woman had awful bright-blonde hair – like a really

bad wig – and her body was disgusting and wrinkled and smelled like rotten vegetables or a dead mouse or something. And then she stood up on the bed.'

Mia white-knuckled her book – like it was a Bible or talisman that might be able to protect her somehow.

My own stomach tightened.

'It gets worse,' Mia panted. 'She started retching all these little foetuses everywhere and they'd bounce on the floor and then scuttle off into the corners of the room where I couldn't see them.'

My head throbbed. Like I was getting the mother of all migraines.

'Then she looked at me and she opened her mouth really, really wide and it looked like a horrible diseased vagina on the inside with all sorts of sores and warts and yellow pus – like those awful photos they showed us at high school about VD.'

She closed her eyes.

'And then she cried out in this really strange voice that was half like a baby and half like an old woman . . .' Mia went quiet for a full thirty seconds.

'What did she say?'

She stifled a cry. 'She said "*You'll see.*"'

Just like that nasty old nurse at Cabrini had said. Although Mia probably didn't even remember her.

'Oh.'

Or perhaps she'd seen our new coolcams catchcry on the layouts I'd brought home from the office?

Either way, the words now filled me with deep, dark dread.

Mia pulled the covers up under her chin, just like she had that terrible night when we'd lost Bubby in the hospital. Her lower lip trembled and she started to cry. I tried rubbing her shoulder, but it was as cold as stone so I stopped.

'We murdered her, Guy!' she cried out. She masked her face behind her book and blubbed for a while.

Finally she looked at me with a great sadness. 'Did you ever have any other names in mind for Bubby? Girls' names, I mean?'

The question took me by surprise. 'Not really,' I replied truthfully. 'You?'

'I was vaguely thinking of "Jane" – for obvious reasons.'

'That would have been nice. And I'm sure Big Jane would have been honoured.'

Suddenly Mia broke into an awful sob. 'You know, Guy, we didn't even have a fucking funeral for her! All we got is this stupid little box with her footprints in it.'

She pulled out a box from under the pillow. She must have hidden it in her luggage somehow and brought it all the way from Australia. It was pink with a little white ribbon tied around it. She buried her head in her pillow. 'They probably just put her in a bin or something . . .'

I had nothing to say. While Mia was still comatose, a nurse had asked me what we wanted to do with the little body afterwards. I'd advised the nurse to follow 'normal procedure', but I really had no idea what that meant.

Mia regained some composure. 'Thank God, I've . . . we've still got Callum. Look after him for me, will you? I'm not much of a mum at the moment.' She put her cold, wet hand over mine, gritted her teeth and put her other hand to her stomach.

I wanted to say so much to her and yet not a single word of love or reassurance suggested itself to me. I felt like I needed to get out of there.

Away from the pain.

'You just take it easy and get some R & R – doctor's orders. I'll come back later with a cuppa.' She didn't respond.

Walking down the stairs, I was reminded of another classic noir in Anthony's collection:

Whatever Happened to Baby Jane?

*

Time seemed all out of whack at Arcadia.

As though the accepted Eastern Standard calibrations had been jettisoned in favour of some bizarre new reckoning system. I soon had no real idea what day we'd arrived, what day it was now and what day we were meant to go home again. After hibernating upstairs for the first few days, Mia finally ventured down on what I guessed to be Saturday morning. She sat on the couch next to Callum vacantly watching either *Toy Story* or *The Powerpuff Girls* on the Cartoon Network with her *Vanity Fair* on her lap. I sat diagonally across from them in the armchair, hidden behind *The Sea-Wolf*, stealing furtive glances at the screen whenever I heard any strange un-cartoon-like sounds.

That same day, after lunch, I ventured upstairs.

Callum was in his room.

'What are you doing, Son?' I asked, sitting on the edge of his bed. It was snowing outside and we were holed up again for the day. Not that any of us seemed to have any real desire to go out.

'I drawing, Daddy,' he smiled.

Having his own room was a luxury after the Three Bears arrangement he was used to at the Olcott. His window looked out onto the side yard and a beautiful snow-capped Atlantic cedar with a low, white wrought-iron seat encircling its base. It would be a lovely place to sit and read or think in the summer.

Callum was lying tummy-down on the floor. Esmeralda had laid out an old blue blanket for him as a drop sheet so he wouldn't mark Susanna's creamy-coloured shag carpet.

'What are you drawing?'

He'd used a number of different coloured crayons and Texta colours. Apart from the usual childish scribbles, I could make out some distinct forms and shapes. 'What's this?' I asked, pointing to a blue and orange rectangle. It had different coloured circles with legs inside it.

'That's us at the Awcott,' he said. 'That's me and Mummy. And that's the TV . . . and that's Melda. Oh, and that's Buzz.' This was good. It was the most animated and talkative I'd seen him in days.

'Where am I?' I asked.

'You was at work. Making your ads.'

'Oh.' The usual absent father scenario.

'This one of you and me at the park.' He held up another picture. There was a small stick figure and a larger one with a lot of white crayon in the background. There seemed to be little blue balls flying in the air between them.

'We having a snow bore fight!'

'And what's this one?' I asked, bending down and picking it up.

Something about the third drawing struck me: I was looking at a red bubble with a little yellow, alien-like figure inside it. The alien's eyes were large and protuberant, the black pupils bulging in fear or anger. A larger figure in what looked like a white coat was attacking the bubble, stabbing it with a large sword.

Callum was tilting his head from side to side, admiring his own handiwork. 'What's this one?' I asked again.

And then I noticed the title: across the top of the alien drawing, Callum had written in big, black, awful letters:

Ded

I dropped the paper and moved back, away from him. 'W-what do you mean "dead?"'

'Nah – that say "Dad", silly! That you!'

'But who's that?' I asked, pointing to the strange little creature in the bubble. My hand was suddenly shaking again.

'That me!' Callum squealed. 'You're like Buzz an' I'm like one of dem little green mans in the machine.'

There *was* a scene in *Toy Story* where Buzz gets trapped in a vending machine filled with little green alien dolls who adopt him as their new yet reluctant leader.

'But he's not green. He's yellow.'

'That cos I couldn't find the green draw-rer!'

The green crayon. Of course.

'Oh. But what are we doing here?' I indicated Buzz's swishing sword.

'We having a swordy fight on my bed at the Awcott!'

Hmmm. I felt momentarily relieved.

It all made perfect childish sense.

Except that the drawing could have been a rough yet faithful depiction of Bubby being extinguished by Dr Hill in the hospital back in Australia, at my request.

*

11 p.m. Saturday.

I rolled upstairs and stopped outside our bedroom door. I heard some movement inside. Mia was still up and turning down the bedspread. I leaned on the doorjamb and studied my wife from behind. She seemed beautiful but different somehow in the golden glow of the bedside lamp. Her back was curved and inviting.

I'd drunk enough wine and JD – now I wanted to swallow her up. I wanted to fuck my way back to forgiveness.

She spun around. 'Guy – what are you doing?' Her tone was fearful and sharp. She pulled her robe fast around her.

It wasn't Mia. It was Esmeralda.

'N-n-nothing, Esmeralda.' I turned away. 'Sorry, I thought you were Mia.' It sounded even more pathetic when I said it.

She looked frightened. 'Your bedroom is further down

the hall, Guy, you know?' She knotted her robe more tightly. 'Maybe you had a leedle too much to drink?'

'Yes, I'm sorry. I am a bit . . . *borrach*?'

There were so many fucking bedrooms. They all looked the same.

'*Borrach-o*. Don't worry about it, Guy.' She gave me an empathic smile. 'I know you had a bad time with your little lost baby and everything last year – and Mia too, especially – and then Mia going to the hospital so sad last week. But maybe you should take it easy you know, Guy?' She touched my arm. 'You know we have a saying back in San Juan del Rio: "You should never swim from the top of the bottle to the bottom by yourself."'

'I know. Thanks, Esmeralda. Sorry. I didn't mean it.'

She put her hands together as if she was about to pray for my salvation and closed her door.

I sloped into the kitchen late Sunday morning, careful not to eyeball the electrical sockets. We'd be going back to New York tomorrow.

Callum was making a red Lego dragon on the bench. Mia – the real Mia – was making Callum some lunch while Esmeralda squeezed oranges. The women suddenly stopped talking as I clumsily plugged in the kettle.

I wondered whether Esmeralda had told Mia about my Peeping Tom escapade the night before. I doubted it. Mia was in no condition to handle any more bad news – and Esmeralda was a kind and smart girl. Maybe I was just paranoid. Their silence made me feel uneasy all the same.

So I grabbed Anthony's heavy coat off the hook and went outside.

There was a short, winding path that meandered down to the sand through a row of neatly trimmed, snow-topped buttonbushes and pitch pines. The midday sun had been obscured by the big black clouds that were swarming across the bay like pirate ships.

I walked tentatively downhill as I'd forgotten to bring my Rockports away with me. All I had were my Nikes and they were already a bit wet. There was a rundown little jetty at the bottom. Some of the pylons had broken away or sunk down into the seabed; it was pretty derelict and decrepit. I hopscotched along the rotted planks and looked out to sea. The wind was picking up – as it seemed to at this time of day – harvesting a fresh crop of white-caps that stretched all the way over to the South Fork ten kilometres away. Specks of boats on the horizon were racing home to beat the storm.

I reached deep into the folds of Anthony's coat and pulled out the bottle of Jack. I took a serious slug of the strong, smoky liquid – Arcadia's wild surroundings seemed to call for something hard and authentic. Hemingway-esque. I coughed and wiped my mouth on my sleeve. I reached down further into the pocket and pulled out my cigarettes and an old Zippo lighter I'd found atop the pot-bellied stove. The booze made itself at home in my gut as I took a long, deep drag. I'd muttered to the women that I was coming out to find some wood for the stove.

I knew that I wasn't really myself. I mean, I was aware of myself being on the end of the jetty but it was as if I, me, my conscious sentient self was standing at the other end, observing the man with the big coat and the bottle.

My heart was beginning to hammer. Maybe it was my alcohol and nicotine breakfast? It started to thump so loudly I could hear it above the quick panicky *lap lap lap* of the waves. I could see myself put my fist to my chest in an effort to calm the runaway muscle. I started to sway and felt nauseous so I sat down. I closed my eyes but that was even worse. My head swirled with a dreadful phantasmagoria of scenes from the last few weeks: I saw myself reading *Jack and the Beanstalk* to Callum at the Olcott; I saw Lucy teasing me at the Royalton; I saw Anthony and me tap-dancing our way through the coolcams presentation in Berkeley; I saw Bill and me playing paper-ball basketball in our office; I saw Mia waking me up that terrible night back in Melbourne in her red-stained night dress – and then my heart began to really gallop – the hospital; Dr Hill; Mia with her legs up in stirrups and her arms crossed above her head as though she was being sacrificed to some pitiless pagan god.

'What have you decided?' Dr Hill asked us from the foot of the bed.
'Have you had enough time to talk?'
He could not have been more solemn or solicitous.
Mia looked at me then looked away.
She hadn't wanted to decide. Or hadn't been able to.
So I uttered the unutterable.
'Intervention.'

I was adrift on a raft of revulsion on a wilderness of sea.

It was nothing like the benign double-bed raft that I'd shared with Mia and Callum that blissful rainy afternoon so long ago.

This time I was on my own. And surrounded by sharks and sea monsters.

I stared at the unforgiving icy water and seriously considered hurling myself into it.

*

Despite my panic-stricken morning, Esmeralda managed to convince me that I should accompany her into Kingsville on Sunday afternoon to buy some seafood. After being cooped up all week, she wanted to get us all out of the house and breathing some fresh air. Mia declined and said she'd stay with Callum, who was happy playing with some of Courtney's old dolls.

I acquiesced more out of necessity than interest: I needed more Jack Daniels.

It was freezing out. I found a tatty old red hunting hat on the coat rack and pulled the flaps over my ears. I let Esmeralda drive because she wanted to practise for her upcoming test. I figured Anthony wouldn't have a problem with letting a novice take the wheel as the Passport already carried quite a few war wounds from the Johnsons' various off-road and skiing-in-Vermont adventures. But I advised Esmeralda to take it easy, just the same, on account of the conditions.

Kingsville was just a few cold minutes away. Aptly named, it could easily have been the setting of a Stephen King novel. It was a typical small, seaside town replete with smelly old fishermen, a harbour full of sad old tugboats and a gap-toothed foreshore broken up by wind-battered lean-to buildings and storehouses.

As we turned down the windy main street, I half-expected to bump into my old maritime nemesis, Captain Olav.

There was a municipal sign in the car park:

Welcome to Kingsville
We are famous for our lobsters,
clams and proud whaling heritage.
Population 1,272.

Esmeralda – who looked like a cute little Eskimo in her big fleecy parka, cap and boots – studied the town map in search of the Kingsville Fish Co-op. I was headed for Larry's Liquor, next to the yacht club. We agreed to meet back at the car in fifteen minutes.

I now appreciated Esmeralda coercing me into town. It was good to get outside, away from the house for a while. Beautiful and comfortable as Arcadia was, it was also a psychological prison of sorts. The change of scene enabled me to start to think a little straighter. To start to process what had happened to us and what was still happening. Mia and I needed to start talking again. We needed to accept all the things that had happened and develop a new emotional strategy to help us move forward.

But I was also concerned about Callum. He wasn't himself. First there was his recent uncharacteristic withdrawal and lack of energy – a subconscious reaction perhaps to

Mia's suicide attempt and the fear that his mother might abandon him.

And then there was the abominable thing I'd seen on the TV screen while he was sitting next to me. I had by now attributed that disturbing episode to a temporary mental aberration on my part. Callum had been an innocent bystander while the VHS momentarily warped and my frazzled mind had played a horrible trick on me. He'd also featured in Mia's awful dream about being in labour and the old woman – another horrible fantasy. But then Callum's drawing had certainly been real enough, hadn't it?

And what about his warning to me back at the Olcott to stay away from the sockets? How could he have known about the sockets? How could he have known about that?

The thought of it chilled me far more than the stiff sea breeze.

As I turned a corner, I passed a grimy, fly-specked window advertising PSYCHIC READINGS – 20 MINUTES FOR $10.

I wondered what psychic disturbance had beset my dear, sweet son recently and how I could help him.

But before that I needed a drink.

Judging by its meagre stock levels, Larry's Liquor was no longer a booze store. It was just a bar down the back of a rat-infested old warehouse.

'D'ya want a drink, pal?' the man on the stool behind the counter asked. I wondered if this was Larry. He was wearing a faded old Cleveland Indians baseball cap and a holey white windbreaker with oil stains on it. His tongue poked through the gap in his teeth when he spoke.

'Ah, no thanks,' I said. 'Just a bottle of Jack.' The room smelled of brine. The once-white, now grey, walls were decorated with life-rings, old nets and water stains. It was like being inside a bilge.

'Here,' he said, filling a tumbler with something rough and brown. 'I hate drinkin' alone.'

I looked at the dirty little glass, which was full to the brim. Then I looked at my watch: 1:45p.m.

'Go on!' he encouraged me, tapping the bar insistently with his gnarled old fingers. He was as crazy as a coot. His tongue was darting in and out of its little hole like a snake.

'Just one,' I said. I drained the glass. Rocket fuel mixed with swamp water. The only thing I'd tasted remotely like it before was the Kava that the natives brew up in Fiji to kill the tourists.

Ahhh, ever-friendly Fiji: land of sun, sand, thousands of smiles and buckets of sex. It was a trip we'd taken soon after we first moved in together: in her crocheted blue and white bikini, brown-as-a-berry Mia had never looked more alluring – like a mischievous, promiscuous mermaid. I looked good, too; I was running and swimming every day and somehow managed to leave my work and my worries behind for once.

On gorgeous Castaway Island, we made love three or four times a day, our orgasmic yelps flying out of our hut window like native war whoops.

Each night, we felt a conservative committee of disapproving eyes settle on us as the waiter with the piano keys smile led us to our torch-lit dinner table on the beach.

We toasted each other with fruit-jammed cocktails under the avuncular yellow moon. 'That's the couple that's always fucking,' we imagined the other guests were saying under their breath. But we didn't care; in fact it made us feel even naughtier.

And even more in love.

We were happy then.

'What *is* that?' I asked, trying to wipe the terrible taste off my lips.

'Larry's Special,' he laughed, banging his chest. 'Mattituck Moonshine' – good for what ails ya – whatever ya got!'

'Only if it doesn't kill you first,' I said. 'Can I grab that bottle of Jack, please?'

He indicated the nearly empty shelf behind him. The few dusty bottles were all empty. 'I got jack. So I ain't got no Jack!' He laughed/wheezed again. 'So how's about another Special instead?'

'No thanks,' I said, standing to leave. 'I'd rather live. Thanks for the drink, Larry.'

I wondered if the small supermarket I'd walked past had a liquor outlet.

Esmeralda was loading the tail of the Passport with her Co-op catch: calamari, scallops, and a live lobster in a new hessian home. Gulls circled and squawked overhead as if we were a trawler about to throw out fish heads. I climbed into the passenger seat and took a long swig out of the bottle I'd finally located in the Kingsville Hotel on the other side of the yacht club. Esmeralda pretended not to notice. The sack started crawling around in the back.

I studied Esmeralda's profile as she lurched the Honda into first. Side on with her new bob cut, she did look a little bit like Mia – anyone could see that. Only slighter and more tanned, like Mia had been in Fiji all those years before.

'Do you know how to cook lobster?' I asked her. 'Another of your grandma's recipes maybe – *Lobster Mexicana*?'

She was concentrating hard. Her small brown hands were white on the wheel. 'No special recipe,' she said quickly. 'The man said just to give him a bath in very hot water.'

'Sounds good.' I thought I might call Anthony later and ask him which of the local whites in the rack might best complement our still-moving dinner.

Esmeralda turned off the main road and onto the beginning of the long unmade one that would take us back through the Christmas-card scenery to Arcadia. Now that we were out of the local traffic and into the trees, she seemed to relax a little. So I asked her, 'Esmeralda, do you think Callum's been OK lately?'

'What do you mean?' She swerved a little to miss an overhanging branch.

'I mean, have you noticed anything different about him? About the way he behaves?'

She negotiated a narrow curve before answering. 'I think he's probly a leedle upset cos you and Mia have been . . . upset, too. Children pick up on these things, you know, Guy? They very smart.'

It wasn't the answer I'd hoped for. 'But apart from that, do you think he's been acting at all strangely?' I snuck another swig from the bottle.

'Not really. Like what?'

Now that I thought about it, there probably wasn't any real reason for Esmeralda – or indeed anyone else – to share my worries about Callum.

He seemed to be reserving his strange side for me alone.

'Shit!' Esmeralda suddenly braked hard. There was a resounding 'whump' as the car ploughed into something soft. Four splayed spindly legs flew through the air, up and over the windscreen. A deer.

'Oh, Guy!' Esmeralda wailed, jumping out of the car and kneeling down beside the broken creature in the snow, 'I think I killed her!' A cotton-tailed rabbit peeked out from under the bushes and then hopped away to spread the sad news. I checked the bull bar. There was a nasty dint in the centre that hadn't been there before. I'd probably have to mention that to Anthony after all.

Esmeralda covered the animal with her parka. It was twitching and foaming at the mouth. Occasionally it shook with a giant spasm and its legs kicked out as if they were electrified. Starting to sob, Esmeralda held her hands above the deer and moved them back and forth, as if she was performing reiki. She seemed scared to actually touch it.

'Oh, Guy,' she turned to me, 'this is really bad, really very bad.' She gave a snort. A white gob of snot was dangling off the end of her cute little nose. She brushed it away with the back of her now bare arm. 'Back home, an animal to die like this is very bad luck. It means cruelty or unkindness is coming. Maybe even worse.'

I nodded sagely at the mad, superstitious thinking.

'What are we going to do?!' she wailed again.

I couldn't think straight – why was she asking me?

I took a squinty-eyed 360-degree scope around us but there were no answers on offer. A small stream of blood was trickling slowly out of the deer's mouth, through the toothpastey foam that was now beginning to congeal.

'Guy?' Esmeralda tugged my sleeve. 'We have to do something!' An owl somewhere hooted agreement.

'It looks like it's on its last legs,' I said, making it up as I went. 'I think it would be cruel to try and move it.' She nodded unhappily. 'Why don't you stay here and I'll go back into town and see if I can track down a vet?' I didn't have the slightest inclination to stay out there in the cold to deliver the last rites. 'Or else we could both go back into town?'

Esmeralda continued her reiki movements. She didn't look up. 'It's OK. I'll stay here, Guy. I was the driver. We can't just leave her out here to die all alone.'

The local vet was apparently in Manhattan having prostate surgery.

So the Kingsville chief of police followed me back out and put a bullet right through the poor animal's brain.

On the way home, I drove a weeping Esmeralda down an overgrown track right to the water's edge, where she let the lucky red lobster back into the sea.

*

Midnight. Our last night in Arcadia.

Mia lay next to me breathing deeply.

I touched her back with the palm of my hand. I didn't want to wake her; I just wanted to feel her there. I wanted to be reassured that she was still there with me, my dear wife. I wanted to tell Mia – and myself – that it was all going to be OK.

That life would improve. That we still had each other. And Callum.

I opened my eyes. I needed to check on him. I padded down the hall to his room, making sure not to glance in Esmeralda's room as I passed.

My son lay crookedly in that way small children do, like a puppet with its strings down. His little chest rose and fell infinitesimally. I touched his cheek and pushed his hair back from his forehead.

He opened his eyes, one at a time. I hadn't meant to disturb him. His eyes glowed strangely in the night light. They weren't his normal blue – they looked more greeny, cat-like – edged with black.

He was suddenly wide-awake.

'It's OK, darling. Daddy's just saying "ni ni". Go back to sleep.'

I lifted the blanket back over him.

He glared at me.

'Sorry, darling – go back to sleep.'

'Bad Daddy,' he said mechanically.

I didn't touch him. I was suddenly afraid to touch him.

Callum's chest started to inflate and deflate rapidly like

104

a blow-up doll's. His fierce, vengeful eyes bored into me. He hissed loudly like a Siamese cat, spitting a big, bright glob of saliva onto my cheek. His chest was pumping up and down as if it was going to burst. I reached out my right hand to keep his thumping heart from suddenly flying out of its cage.

'*Cunt Daddy*,' he hissed again.

I screamed. 'Mia! Esmeralda!'

He smiled lopsidedly at my panic, threw his head back and lifted his little Elmo T-shirt to show me his tummy. The wild thumping seemed to have moved down there. His belly was now stretching violently as if it had a steel piston pushing up underneath it.

'Mia! Esmeralda!' Where the fuck were they? I stepped away from the thing in the bed. This wasn't my son. It was a beast from another world.

He rolled onto his side to face me, still grinning like a mini Jack Nicholson. He looked down at his bare tummy again and – almost as if he was willing it – forced his gut to slowly tear open. I put my hands up and covered my eyes. But I could still hear the sound of his skin, sinews, fibres, vessels, ligaments and nerves being ripped apart.

The stench in the room was diabolical: a mixture of shit, urine and vomit; the extra-cheesy bolognaise sauce Callum had eaten for lunch, and a deeper, older, mysterious smell that I hadn't encountered before. Sickly sweet like old maggot-ridden meat that has been left out in the sun to die a second time.

'Mia!' I howled. But my voice had been stolen by

disbelief. I covered my eyes and made a tentative V open-ing between two twitching fingers. Because I didn't really want to see.

Callum's bed was now a red sea; spider threads of blood were running down the bedspread onto Susanna's white carpet. I gagged and fell into a wicker chair near the door. Callum fixed me with his baleful eyes, reached down with his hands and pulled the horrendous hole in himself even further apart.

There was something inside him.

Something moving.

I closed the V and then opened it again a knife's edge.

The little rubbery-looking limb rose perpendicularly out of my son, fighting for freedom.

It shook with anger.

Its half-formed index finger pointed towards me as if it wanted to make a soul-destroying accusation.

Mia and Esmeralda burst into the room as one.

I pointed back at Callum, jabbering jibberish.

But he was suddenly asleep, completely intact and smil-ing like an angel.

Mia led me back down the hall and put me back to bed.

At least that's what she told me the next morning.

Logical hat

Tuesday, 9:15.

'Welcome back,' Anthony grabbed my shoulder in the Brave Face corridor. 'How was it?'

I felt like shit.

And I didn't really feel like telling anyone about all the fucked-up things I'd seen and experienced in Arcadia because I was still trying to fathom them myself.

'It was . . . quiet. And beautiful. You're very lucky to have a place like that.'

'I know. I wish we could live there full time,' Anthony grinned. 'Away from the madding crowd.'

'Um, we had a bit of a bingle in the Passport I'm afraid. Ran into Bambi's big sister.'

'Christ! Was anyone hurt?'

'No, it was just me and Esmeralda in the car. Esmeralda was driving, but it wasn't her fault – the fucking thing ran into us. We were fine. But the chief of police will have turned it into venison pie by now.'

'Well if you hadn't hit it, some hunter probably would have. They're a local menace.'

'There was a bit of a dint in the bull bar. So I dropped the car off at a body shop in Queens yesterday. Should be ready by the end of the week. Sorry, mate.'

'You idiot,' Anthony rolled his eyes. 'You shouldn't

have worried about that. It's already had a few knocks anyway – adds character. Anyway, as long as you guys are back in one piece. How's Mia?'

'She's . . . improving,' I lied.

'And the boy?'

'Fine,' I lied again. 'The natural surroundings helped inspire some of his artwork.'

'Not another bloody creative wanker in the family? Speaking of which,' he looked at his watch. 'It's only 9.20 so Baldy Bill won't be in yet. But I think he and his mate Jay have come up with some quite nice stuff on coolcams.

'I didn't want to look at it before you'd seen it, of course, but we weren't exactly sure when you'd be back. And I had to make sure that some progress was being made because the boy wonders in Berkeley have been hassling me for it.'

'That's OK. I'll get Bill to run me through it. When are we meant to re-present?'

'Friday. It doesn't leave much time for you to change things if you need to.'

'Waddya mean? We've got a whole three days.' I feigned light-heartedness. 'Am I going with you?'

'See how you're feeling. Probably not. Lucy told them that you'd had an accident in the family so they'll be fine if you're a no-show.'

An accident in the family. That was one way of putting it.

He clapped me on the shoulder again. 'You've been through a lot, you and Mia. So if you need any more time off—'

'Thanks, mate,' I said. 'But I think some good hard work will be the best medicine for me.'

I meant it. Work meant that I could fill my mind up with stuff I could handle and understand. Work meant I didn't have to think about things that were painful or disturbing. Or terrifying.

By now we were in his office. Anthony nodded at the latest *Advertising Age* lying open on his desk. There was a cheesy photo of him shaking hands with one of the coolcams VCs outside their funky little building – he'd flown back over while we were away in Arcadia to negotiate terms and sign the contracts.

'Look – we made the big time, Girly!' He indicated the equally cheesy headline: *COOLCAMS: capitalism with a capital 'see'*.

*

'*So wadidya get up to on your va-ca-tion?*' Bill parodied the nasally voiceover to a recent TV campaign for a chain of travel agents. I supposed it was easier than asking, 'So how have things been since your wife tried to top herself?'

'Well, I went drinking with Buzz Lightyear and the Powerpuff Girls a lot.'

'Ah, my little Blossom, Bubbles and Buttercup,' he riffed nostalgically. 'Do you know what makes the PPG so fucking great?' He was going to tell me whether I wanted him to or not. 'Well, as well as dealing with standard superhero shit like defending Townsville against villains or monsters, the Powerpuff gals also have to deal with genuine childhood issues like bedwetting and security blankets.'

I just looked at him.

'The PPG's also got a fantastic fifties futuristic slash minimalist design that makes it look like a gorgeous Hockney painting. Plus the violence is a whole lot more brutal than your average kids 'toon.' He was excited now, and obviously an aficionado. 'Best ever episode?' he pretended he was being interviewed. 'The one where the girls have to battle it out against evil cloned versions of themselves called the *Puffpower* Girls. Get it? It's the girls in reverse.'

'How do you know all this shit?'

'Lifelong cartoon addiction. Plus a few years back, I did the UCLA Animation Workshop. It was awesome!'

Bill was a bona fide pop culture vulture – and his fascination with 'the rich, the famous, and the fucked-up' as he called them, extended way beyond cartoons. In fact, when I'd first mentioned to him that we were staying at the Hotel Olcott, Bill claimed that as well as Mark David Chapman having briefly been a guest there, that other world-famous assassin and former resident of the Bronx, Lee Harvey Oswald, used to wash dishes in the Olcott kitchen in the fifties as a teenager.

'Yep,' Bill had laughed. 'Then, when he got his weekly pay check, little Lee would hotfoot it out to the gee gees at Belmont and try to win some money for the Communist Party. Trying to turn capitalism against itself even back then, I guess.'

I found the story hard to believe and decided I'd check it out with Michael – our unofficial Olcott historian – at a later date.

But the Oswald story was easier to stomach than Bill's Oswald joke.

'Hey, did ya know that some very reliable witnesses placed Lee Harvey Oswald in a Dallas cake shop at the exact time of the assassination?'

'Really?' I'd taken the bait.

'Yup, which proved beyond doubt that he didn't do it . . .' Bill paused for comic effect. 'Oswald was just a *pastry*!'

7.30 p.m.

Lucy gave me a long, hard, meaningful hug in my office after everyone else had gone for the night.

'I'm so sorry, Guy. Really sorry for you and Mia.'

'Thanks,' I said. I should have let go of her. But it felt so good holding her.

I felt her nipples stab into me. She must have felt me harden, too. 'If you need someone to talk to . . . have a drink . . .'

'Thanks,' I said, finally pulling away. 'I'll let you know.'

The next day, at lunchtime, I found what I'd been looking for on psychquestions.com. It was an article by a Dr Georges LaFargue from the International Institute for Sleep Disorders, Zurich, Switzerland:

SLEEP PARALYSIS AND RELATED HYPNAGOGIC AND HYPNOPOMPIC CONDITIONS

Sleep Paralysis is a condition in which a subject awakens and becomes fully aware yet remains unable to move any part of their body, except possibly their

eyes. It occurs at the nexus of the sleeping and waking state, generally when the subject is emerging
from the unconscious state. Technically the subject
is mentally awake but discovers their muscles are
immobilized.

That didn't sound like me – I had walked right down the
hall to Callum's room at Arcadia. I hadn't felt paralyzed
at all.

Subjects may also experience a wide range of visual
and auditory sensations known as hypnopompic
hallucinations . . .

This sounded more like it:

The associated experiences that come with the hallucinations can be distressing and/or terrifying to the
subject. Some subjects feel a threatening presence, 'the
intruder' (sometimes armed), in the room, some have
out-of-body experiences – e.g. flying through a series of tunnels – while others feel they are being
chased by assailants or are, in some extreme cases,
under alien attack. Subjects may also feel a sinister
weight crushing down on their chest or a choking
sensation.

Relatively little is known about the physiology of
sleep paralysis, but it has been attributed to sexual abuse,
stress, irregular sleep patterns or sleep deprivation,

excessive use of drugs or alcohol or lying in a supine position.

A perfect description of my life in advertising.

Sleep paralysis is widely documented across many different cultures and is well represented in art, music and literature. For example, Edgar Allan Poe wrote frequently about the condition while Ernest Hemingway included a sleep paralysis scene in his famous short story, 'The Snows of Kilimanjaro'.

Oh, Papa, I suddenly felt a whole lot better!

I was obviously completely normal.

I also read a little about nightmares, night terrors and sleepwalking. Maybe I'd been sleepwalking and sleep-paralyzed at the same time in Arcadia?

And of course, the next day, there was nothing on Callum's tummy that I could see, apart from a strange little rash that looked like a smile. But that was most likely a minor allergic reaction to the calamari he'd had for dinner that last night or to the laundry detergent at North Fuck.

So it had all just been a nasty if incredibly vivid dream; it was as simple and reassuring as that.

If only.

I shook my head violently and clenched my eyes tight shut: but what about the things I'd seen during the *day* at Arcadia, and even before that, too.

The image on the TV?

Callum's drawing?

Those too, I knew could be explained if I put my logical hat on. But the screaming electrical sockets? How could Callum possibly know about something I was unable, or unwilling, to revisit myself?

I'd certainly been fully awake, cogent and alert on those occasions, hadn't I?

Yes. But then I put my logical hat back on: maybe Callum had acquired his own infantile fear of the different, face-like sockets in his new bedroom at the Olcott? Plus my wife had just tried to commit suicide and I was undoubtedly a little stressed about the responsibility of taking on a brand-new job in a brand-new country.

So it was no wonder I'd been a little jumpy and suggestible lately.

Give me the daggers. The sleeping and the dead are but as pictures; 'tis the eye of childhood that fears a painted devil.

The article finished with the fact that Lady Macbeth had been a sleepwalker, too.

*

It felt strange being back at the Olcott.

The same but different somehow.

There was a strong undertow of something missing. Of things unspoken. Of issues unresolved.

Or unresolvable.

The lingering scent of Susanna's tulips was now sour and fetid. As if a small animal had died somewhere in the apartment.

Mia and I both made an effort to be 'normal' – for Callum's sake, more than for each other. Because despite the resolution I'd made in Arcadia to resurrect our relationship, my emotional fuel tank was running at an all-time low. I just didn't have the energy or inclination to talk about us or what we'd been through.

And if I couldn't talk to her about us, how could I possibly talk to her about Callum?

And by Mia's standoffishness, I could only conclude that she felt the same reluctance to reconnect with me. We went through the motions: ate dinner, traded small talk, did the dishes. But we rarely touched or kissed. And we never went to bed at the same time.

She had also avoided getting dressed or undressed in front of me for months now. Although one day she came out of the bathroom when she didn't realize I was there, wearing only a towel around her head. Under her long-lost breasts, I took in the scar on her belly. It was thin and livid, razor sharp. And although it was shaped like the smile that Callum used to draw there, it now seemed more like a mocking leer.

That week we got back from Arcadia, Mia began apartment-hunting again with Susanna. But then Susanna had to go away on a school skiing trip with Courtney to Vermont for a few days and Mia lost the momentum.

I didn't really know what she got up to during the day. But Esmeralda told me she spent a lot of time flicking through her now dog-eared copy of *Vanity Fair*. Or just looking out the window with a tissue scrunched up in her hand.

I wondered what she looked at: there was no view to speak of; just the side façade of the drab, ugly apartment building next door to the Olcott – a grey, congealed, meaningless mess.

As I'd promised Anthony, my coping mechanism was going to be to throw myself back into work. We took the kernel of Bill and Jay's *Rear Window* idea and refashioned it into something more stylish and self-consciously 'super-cool'.

TVC Scenario
45 seconds (30 second
   cut-down)
<u>Client</u>: www.coolcams.com
<u>Title</u>: 'To catch a thief'

Brave Face

Put your best face forward

<u>Music (under):</u> 'Watching the Detectives' by Elvis Costello (instrumental re-record, more contemp and chilled)

We open on a sloppy-looking, mid-50s detective. He is studying grainy CCTV footage of a beautiful female jewel thief in a figure-hugging cat-suit, committing a daring midnight robbery in Tiffany's. Just before making her exit, she winks tauntingly at the camera – as if to say *Catch me if you can!*

The tech-challenged detective scratches his bald, perspiring head in frustration.

He then deploys a motley arsenal of shoddy old surveillance cameras, manned by a team of clumsy, clodhopping officers who try to monitor the elusive thief's unpredictable movements.

They tail her:

– To a secluded bench in Central Park where she exchanges the jewels with a man in dark glasses and a trench coat for a suitcase filled with cash.

– Back to the fashion pits of 5th Avenue where she spends her ill-gotten gains on expensive clothes, shoes & yes, jewellery.

– To the finest restaurants and nightclubs where she celebrates her crime with a couple of very good-looking admirers: one male, one female–

Until finally the detective tracks her down to her large loft hideout where the three revellers share her bed.

However, when we close up on the thief sitting at her computer the next morning in her silky Japanese bathrobe, we realize that she has, in fact, been using her own network of superior-quality, crystal-clarity <u>coolcams</u> cameras to watch the detectives watching her!

When the detective finally pounces, all he finds in her hideout is an empty safe with a red rose and a little note inside that reads, *So long, sucker!*

Over this final scene, we hear an ironic female voice over: *coolcams.com. You'll see.*

Anthony flew over to San Fran with the storyboard on the Friday red-eye and the coolcams kids lapped it up.

'That's great, bro,' Bill smiled when I relayed the news to him. 'Here, I got you a little something to cheer you up.'

It was a video: *The Powerpuff Girls* Season 2 – featuring the famous 'Puffpower' episode.

*

While the coolcams TV storyboard approval was great news, the huge amount of work that came with it over the next week wasn't so great.

Not only did we need to start meeting with directors and production companies to see who'd be right to produce the spot, we also needed to review, and adjust where necessary, all the other print and online material we'd already presented in order to make sure all the disparate campaign elements still, as Anthony liked to say, 'sang from the same song sheet'.

On top of coolcams, Anthony also wanted a couple of 'quick' spec campaigns churned out for a microchip manufacturer and the Silicon Valley Bank.

'So you mean "quick and shit"?' I asked him testily one night at midnight.

Bill gave a tired snicker behind me.

Anthony was swaying in the doorway: he was exhausted, too.

'Oh don't give me that "woe is me" creative prima donna routine, Guy. I know you're fucked – we all are – but just do your best. I've gotta show these guys something next week.'

Secretly though, I was kind of happy to be stuck at work: it meant that I wasn't spending much time at the Olcott or, more to the point, near Callum.

All the weird Callum-related stuff that had gone down at North Fuck had sent my head spinning.

I still didn't know what to make of it all. I needed some space and time to gather my thoughts and shake off the sense of dread I'd brought home with me like a bad flu.

In the meantime, work was an effective if debilitating diversion.

But, smack dab in the middle of this week from hell, some genius decided it was the perfect time to hold the Brave Face Family Day.

At the point when it became too busy and noisy to do any work, with all the extra civilians milling around our office, I resorted to checking my emails. There was a surprise message from my Australian friends, Jim and Nadine, who were threatening to come to New York in a few weeks to spend a 'wild weekend with good old Guysville' on their way back from Ibiza. If they were relying on me to provide their NYC entertainment in my current stuporous condition, they were going to be sorely disappointed.

Meanwhile, Callum was pulling the tops off markers at Bill's desk and sticking Post-it notes to his face. But Bill didn't notice because he was showing his new girlfriend, a Japanese photographer's assistant, his favourite Jasper Johns book.

Mia was leaning against my desk while Lucy lingered dangerously in the doorway. I felt like Michael Douglas in *Fatal Attraction*.

'So this is the seat of power,' Mia said, surveying my well-ordered workstation.

'Power sometimes,' Lucy said quietly. 'Pain more often. Especially if he can't crack my briefs. I'm Lucy,' she said without a fraction of her usual confidence. She walked forward extending her hand.

'Mia.'

There was a long, unpleasant pause. Bill and his girlfriend looked up at the silence but then quickly buried their heads back in the Johns.

'So you work with Guy on coolcams?'

'Coolcams, other new business prospects – you name it, we're a team!'

Mia frowned. Lucy bit her lip and soldiered on. 'I get to do all the boring grunt stuff: background research, client liaising, writing the brief. Then these boys here get to play.'

'I see,' Mia said coldly. After living with me for years, Mia already had a pretty good idea what account service did. Plus from what Susanna had no doubt told her, this woman seemed to be overly friendly with her husband.

And the antipathy appeared mutual. 'And what do you do, Mia?' From me, Lucy already knew full well that the only thing Mia had been doing lately was keeping the vineyards of California in rude financial health.

Mia answered without looking at her. 'Um. I was an art broker back in Australia but—'

Susanna Johnson suddenly appeared in the doorway in a crisp Donna Karan charcoal suit with a bottle of Krug in one hand, making a drinking motion to Mia with the other. Susanna looked straight through Lucy, too: the snippy solidarity of the First Wives' Club.

Mia dutifully followed the boss's wife out with a not-at-all convincing 'Nice to meet you.'

Safe at last, Lucy rolled her eyes, wiped metaphoric sweat from her brow and trudged back to her office.

Bill finally looked down at his desk, to notice that Callum had added big pink, purple and black flowers to the detailed Yo digital layout he had been working on all morning.

'Family Days,' he snapped his big photo book shut. 'God love 'em!'

'Do you still love advertising, Guy?' Mia looked at me that night with pity.

As if she was asking whether I was still doing crack.

I looked up from the *New York Times*. 'It's a living.'

'Seriously, Guy.'

I wasn't sure where this was going. 'It's my job,' I said. 'It's what I'm good at. It pays the bills. Why do you ask?'

'Do you think advertising's good for society; for the world, I mean? For people? For us?' She looked positively nun-like now, asking for my confession.

Saint fucking Mia.

'What's this all about?' I was annoyed. Surely there were so many other more important things we could be talking about. Things we hadn't even broached.

'It's this fucking No Hopers book, isn't it? Filling your head with a lot of nasty, negative No Ideas.' I picked *No Logo* up from the coffee table and turned it over. 'Naomi Klein? She should be called No No Klein!'

'Why do you hate strong women, Guy?'

'I don't!'

She remained irritatingly serene. 'Why are you so angry? I was just asking a question.' She snatched the book back out of my hands. 'I just wondered whether you ever thought about the repercussions of what you do every day.'

'Look, Mia, I know you've had a rough time lately. But so have I. And I'm sorry I've been so busy since we got back from Anthony's place. But advertising – my job – pays for our life. Where we live, where we go, what we eat, what we buy, what we do. Especially since you're not working.'

'But it doesn't have to be our life,' she countered. 'In fact, I'm not even sure I want it to be our life any more.' She looked lost and empty. 'I think we should go home.'

There, she'd finally said it.

I'd already thought about my answer to this inevitable proposal many times over the last few weeks. 'Look, sometimes I feel like going home, too. But I've made a commitment to Anthony. We've really only just arrived. I can't just turn around now and say, "Sorry, mate – didn't work out, so we're off home." Plus it'd be like giving up.'

'But what about your commitment to *us*, to me and Callum? To your family, Guy? If we're not *all* happy here, then what's the point of being here? Are you telling me we're staying here for advertising's fucking sake?'

She still didn't get it. 'It's not for advertising's sake, Mia. I just don't want to feel as though I've been beaten by New York. I can't go back to Melbourne with my tail between my legs. I've gotta give it a go.'

'I think this is really all about your ego, Guy.'

'Maybe it is. But at the moment, it's my ego that allows us to eat.'

'You could do something else,' she persisted. 'We could go back and you could become . . . an English teacher or something! I could get back into my buying—'

'An English teacher?' I was incredulous. 'A fucking *English* teacher!' She may as well have said street sweeper. 'Do you honestly believe that we could survive on an English teacher's wage? For a start, I'm not trained as a teacher – so there's three years' study before I could even start. Then, when I do finally graduate and get a job in some dead-end school, my wage would cover exactly four-fifths of fuck all of the mortgage. Let alone little extras like private school fees or . . .' I wavered.

'Or what?' she shouted.

'Psychiatric treatment.'

'For who? I'm not mad, Guy. I'm just very sad. It's normal after you've lost a baby, you know.'

'Not for you. For *Callum*. He's not normal, Mia!'

'Maybe he hasn't been himself lately because his mother's been very depressed and his father's been acting like—' She fluttered her hand.

My problem was that even though we'd only been back a few days, the whole week up in Long Island had by now assumed a muddy, inchoate quality in my mind. Now we were back in the relative sanity of New York, it was difficult for me to articulate all the bizarre and disturbing things that were seeming to happen whenever Callum was around without sounding like a complete maniac. And if I knew that if I tried to, Mia would simply laugh in my face.

So I attacked instead. 'You just haven't noticed it because you've been so fucked up yourself!'

'Maybe you're the one who's a bit unhinged lately, Guy. By booze. Or coke? Please tell me you're not snorting that shit again. It turns you into a monster – I couldn't bear it!'

I'd had a bit of a coke relapse the year we lived in Sydney. Mia hated Sydney.

'Maybe you're the one who's fucked up, Guy. Maybe you're the one who needs to see a fucking shrink!'

I rolled my eyes. 'Can you honestly say you haven't noticed anything strange at all about our son lately?'

'Can't blame him if he is a bit out of sorts. No wonder. For the past few weeks, his parents have been on another planet.'

She was right on that score at least: together, we'd boarded a starship to a hostile, uninhabitable world where all the usual laws of reality seemed to have been completely reversed.

The face of Satan laughing

After a couple more energetic debates with Mia, Susanna pulled a few strings and we managed to get an appointment for Callum on the Tuesday of the following week.

According to Susanna, Claude Lavelle was one of the finest child psychiatrists in the city. He'd cured Courtney of her bed-wetting a couple of years back and had helped relieve another little girl the Johnsons knew of her pre-school anxiety.

But he didn't come cheap: Upper East Side, upper price bracket.

His waiting room was more like the library in a magnificent French chateau. There was a De Kooning lithograph; a dozen fresh white roses in a very expensive-looking Chinese porcelain vase; a tank filled with a kaleidoscope of tropical fish; and a vast mahogany reception desk with a glossy secretary pouting behind it – totting up Dr Lavelle's invoices on a sleek new Dell. Mia was right: I was definitely in the wrong profession.

We sat on a pale-mauve leather couch while Callum, despite our quiet admonishments, ignored the children's playpen and pressed his face up against the glass of the fish tank.

Mia was there under sufferance. Callum thought he was going to see a man to talk about his drawings. The *Sports*

Illustrated secretary brought us freshly roasted coffee in bright new Terence Conran cups.

We didn't have too long to wait. 'Callum?' Dr Lavelle marched out, bent down and shook Callum's hand. 'Oh good, I see you brought your drawings with you. Would you like to come in and show them to me?'

Callum looked uneasily at Mia. 'It's OK, darling,' she said. 'Mr Lavelle looks at lots of drawings from boys and girls. He knows all about them. Mummy and Daddy will stay right out here and wait for you.'

'Can I bring my Buzz, too?' Callum asked, showing Lavelle the doll in his other hand.

'Of course you can. I've had Buzz in my office once or twice before, you know.'

'Woody too?' Callum asked as Lavelle led him away.

'Oh yes, Woody the cowboy often visits me, too.'

Fifty minutes later, Mia and I were sitting opposite Dr Lavelle's desk ourselves, waiting for the debrief. That's what we called it in advertising anyway. I wasn't sure what the technical psychiatric term for it was: Diagnosis? Hokum? Bunkum? Meanwhile, Callum was back outside with the secretary and Doctor Seuss.

'Callum is a very bright and slightly sensitive little boy,' Lavelle began. I waited for the 'But', but there was none forthcoming. 'Aside from that, he seems completely normal. And he seems to have adjusted very well to life in a strange new country.'

Mia leaned forward. 'I lost a baby last year. What sort of effect would that have had upon him?' She didn't mention her suicide attempt: we thought we'd managed to hide that horror from Callum.

'Ah yes, he mentioned the baby. He said that Mummy was very sad that "Bubby" was gone. And that Daddy was too. At this early age, he was probably very jealous at the thought of a sibling he'd have to compete with. So he's probably actually secretly happy and relieved about the loss at some level. Children are selfish and often perverse that way. They take self-preservation to extremes. As long as Mummy eventually recovers from being *sad* and Daddy stops being *upset*, it probably won't cause him too much trauma down the track – even if you have another child at some stage. Because he'll be older then and better able to cope with the competition.'

Mia nodded. I shook my head. Another child certainly wasn't on my agenda at this stage.

'And his drawings?' I asked.

'His drawings are fairly typical of boys his age: filled with adventure scenarios from TV or videos or books, interspersed with people from his own real-life experience. It's a way of making normal life seem more exciting. Or the opposite: making a fantasy world seem more real.'

'But what about this one?' I persisted. I held up the DeD alien picture.

'He told me it was you and he having a sword fight. Except that you had assumed characters from the *Toy Story* movie that he likes.'

Undeterred, I then told Lavelle about Callum's dream about the electric skeleton.

He volleyed back again with the bleeding obvious. 'Yes,

all children have bad dreams from time to time, just as we do as adults.'

Mia butted in. 'So is there anything to really worry about?'

'Not that I can see,' the good doctor decreed. 'Just keep monitoring him and look out for any changes in behaviour.'

I rolled my eyes.

'I told you!' Mia spat. 'This has been a complete waste of time. Sorry, Dr Lavelle, my husband works in advertising – he has an overactive imagination.'

'Oh, no problem, I assure you. Better to be safe than sorry.'

Yeah, right, especially at $325 an hour.

On our way out, I screwed up Callum's drawings and tossed them into the secretary's shiny gold wastepaper basket.

*

'I want to put your big, hard cock in my mouth until I've sucked it dry.'

Lucy hadn't said anything remotely like that. All she'd said was, 'So how you feeling?' But her eyes were so bright and bewitching that they made me feel that any fantasy was a possibility.

Ever since we had entered March, work for once was slow. There were lots of irons in the fire, lots of submissions under consideration, lots of results we were waiting to hear back on. But it was one of those strange limbo times when the hours plodded past in slow motion and nothing much seemed to be happening.

Anthony was out on the west coast again, trawling the conferences, flicking out business cards and looking under rocks for new clients. But unlike the liquid excitement that had flowed fast and furious when I'd first arrived in town, I now sensed the pale ghost of recession hovering in the wings. Everybody seemed to be waiting for something to appear or change, but no one was exactly sure what it was. Had we finally reached the limit of greed and 'gimme more'? Were the tech stocks, with their ludicrous names like why.com, yo.com, zi.com and whatthehell.com – and the faceless companies they propped up – really going to change the way we lived our lives and make the world a better place? Or were they really just opaque and ultimately unworkable sophomoric scams?

Yet the market kept climbing, the nebulous never-ending ticker kept unspooling its digital hopes and dreams and lies and the NASDAQ continued to *boing! boing! boing!* like an overworked pinball machine on its last legs. Yes, the dotcom bubble was still floating high above us like a beautiful crystal ball. But how long before it lost its lustre and burst into the 'now you see me, now you don't' nothingness that it really was.

'So?' Lucy repeated.

It was dusk. The side bar was dark but warm, not gloomy. Not with Lucy's dancing eyes to brighten it up.

Work may have slowed up, but I still didn't really feel like rushing home to the Olcott at the end of the day.

'I've been a little bit down lately. Lousy, actually.'

'I could tell. Want to talk about it?' She uncrossed her legs, then recrossed them the other way.

I didn't really want to talk about it. I really just wanted to go to Lucy's apartment and fuck her brains out. I was sure that would be a lot more therapeutic than just talking.

'It's just . . . Mia. Not just Mia – me and Mia . . .'

I didn't want to mention my feelings and concerns about Callum. I wanted Lucy to think I was vulnerable and sexy. Not insane.

'What about you and Mia? Have things been bad between you since . . . ?' I wasn't sure whether she meant the lost baby or the suicide attempt – but both were relevant. She put her soft, silky hand on my knee.

'Yeah, we're not really communicating. I'm not sure that she loves me any more. I think she even blames me in a way for what happened.'

'Oh that's ridiculous, Guy. She's probably just still depressed and all fucked-up like you are. You've been through an awful lot, you two.'

I sipped my Red Star, thirsting for sympathy. 'Perhaps we *hadn't* been getting on even before this. Different priorities. Moving in different directions. Maybe it was really just Callum – and maybe the new baby – that was holding us together.' I trotted out the old *my wife doesn't understand me* shtick, yadda-yadda-yadda.

'So how's he doing, the little guy?'

It seemed I'd have to talk about Callum after all. 'He's . . . doing OK. Fine. He's got a great nanny, which is lucky because Mia and I obviously haven't been looking after him as well as we normally do. We've been a little emotionally . . . distracted.'

Cue the violins. Cut to her other hand on my other knee and a delicious red open mouth whispering into my ear.

'I'd like to distract you, Guy.'

At least that's what I imagined she said.

*

Saturday April 1: April Fool's Day.

There was a fat little oblong packet on the table.

'What are these?'

'They're the photos from our first weekend,' Mia sighed. 'Back when we were happy to be here.'

I started to flick through them. There we were – lording it round Central Park in the carriage, Callum exultant on Balto's back, dodging the crowds in Times Square, hamming it up in the Warner Brothers Store, chowing down in the Muffins Cafe, terrorizing the Olcott lobby. Smiles, laughter, joy and excitement. Mia was right: it looked like another family.

The following Tuesday morning, I was sitting in Lucy's office staring at the crossed soles of her bare feet up on the desk, wondering where her legs ended. The night before, over a drink, she'd been telling me about her childhood down south. Now she was telling me some more.

' . . . and before the ranch, we were in Dallas.'

I told her Bill's Lee Harvey Oswald joke and she

chuckled with recognition. 'Yeah, I remember hearing that one when I was back in grade school.' She recrossed her feet and I tried to look away from the split second revelation of her inner thighs. 'My Daddy was there that day, you know.'

'What? At the Kennedy assassination?'

'Yeah, he used to be in commercial real estate and he had a meeting with the building supervisor of the Dal-Tex Building the afternoon that Kennedy was killed.'

I shook my head. 'Sorry, I'm not an assassination buff – does Dal-Tex mean something?'

'Well, the Dal-Tex building was just across the street from the Texas School Book Depository – adjacent to it, in fact. Daddy was early for his meeting that day so he decided to stand on the corner right opposite the Depository and check out the motorcade.'

She suddenly reached for her pad and scribbled a note. 'They have an earthcam up on the sixth floor there now, did you know? Maybe coolcams should put one over the Triple Overpass so you can see it all from the reverse angle?'

'Good idea!' Lucy never stopped thinking.

'Anyway, Daddy was standing on the little wall of the long water fountain that's there, the 'reflecting pool' I think they call it, so he could watch the cars go by.'

'On the corner where the car turns and starts to head down to where the shots are fired?'

'Exactly.'

'Wow! What a place to be: your old man's part of history!'

'I guess so.'

I looked over her toes. 'Did he see anything?'

'Well, first up, this young black guy had an epileptic fit right near where he was standing.'

'Really? Is that well documented?'

'Yeah, all the conspiracy nuts say he was an actor just pretending to have a fit to divert attention from all the open windows around the Plaza. But my father said he saw this guy hit his head pretty damn hard on the low concrete wall of the pool.'

'Maybe he was an early De Niro method actor type?'

'Maybe. Anyway, a cop called an ambulance and they put a stick in the man's mouth to stop him choking and then they took him away just a couple of minutes before the motorcade was due to arrive.'

'So did your Dad see anything else? Anything interesting? Like rifles sticking out of windows or anything?'

Lucy looked thoughtful for a moment. She suddenly seemed a little reluctant revisiting the family lore. 'Well, he was wearing his big, wide-brimmed Stetson – just like Governor Connally was that day. In fact, Daddy's sometimes referred to as "Reflecting Stetson Man" or "Connally 2" in those lunatic conspiracy books. Anyway "Reflecting Stetson Man" had his hat on as usual and he didn't have any reason to look up in the air at that point because he was probably really just trying to see through the crowd, smoking his cigar and turning around to see if the motorcade was coming.'

'Oh.' Disappointing.

'Then the cars went by and I imagine Daddy would

have tipped his hat to the president and then, right after that, all the shooting started.'

'Did he say where the shots came from?'

Lucy shook her head. 'He said the sounds were ricocheting all round the Plaza – like firecrackers he said. Dealey Plaza is actually quite small, like a box canyon, so the sound bounces from building to building, apparently. And people were looking around wildly in all different directions. And everyone was screaming at the tops of their lungs like it was a horror film at the drive-in.' She pulled her feet off the desk and sat forward.

'Daddy finally did look up and he saw a huge flock of pigeons fly off from the roof of the Depository. Then he jogged a few yards down towards the grassy knoll because that's where most of the crowd seemed to be running and . . . It was just chaos all over.'

'I can imagine – I've seen some of the film clips.'

'But then Daddy turned around and looked *back* towards the Depository Building and he saw something that he still doesn't really like talking about.' She seemed uncomfortable with the detail herself, dragging deeply on her Dunhill as a delaying tactic. 'Because he's not really given to "fanciful notions", as he calls them.'

'Try me.'

'Well he said that that same group of pigeons had flocked together up in the sky . . .' She stared intently at the orange tip of her cigarette for a few more seconds '. . . and that it looked just like the face of Satan laughing.' She shuddered.

'Jesus!' I suddenly felt like a cigarette – and maybe a drink – myself. 'Did your dad ever hear any local Dallas rumours about who might have been responsible for the crime?'

'Lots of them. But the one he liked the most was that Frank Sinatra had ordered the hit.'

I gave her an incredulous look.

'Well, the theory goes that Kennedy had snubbed Sinatra earlier that year by staying at Bing Crosby's house instead of Sinatra's house out in Palm Springs. So to pay him back, Sinatra had the president whacked.'

'What, so was it Ol' Blue Eyes himself up on the sixth floor?'

'Close. It was Jack Ruby! Sinatra allegedly knew Ruby through his own casino at Lake Tahoe in the fifties – the Cal-something. So he asked Ruby to do it and Ruby said yes because he had big gambling debts at the time and had some Mafia heavies chasing him for them.'

'So was Oswald in on it or not?'

'According to the Sinatra theory, Oswald both was . . . and he wasn't.'

Just then, Terry the Terrible walked past Lucy's open doorway and glared at me. He'd been wanting to brief me on a new corporate brochure for a big satellite communications client that our UK office usually handled. I knew it would be a long, dull job, so I'd been putting him off. 'Well, it's been fun, Luce, but I guess I better go and assassinate Terry before he gets me first. You're better than the History Channel!'

And a hell of a lot sexier.

She smiled. 'If you're really interested, I'll ask Daddy to email me what he remembers.'

I paused in the doorway. I wished I could stay in there all day shooting the breeze and studying her legs. 'See you this afternoon for our exciting new yo.com meeting.'

'Yo, Bro,' she smiled.

'By the way, is it true you were seeing JFK Junior last year?' The thought of the two of them together had me very excited.

'Is that the rumour?' Lucy scoffed. 'We were trying to get JJ on the board at Highcams. I met him at a company cocktail party and took him up to see a camera we'd just installed on top of Trump Tower. He was nice – and very flirty of course – but a little too . . . Hyannis Port for me.'

She looked me straight in the eyes. 'I prefer my men to be a little more "real".'

I went back to my desk, trying to hide my hard-on underneath it.

As I skimmed the client brief, I wondered whether one of their many satellites could have picked out the killer in the Depository's sixth-floor window back in November '63.

I seemed to remember that Lee Harvey Oswald claimed he'd been in the first-floor lunchroom of the building at the exact time of the assassination. And when a cop accosted him on the second floor getting a Coke out of the machine no more than ninety seconds after the shots rang out, he'd acted completely normal.

Not at all out of breath.

As cool as a cucumber.

I wondered whether the sockets in that lunchroom had been screaming.

Yo.com was a nifty new back-end personalization provider for other online businesses. So when one of the big online retailers told you which books you were likely to enjoy reading next, it was Yo who had already done the algorithmic homework for them.

Anthony was away at a new media conference in San Jose, to which he'd invited the coolcams kids and a couple of our other west coast clients – or our 'faultline confrères' as he called them.

So it was just Lucy and me today.

But our scheduled mid-afternoon meeting downtown turned out to be more of a 'no' than a 'yo'. Their blue-haired teenage receptionist, who had more metal in her than an aircraft carrier, told us that the marketing director we were meant to be meeting was still up in the air somewhere on a foggy flight out of Chicago.

'Sorry, guys,' she explained through her gum. 'I woulda called ya but Ben didn't leave me no numbers.'

'If only there was a Yo for your personal life that could tell you what you were going to do next.' I was holding my folder over my head as we trotted out of their lobby into the rain.

'Not very personalized of them to not even show up!' Lucy complained from under her red Levis jacket. A taxi splashed past, soaking the cuffs of my Diesels and completely drowning Lucy's Blahniks. 'Shit!' she cried. 'These shoes cost me a month's salary. And that taxi's just gone and pissed all over them!'

The rain intensified into artillery fire: small, stinging ball bearings battering us into an early retreat. The wind also brought out its icy whips. So we holed up in the cosy entrance to a Jewish cake shop called Levin's, a fragrant foxhole against the marauding elements. With the heat venting out from the deli inside, it was a small, warm, moist place to take shelter.

We stared through the steamy window at the bar mitzvah blintzes and freshly minted matzah balls. But as the rain intensified and we remained trapped under the awning, eventually we had nowhere else to look apart from at each other.

She really was good enough to eat.

'Olcott Races, Callum's Day, doo dah, doo dah . . . Olcott Races, Callum's Day, oh–the-doo-dah-day . . .'

It was funny, but apart from the occasional maid pushing a vacuum cleaner, we hardly ever seemed to see anyone else on our floor.

Home from work, I raced Callum down the long, deserted hallway. But he was slower than usual and not really into it.

'I wanna see Mummy,' he said.

'OK. It's time for dinner now anyway.'

I sat down with a Red Stripe. 'So how did it go?'

Mia had had an interview at a gallery in Soho.

'So so.'

She sipped her Chardonnay. I could tell there was more in her than in the bottle. She hadn't drunk like this since after she'd had the abortions all those years ago.

'They said they'd call me if anything came up. And they gave me the numbers of some other galleries downtown and out in Brooklyn.'

'So it was a worthwhile meeting?'

'Who knows?' she slurred a little and the wine sloshed dangerously around her glass.

'How was Callum today?'

'Fine. Esmeralda took him to a Peter Pan puppet show up in Harlem. Now he wants to learn how to fly.' But it wasn't Callum or flying boys she really wanted to talk about. 'You've been getting home even later the past few weeks? Eleven last night?'

'Yeah – well we've been busy.'

'Funny. I spoke to Susanna today and she said you'd actually been pretty quiet. That's why Anthony's out in California trying to drum up more business.'

She kept staring at me: I was a rabbit in a headlight. A couple of nights the week before, I had genuinely been working with Bill on new business pitches that Anthony had briefed us on remotely. But last night, Lucy, Bill and I had gone round the corner for a drink and then Bill had left round nine.

And Lucy and I had stayed on a bit longer.

But I really didn't feel like going into the details right now. 'Busy, not busy – it's all relative. With respect, Susanna doesn't know a lot about the day-to-day business. Just how to spend the profits.' I started to clear the dishes.

'Daddy read me a story!' Callum demanded, thrusting his Paul Hamlyn fairy tale book into my belly. 'Come on, Dad!'

'Read your son a fairy tale,' Mia said drily. 'After all, you've been telling me a few lately.'

Oh yeah? I felt like saying. *And with the amount you're putting away these days, you could give my father a run for his fucking money and that's saying something.*

But I said nothing: there was no point. Especially when she was like this.

I closed the book, tucked Callum in and switched on his Noddy lamp.

I noticed a blob of blue clay on the side table next to him.

'What's that?'

'Play-Doh, silly! Don't you even know?'

I picked it up. 'Yes, I know it's Play-Doh. But what have you made out of it?'

'Don't tell Mummy,' he lowered his voice to an excited whisper. 'But I made Bubby!'

I turned the little blue sculpture over in my hand.

My heart froze.

Complete with froggy feet and hollow eyes, although slightly smaller than life-size, it was a pretty good facsimile of a baby in utero mid-term.

Because I intentionally hadn't been home early these past few weeks, I'd managed to avoid any awful Callum/Bubby mind-fucks. In fact, I'd almost managed to convince myself that the shocking events at Arcadia had been mere figments of my fevered imagination. But now it seemed as though the whole sequence was starting all over again.

'Talking 'bout Bubby makes Mummy sad,' Callum explained solemnly. 'So I just showing her to you, Daddy.'

I was still turning the thing over in my hands.

'You know what, Son? I do think it's a good idea not to mention Bubby to Mummy. It does upset her. But this little Bubby you've made' – it felt very cold in my hand – 'is *so* good, I'd like to take it to work with me. Can I do that?'

Callum lapped up the praise. 'Oh yes, Daddy! You can keep her on your work desk, next to your 'puter. I can easy make another Bubby for home!'

'We-ll, you've made a good Bubby already,' I demurred. 'So maybe next time, make something different, eh?'

Callum pondered this new challenge for a moment. 'Maybe a Balto instead – or a Buzz or a Woody!'

'Great idea, Son!'

I slipped the sinister little effigy into my pocket.

'Good night, darling.' I kissed his forehead and switched off the bedroom light.

For the next ten minutes, I sipped on another Red Stripe and kneaded the Play-Doh in my pocket until my fingers were raw.

Then, once Mia had also safely gone to bed, I walked down the passage to our front door, opened the heavy stairwell door to my left and hurled the nasty little blue ball down into the abyss.

Like a copse

'Guy, Esmeralda's in hospital!'

'Esmeralda?'

'Yes. They've taken her to Mount Sinai!'

Mia was yelping loudly at the other end of the phone. As if she couldn't draw breath.

'W-what happened?' Bill heard the catch in my voice and looked up from his layout.

'I-I don't know. I had a coffee with Susanna at Isabella's. Then I went to Fairway to do the shopping . . .'

'Yes?'

'And then when I got back to the Olcott, Michael came rushing up to me and . . .' She gulped.

'Keep going. Take your time.'

'Told me that she'd fallen and hit her head.'

'Fallen where? Off what?'

'The couch. You know how she's always fiddling with the curtain cord because she says the room's so dark during the day?'

I remembered I had seen her do it that one time. And I hadn't liked her doing it. 'Yes?'

'She was always fiddling with the bloody cord and sometimes it got stuck and she used to stand on the arm of the couch—'

Mia began to wail. I'd never heard her sound like this

before. Even after she'd lost babies, her crying had been quieter, private, human. Now she sounded like an animal caught in a trap.

'Where's Callum? Is he all right?'

'He's here with me. He's fine but a bit shocked. One of the Irish maids found him wandering up and down the corridor. He was the one who found Esmeralda lying there, poor little thing. He'd been having a nap and then he wandered out to the lounge and saw her lying there on the floor with blood coming out of the back of her head. One of the ambulance guys also noticed some blood on the window sill, so maybe she cracked her head on that on the way down.'

'Jesus. What do the doctors say?'

There was a long, terrible pause.

'Guy, it doesn't look good. She's still unconscious – that's all they'll tell us at this stage.'

*

We'd told Callum that Esmeralda had been taken to hospital with 'a really bad headache' but that she'd probably be OK and back home before he knew it. That was two days ago and he still needed some serious cheering up.

'Come on, son. I'm taking you down to Texas, boy!' I put on a lame John Wayne drawl.

'Wh-at?' Mia slurred from the couch. It was dinnertime, but that event didn't seem to have crossed her addled mind yet.

'It's all right, Mia. I'm taking Callum downstairs to

Dallas BBQ. Do you want me to bring you back anything? Some nachos with guacamole? Or some tacos maybe?'

'No thanks.' My wife didn't eat much these days. The only nutrients she was getting were from fermented grapes. Maybe the anti-depressants were killing her appetite.

Despite what we'd told Callum, we really had no idea when Esmeralda would be rejoining us. The day after the accident – as soon as she'd been allowed – Mia had visited her at Mount Sinai. Apparently Estella was there, too, maintaining as much of a vigil as her duties at the Johnsons' would allow her.

'What did they say?' I had asked as soon as I'd got home from work.

Mia was trying to make *pozole* in Esmeralda's honour. She was dropping occasional tears into the frying pan along with the olive oil.

'They've put her in a medically induced coma. The doctor I spoke to said they had no idea about how long she'll be like that. Oh, it was horrible, Guy. She's just lying there like a corpse.'

Or *copse* as Esmeralda would have said.

'So no prognosis, then?'

'They're running "tests" – they always say that, don't they? But they can't offer anything conclusive.'

Mia was leaning against the kitchen bench, wiping her eyes with a tea towel. 'I'm not sure I can go back there till she's better. Mount Sinai is such a sad place for me.'

I held her, but again there was that stiffness.

'Estella said she'd call us as soon as there was any news.'
I let her go.

'This place is a bit like where Esmeralda comes from,' I
explained as Callum and I entered the Dallas BBQ and
slid into a red booth behind a noisy bunch of teenagers.
'Sort of like Mexico.' Actually I was pretty sure it was
nothing like Mexico – I was just trying to make conversation with my sad and distant son.

Callum seemed neither impressed nor interested. He
looked up at the sombrero hanging on the wall. One of
the teenage boys said 'shit'. I glared at him and his friends
all laughed nervously.

It must have been Michael's hour off. He was sitting
over at the bar with his boyfriend, Enriquo – the moustachioed bartender who'd served me my first beer in New
York. Callum liked Michael, not only because he wore ties
that featured cartoon characters but because he also
expertly mimicked their voices for Callum whenever we
stopped by the front desk.

'*Here's your mail, Cawwum,*' Elmer Fudd might say, '*It's
vewy vewy interesting.*'

But today I doubted that even a note-perfect '*sufferin'
succotash*' could make Callum smile.

I tried to enthuse him: 'You can have some of the
yummy food that Esmeralda makes for you. Like tacos!'

He just looked sad.

'You miss Esmeralda, don't you?' Of course he did. His
favourite new person in New York, perhaps the only stable constant in his life, and now she'd been taken away

from him in an abrupt and violent fashion. Plus he wasn't enjoying the local playgroup nearly as much as that first time with the Play-Doh: he'd told Mia one of the Puerto Rican boys had started picking on him.

He avoided the question but asked, 'Daddy, can I have a drink of water, please?'

'Of course you can. And I'll get a Bud for Daddy.'

Michael was drinking a Fluffy Duck at the bar and laughing with Enriquo. Someone put 'Blue Bayou' on the jukebox and I suddenly missed our nanny, too.

2

Without a rope

I was holding Callum's mittened hand as we walked through the park.

Up ahead I could make out the mime artist in his black-and-white striped tunic, his pancaked face wrapped in the swirling winter mist.

A menacing Marcel Marceau.

He signalled flamboyantly to Callum, who broke my grasp and ran towards him. 'No, Callum!' I cried. 'Wait for Daddy!'

But Callum ran and ran and ran while I was strangely flat-footed and unable to get up any speed. The mist thickened and swirled like steam off a witch's cauldron.

When I finally arrived at the place the man had been standing, he had shrunk to the size of a child. He had become Callum.

'Come on, Son,' I reached for his white-gloved hand.

'You'll pay for this,' he rasped.

He pulled a long knife out of his sleeve and sliced off my hand. Blood started to spew from my stump.

'You'll see.'

Behind the white mask, an old lady cackled.

I yawned, groaned, then yawned again.

Saturdays kept rolling round like carousel horses. They seemed to be spinning faster and faster, and lately it was taking all of my depleted energy just to stay in the saddle.

Speaking of energy, I needed to get fit again: my gut was becoming a bagel.

With his many commitments, Anthony and I couldn't seem to lock down a mutually agreeable time to visit the New York Health Club. He often went at 5.30 a.m. But I often had trouble sleeping these nights, so that didn't really work for me.

I shuffled out through the lobby and nodded to Michael, who today had Pepé Le Pew and matching French cologne around his neck. Michael seemed to favour Looney Tunes over Disney, but he did occasionally wear a sparkly Tinker Bell tie that Callum found particularly endearing.

This Saturday was still rubbing its eyes, too. The snow was starting to slip off the sidewalks and trickle down the drains. But there was still a sharp nip in the air, especially when the sun strained to peep over the tops of the buildings.

I ran lightly past the Dakota, dodging the early-bird tourists and the slushy puddles. I hung a left at Strawberry Fields and followed the path through the bare tree arches all the way up past the 79th and the 86th Street Transverses to the reservoir. It was less than a kilometre and a half from the 72nd Street entrance to the reservoir. And a lap of the reservoir itself was just over 2.5 km. So, from the front door of the Olcott and back again was roughly a 6.5 km round trip.

I couldn't possibly run all that way in my current gone-to-seed condition. But if I could just make it round the reservoir itself without having a heart attack, that would be a start.

Michael had told me that it was officially known as the Jacqueline Kennedy Onassis Reservoir. I imagined the Queen of Camelot trotting around it in her jodhpurs in the sixties with *Life* photographers snapping at her heels.

And then I remembered Dustin Hoffman obsessively lapping the reservoir in that great old movie, *Marathon Man*. I also recalled Dustin running bare-chested – with a serious limp and with his mouth gushing blood – along a dark freeway in his stripy pyjama bottoms. If Dustin could run injured in his PJs, then surely I could stagger a few pissy kms in my nice warm Diadora tracksuit.

Jogging always spurred my mind into action. I began to think about our current domestic situation: what to do about me and my forlorn little family?

Mia and I were both really struggling. Holed up in our individual hells.

And Callum was certainly far from the same normal little boy we'd brought over with us from Melbourne.

Big black birds tailed me from high above. The same muttering bag lady I'd encountered that first morning out-side the Dakota stopped and stared at me, wheezing and smelling of urine.

A couple of fully Reeboked joggers flashed past me like spectres in the mist. A booby trap of snow dropped from a branch above onto the path, forcing me to swerve at the last second. I staggered to a stone bench on the per-imeter of the little lake. I'd made it to the reservoir, but there was no way on God's earth I was able to go any further. I sat, wheezing louder than the bag lady. Another skinny, annoyingly fit-looking runner sped by, making me feel fat, fucked and old.

From somewhere far off, a church bell counted to seven.

I coughed like a consumptive.

Marathon Man?

I was running just to stand still.

*

At the beginning of that week I told Bill – knowing of his interest in such things – what Lucy had said about Frank Sinatra being responsible for killing Jack Kennedy.

'Wouldn't surprise me,' Bill replied, slurping his latte. 'First of all, Sinatra organizes all the entertainment for the big '61 inauguration gala – as well as the high-class DC hookers for the after-party at the Statler-Hilton, mind you. Then, two years later, he's bumped off the Kennedy Christmas card list by brother Bobby for pimping the president a Mafia moll called Judy Exner who's a dead ringer for Liz Taylor – except you didn't need to marry her to get laid. I mean, where's the gratitude?

'Plus ya know Ol' Blue Eyes was pretty fucked up from when he was a kid. His mother was the Hoboken rabbit catcher. She used to perform abortions for all the knocked-up girls in the neighbourhood. Her nickname was 'Hatpin Dolly'.'

Hatpin. That was a word I hadn't heard in decades.

'Plus little Sinatra wasn't breathing when he was born,

so his grandmother had to hold him underwater to get his little lungs pumping.'

While that little titbit reminded me of something else that I really didn't want to revisit either, and which I had spent most of my life trying to forget.

'Really?'

'Yep, and that's why he could hold his breath so long as a singer: it was the secret to his success, apparently. Anyway, Dolly was a tough little Democratic ward boss with a mouth on her like a longshoreman. She had a lotta enemies, did Dolly. So when little Frank pops out with no lungs, a perforated eardrum and a big scar on his cheek from the forceps, her enemies laugh behind her back that it's one of her abortions gone wrong!'

'Nasty.'

'Uh huh. Ya know "Sinatra" is Italian for "sinister", right?'

Bill wiped foam from his lip. 'Forget JFK, it's a wonder Sinatra didn't end up as a serial killer.'

'"The Stranger in the Night"?' I suggested.

'I knew you'd say "Somethin' Stupid".'

'You guys sure haven't had much luck since you got to the Big Bad Apple.' Lucy drew back on her Stuyvesant and rubbed my shoulders.

'I used to think you made your own luck. Now I'm not so sure.'

Her tiny, art deco apartment was down in the West Village. So were yo.com and a couple of our other Silicon

Alley clients. The perfect alibi for our afternoon 'briefing sessions'.

'How's your wife?' She cracked a Diet Coke.

'Don't ask me about her.'

'Don't be guilty,' she ruffled my hair. 'We're not hurting anyone. Just having a little fun.'

'I think it's called infidelity, actually. I'm married, remember.'

She stubbed out her smoke. 'I try not to put a label on stuff. Helps me sleep at night.'

'Good for you.'

'Oh come on – don't I at least bring you some pleasure?'

She did actually. And it was the only pleasure I was getting in my life at the moment. But it was a horrible, guilty pleasure that, since it had begun a few weeks before, made me feel dirty and disgusted with myself afterwards.

'Well, can I ask about your little boy then?'

'What about him?'

'Well you said that while you were away that he was acting strange and doing weird things?'

Had I? I must have been very drunk at the time. It worried me that I couldn't remember telling Lucy about my experiences out at North Fuck. I usually kept my crazy Callum thoughts to myself. If Lucy thought I was going loopy, she might stop fucking me.

'Hmm. I think he's just like Mia and me: a bit overwhelmed by the city and all the stuff that's happened. He's only three, remember. Well, three and a half now.'

She shook her Jennifer Aniston coif in disagreement.

'That's not what you said, Guy. When we were at Chumley's that night, you said that when you were staying out at Anthony's house on the island that Callum did some kind of nasty drawing and showed you some weird creature on the TV or something that really freaked you out? And that you had some terrifying experience when you went sleep-walking or something?'

Chumley's. I remembered now: it wasn't too long after we'd come back from Arcadia. Another occasion when Bill had gone home early, leaving Lucy and me to our own, dangerous devices. I had been very drunk that night. And no wonder: I had the ghosts of Hemingway, Steinbeck, Faulkner, Mailer, Fitzgerald – all the Big Fish – glaring down at me from the walls, asking me why I was wasting my life writing poxy little banner ads instead of a proper book.

(I had actually tried to write a novel a few years before. I used the Subaru Australia ad pitch as a plot skeleton and called it *Car Toon*. I sent the first three chapters of my comic masterpiece to an agent but he felt that satirising advertising didn't really work – given my often immoral profession was such a joke already. Then Callum arrived and, apart from a few desultory short stories, my literary career was aborted before it even began.)

'Did I?' I finally answered. 'I was quite pissed that night. I can't really remember what I said.'

But my switched-on southern belle wasn't going to let me off that easily. 'You seemed *very* scared,' she insisted. 'Terrified, actually. For the both of you. And you said he had recently started behaving weirdly again. You said that he also made some freaky little sculpture? Guy, you said you thought he might be *possessed* or something.'

She probably did think I was mad. I hoped she hadn't said anything to Bill or Anthony about my crazy suspicions.

I put my shirt on first, then my briefs – today we really did have a new business meeting at five. 'Hmm . . . I was probably just trying to be dramatic or something to impress you . . . interest you . . . I don't know. Callum's fine . . . Where are my socks? . . . I make things up. For a living, remember.'

Lucy looked at me with sceptical eyes. 'I think you're a little fucked-up, Guy. I think maybe you should go talk to someone.'

She hooked up her purple Wonderbra, then poked her finger forcefully into the back of my head. 'There's some strange shit going on up here.'

*

'Guy, we're going home.'

I'd just tucked Callum into bed.

'Home where? Who's going home?'

'Callum and I. We're going back to Melbourne.'

Although I'd been half-expecting this announcement for weeks, the bulletin still rendered me speechless.

An old movie was playing on the TV – gleaming San Francisco cable cars rattled across the screen in glorious Technicolor. Mia was sitting on the couch. The same one Esmeralda used to stand on to wrestle the curtain cord. She took a long, sad sip of wine. 'I wouldn't imagine you'd want to come back. I thought you were so happy here. What with your new job. And your new work *mates.*' She wiped her lips with the back of her hand. 'Susanna's helping me make the arrangements.'

Callum's *Three Blind Mice* book was on the floor at my feet. I kicked it away.

'Fucking Susanna!' I stood up. 'Does Anthony know anything about this?'

The phone rang. Mia raised her glass to the timing. It was the great man himself.

'Mate, I'm so sorry to hear about you and Mia. Is there anything I can do?'

'I-I don't know,' I sat down again. 'I only just found out "the news" myself.'

Mia walked past me into the bedroom and closed the door.

'Do you need any more time off? We can always get Jay back in.'

And fuck fucking Jay. I was sure that slick Ed Norton-lookalike arsehole was after my job.

'No, I don't think so. I can work it out. We can work it out.'

There was a long, un-Anthony-like pause. 'I hope we can. It's a prick me being your boss as well as your mate.' He went agonizingly quiet again. 'But I have to support my business as well as my friendships.' The consummate diplomat: it was by far the worst thing he had ever said to me.

'Give me a week, Anthony. Please.'

'OK. But, Guy. . .' He hadn't called me Girly in ages.

'Yes, mate?'

His voice had an edge to it I'd never heard before. 'Maybe I'll start coming along to those downtown meetings as well.'

I went up to the roof to have a smoke.

I could just make out the treetops in Central Park over the fractured foreground of washing lines, satellite dishes, TV antennae, air-conditioning units, and water towers that ran along the rear of West 72nd. A phalanx of pigeons or doves flew as one big slow 'V' above them.

I drew back, drowning in the nicotine. The moon was pale and sickly-looking, a timid reflection of itself. I flicked my butt over the edge and went back down.

It was only 9.15. Mia was already slumbering, or at least pretending to be. Callum was talking in his sleep with his arm flung over his face next to her. I put my ear to his mouth and thought I heard 'mice' and 'knife', but I couldn't be sure.

'Mia?' I put my hand on her shoulder.

She didn't answer for the longest time. Without turning around, she covered my hand with hers. 'If *you* want to stay, maybe you should. Maybe the break would do us good. You could come home and visit us after a month or two.'

'I don't want you to leave.'

'I just don't want to be here any more.'

'I know. I feel that way as well sometimes. Like it's all been one long, horrible nightmare.'

She turned around. 'Well, why don't we just fucking *go*?'

Part of me agreed with her. But I also felt that if we ran back home now, that nothing would really ever be resolved between us.

I remembered reading a Zen parable once about a dog that keeps moving from place to place to get rid of his fleas. But wherever he goes, no matter how far he travels, the fleas are still always with him. I feared it would be like that with us: if we went back to Melbourne, we'd still be scratching the fleas.

I tried the soft approach. 'Look, they say it takes a good year before you settle into a new city. Plus, we've had our ups and downs.'

'Ups and downs?' Mia sat up. '*Ups and fucking downs*?!' she hissed through gritted teeth. Callum stirred, but then went back to his nursery rhyme dreams.

'Guy, since we've arrived in New fucking York we've had hospitalized nannies, depression' – she flicked her thumb at herself, then back at me – 'paranoia and, unless I'm an absolute idiot, regular fucking infidelity as well!' Her mouth was a machine gun. 'Plus, we've been stuck here for months at the Bates Motel. So there really hasn't been much of a chance to "settle in", now has there, *darling*?!'

'No,' I admitted. 'Maybe there hasn't.'

In the next room, I could hear the movie Mia had left on. Jimmy Stewart was in some kind of trouble and getting all tongue-tied. I knew exactly how he felt.

'Callum and I are leaving at the end of the month,' Mia said. 'Non-negotiable, Bucko. And at this stage, I don't really give a rat's arse whether you're on the plane or not.'

She was immoveable once she'd made up her mind. Hot-tempered like her mother but bull-stubborn like her father – the worst of both worlds. She turned over to face the wall. Conversation over.

I shrugged and went back out to the couch to share a Jack with Jimmy.

It was *Vertigo* – my favourite Hitchcock. The action was up to that crucial plot point two-thirds of the way through the film where Jimmy's dream woman, the brittle blonde Kim Novak, bungee jumps off the San Juan Batista Mission belltower. Without a rope.

But then, of course, the story goes on. Jimmy has a kind of a breakdown and, after a while, comes across another woman who looks very similar to the Kim Novak he's just lost – except this new one's a brunette and a lot less crazy. So he starts dating her (who wouldn't jump at a second chance at dating Kim Novak!), but then, gradually, he begins to wonder whether the doppelgänger is more than just a doppelgänger?

If it were me being deceived, I couldn't have cared less. I'd just lay my weary head on Kim 2's big, beautiful breasts and let her stroke all my troubles away.

Callum moaned loudly in his sleep from the bedroom: probably something about a farmer's wife.

I was very tired now. But not nearly tired enough to go to bed.

Bye bye birdie

Last week of April and the coolcams TV spot was finally going into production. The budget had been approved, we'd selected a director and a production company, cast the talent and scouted the locations. Under normal circumstances, I would have been very excited about the project.

'Should she be more like Catwoman or Batgirl – her costume?'

'What's the difference?'

'Here, look at these.' Bill held up some pictures.

'Just so long as it's a sexy, slinky black latex jump suit. She's a jewel thief, not a superhero. We don't want any confusion.'

'So what about the mask? We have to see that she's gorgeous from the get-go, right?'

'Latex or black plastic. Whatever gives it that sexy, slick sheen. And bigger cut-outs for her eyes. The eyes are very important.'

'Eye eye, Captain!' He paused with a mischievous smile. 'But what about the MacGuffin?'

'Oh don't start that again, for Christ's sake!'

Bill and I had been debating earlier whether a bag of stolen jewels constituted what Hitchcock would call a

'MacGuffin': an arbitrary object that helped drive the plot of a film forward – like a secret dossier or a computer code or a treasure map – because of the way characters reacted to it but which was, in itself, actually unimportant to the overall story.

I'd done some research on famous MacGuffins in film history and printed out a list, which I now handed to him:

- The eponymous statuette in *The Maltese Falcon* (1941)
- The letters of transit in *Casablanca* (1942)
- The uranium in *Notorious* (1946)
- The case with glowing contents in *Kiss Me Deadly* (1955)
- The government secrets in *North by Northwest* (1959)
- The Ark of the Covenant in *Raiders of the Lost Ark* (1981)
- The contents of the briefcase in *Pulp Fiction* (1994)

'Yes, yes, yes,' Bill raised his index finger. 'But the main difference is that our chick is an actual jewel thief. So, in this case, I'd say the jewels are more of a MacSomethin' than a MacNothin', wouldn't you?'

Lucy walked past our office and gave me a greasy look. I'd become distant and uncommunicative since Mia's recent outburst. The reality was, I still liked Lucy a lot – too much, in fact. But since Mia's threatened departure, I was doing my best to lock Lucy out.

Bill looked at Lucy looking at me. 'I guess that's the end of the New Algonquin Club for a while.'

'Don't even joke.' I put my head in my hands. 'I don't know if I can go on, Bill. My life is shit. All of it. I wish I'd never come to this fucking fucked-up country.'

'Buddy, I really think it's time for you to go get some help. From someone who cares, I mean.'

I shrugged. 'You mean a shrink? You sound just like bloody Golden Girl.' I looked towards Lucy's office.

'There's no stigma, man. Especially in your case. My ex-wife will have me on the couch for decades. But I'd rather be on the couch than under the ground.'

'Yes, but you are actually crazy.'

'Welcome to Noo Yawk, Kangaroo Boy. Everybody's crazy!'

I didn't really have much time to dwell on the vicissitudes of my mental condition because, half an hour later, Mia called saying she would be dropping Callum into the office for a couple of hours while Susanna helped her 'sort some important things out' downtown. Things like heading back to Australia, no doubt.

This time Bill was fully prepared for Callum's visit: he cleared all of his important work off his desk and placed it in a folder on top of the bookshelf, well out of Callum's reach.

'Hey, little man – take a seat right here. Your Dad never does any work anyway, so you may as well have his chair.' Bill lifted Callum up and put a pad and some markers in front of him.

'Do you like to *pretend* to write like your Dad or draw *brilliantly* like me?'

Callum picked up a pink marker and took the top off. The powerful solvent smell made him crinkle his nose.

'I'm going to see Anthony about those changes to the document,' I told Bill. 'Back in a tick.'

Anthony's PA told me he was out. And I was trying to stay away from Lucy's office. So I went into the kitchen to make a coffee. The old machine had now been replaced by a gleaming, bean-fuelled Lamborghini.

Terry the Terrible was sitting at the kitchen table with a pizzaman.com menu in front of him, no doubt making notes for an upcoming travesty pretending to be a brief.

I ignored him, made the coffee as quickly as I could and then went back to my office carrying two cups.

'So what have you two been up to?' I put Bill's coffee on his layout pad.

Stephen Cummings was lamenting quietly in the background.

'It's the darndest thing,' Bill said. He looked almost white.

'What is?' Callum was clicking the mouse to Bill's Mac and making Super Mario leap tall buildings. Bill looked at the top of Callum's head then back up at me.

'What is?' I asked him again.

'It's just weird is all.' He then looked out at the big shiny needle of the Chrysler Building, piercing the clouds.

'What is?'

He reached out for his coffee, but his hand was

trembling a little. So he used both hands. 'Oh really, it's probably nothing.'

I'd given up asking, so I just sat down and waited. I looked at him.

He finally spoke. 'Well, you know that last little baby bird out there?' He pointed to the window.

Of course I did – we'd been watching the little bird family outside on the ledge for weeks now. Only one baby was left – the runt or whatever the ornithological equivalent of the smallest sibling was. The other three babies had all grown up and flown the coop. 'Well, I pointed it out to Callum and just as we were looking at it' – he paused and put his cup back down because his hands were still shaking – 'a big black bird much bigger than the mother swooped down, bit the little bird's head clean off, then flew off with it.'

I looked out the window and walked a little closer: the brown nest was now completely red. The baby bird was still convulsing in the middle of it, blood spurting out of the hole where its head had just been.

'And then little Callum here—' Bill's voice trailed off and he licked his lips nervously.

A shiver sprinted up my spine. 'What did Callum do?'

Bill gulped, then frowned as if he couldn't quite believe what he'd just experienced.

'He said *Bye bye birdie*.' He snorted at the ridiculousness of what he was telling me. 'Then he just giggled. Like it was a game or something.'

'A game like Mario!' Callum squealed as the little Italian cyber-plumber jumped off a building into the great unknown, all the while keeping his glinting blue eyes fixed firmly on mine.

When Bill took Callum over the road to Café Europa for a hot chocolate (and to calm his own jangled nerves, no doubt), I did a quick mental recap. With the thing on the screen at Arcadia, the DeD alien picture, the Play-Doh sculpture and the sockets, it had been just me who'd borne witness to Callum's strange and disturbing behaviour. He never seemed to reveal his other more sinister self to Mia, Esmeralda or anyone else. But now it seemed I finally had another witness: Bill.

It seemed that the 'other Callum' was finally coming out into the open.

Perhaps now the time for playing games was over.

I don't think we're in the Gamma Quadrant any more

Another bad day at Black Rock.

Black Rock is the wind-blown bayside suburb where I am incarcerated as a child.

I have wet my bed again the night before and my mother greets me at the back door as I arrive home from school.

The grey/golden sheets flutter accusingly on the line: traitorous, urinous.

'Don't you think I already have enough to do with your bloody sister without you pissing your fucking pants almost every night?' she screams from the top of the back steps.

There's really no answer to this question. Not one I can ever think of anyway.

'Take those off – they're probably all pissy, too,' she indicates my school shorts, 'and go and stand on the washing chair.' A rickety broken old thing under the clothes line where she rests her basket as she trades wet clothes for dry.

My father takes up residence in this chair during the summer months – when he's home that is – to smoke cigarettes and drink beer as he watches my sister stomp on snails and pull the heads off the wild daisies we call a garden.

One of my mother's many unique qualities is the stentorian range of her voice. The kids who live either side of my house easily hear her reproach float over the fence as they, too, begin to arrive home for the day.

For afternoon entertainment, there's nothing they like better than to take up positions in the trees overlooking our yard, nibbling their freshly baked biscuits or shiny washed fruit. Sometimes they throw apple cores or stones or acorns at me. They always throw insults.

'You can stand up there till the bloody sheets are dry,' my mother decrees, slamming the door shut like a slap. That always gets a big laugh from the Greek chorus either side.

And there I stand, centre stage, trying to pull my school shirt down over my underpants, my bare legs shivering whether it's windy or not.

Sometimes in the colder weather the sheets won't dry, of course, and I'll have to stand there till bedtime.

My father used to describe this peculiar punishment as 'enjoying the wee breeze'. 'Show some heart, Son,' he'd say when he'd arrive home and discover his son standing like a scrawny scarecrow in the back yard with his knees knocking together. Then he'd shake his head with disappointment, 'Get out of the wee breeze and show some fucking heart.'

Perversely, this vain admonishment sometimes loosened my accursed bladder a second time. And as the hot yellow liquid ran down my legs, I would stare up into the heartless sky and pray for some kind deity to deliver me the organ I so sorely lacked.

'Why do you think you're telling me this story, Guy?' Dr Blakely asked.

At the same time that coolcams was hotting up, and as a result of my recent conversations with Lucy and Bill, I'd selected another name off Susanna's shrink list. But this time the name was for me.

'Because you asked me about my mother.'

Jesus – Psychotherapy 101! I wondered if she was going to ask me to draw a picture for her as well: '*Here's me and here's my big, bad mommy.*'

'Yes, Guy, but you could have told me any number of stories about your mother. Why did you choose that particular one?'

How should I know? She was the professional – why couldn't she tell me?

Still, she was kinda cute in a prissy, well-groomed sort of way. Like Tony Soprano's shrink.

'I suppose it seems sort of dramatic and memorable. I don't know – it's just stayed with me for some reason. Like a bad penny.'

I took a sip of water.

'And how do you think having a mother like that has affected your relationship with other women? With Mia, for example?'

Wow! She didn't waste any time, this one. 'Um, well . . . Mia's entirely different, of course. Or else I wouldn't have married her.'

I smiled. But she didn't smile back. She'd no doubt already heard all the stupid wife and mother jokes in the universe.

'Different how?'

'Well obviously Mia doesn't torture or beat me . . .' I paused. Mia had, in fact, hit me on a few occasions when her temper had got the better of her. With her fists flailing like a little ninja warrior, she'd once even given me a black eye. And I was sure she felt like beating the shit out of me lately.

Doctor Blakely raised her eyebrow like a drawbridge going up. 'How about beating you up *emotionally*, then?'

I looked at my watch: fortunately there was only ten minutes to go.

'Um, well I suppose we have had a rough time lately . . . with the lost baby and her um, you know, *attempt*. And Esmeralda's accident, of course. Mia's been a little temperamental. I suppose we both have.'

'So how *has* Mia been treating you then?'

It took me a full thirty seconds to come up with 'Hmm . . . A walking Finland springs to mind. She used to be Fiji.'

But Blakely didn't go for the national metaphors. She clicked her tongue. 'Guy, I should say from the very beginning here that if we're going to make any real progress in these sessions, you're going to have to learn to trust me.'

She locked a strand of auburn hair around her ear and powered on. 'Because if you're just going to keep meeting me with a wall of wordplay, jokes and sarcasm, then there is only so much we will ever be able to achieve together.'

I squirmed. I knew she was right, but it was hard for me to talk about my feelings. I'd never really done it before – even with Mia.

I tried again – just for her. 'Um OK, sorry. Well then, I would say that Mia's been uncommunicative, cold . . . antagonistic, and even hostile sometimes.' I blew out a big lungful of air.

'Good. Go on . . .'

That was *good*? I soldiered ahead. 'A-and I think she blames me for a lot of stuff. I get the feeling she thinks that we would have been better off staying at home. In Australia.'

She leaned forward. 'Perhaps if she is – and you may just be experiencing it that way – she's blaming you unfairly?'

I suddenly felt about Dr Blakely the way I felt about Kim Novak: warm, loving, needy.

I wanted to float over and nuzzle her.

'Even more importantly, you seem to be blaming yourself for things you had absolutely no control over, Guy.'

It was love: pure, unadulterated, unbridled affection. I wanted to stay talking to her for ever. She was like a drug in a dress.

'Um, Dr Blakely, there's something else I wanted to discuss with you. Some things about my son.'

'I'm sure you do. And I'm sure the way *you* are at the moment will be having a major effect on how *he* is. So we need to get you healthy so you can be a good father for him.'

She stood up and reached for her invoice book. 'But I'm afraid that'll have to wait till next week.'

*

I was looking after Callum again while Mia was out seeing a Broadway revival of *The Real Thing* with Susanna.

Presumably they'd be making some more 'Mia leaving Guy' plans during the interval.

I wished I could have gone to the play myself and lapped up Stoppard's dazzling bon mots and dramatic tricks. But here I was, home alone with my son instead.

He was standing on the arm of 'the Esmeralda Sofa' as I now thought of it.

'Get down please, Callum.' I raised my glass at him, sloshing a little Jack Daniels on the carpet.

Without Esmeralda around to supervise me any more, I'd been 'swimming from the top of the bottle to the bottom' rather more frequently these past few weeks. 'Please, get down from there.'

But he was muttering something to himself. It sounded like 'Daddy gotta pay Daddy gotta pay Daddy gotta pay Daddy gotta pay Daddy gotta pay.' He didn't seem to hear me.

He was holding the new curtain cord in one hand – we'd asked the Olcott for a new, more user-friendly curtain set-up – and his beloved Buzz Lightyear doll in the other. Buzz also had a cord: you pulled it and it made him say things like 'Never tangle with a space ranger, my friend' or 'I don't think we're in the Gamma Quadrant any more'.

'Get down please, Callum.' I raised my voice.

Callum blinked. But it was Buzz who responded: 'I could fly around this room with my eyes closed!'

Through the dim light from the ever-flickering art deco lamp, the doll's eyes suddenly glowed hot chartreuse with an evil black pit burning at their centre. The thing shot out of Callum's hand and rocketed across the room toward me, arms outstretched, just like in *Toy Story*.

Callum laughed to see Buzz fly. '*To infinity and beyond*!' he cried, echoing the doll's famous catchcry.

'Shit!' It knocked the glass clear out of my hand,

smashed into the wall behind me and fell to the floor. 'Callum – stop it!' I screamed.

He climbed down off the sofa and looked up at me, frightened. His lower lip was trembling. 'Don't yell me, Daddy. It's just Buzz flying . . .'

I turned around to where the doll had fallen. Its eyes still on fire, it looked like it was sizing me up for a second attack. Then it spoke again: 'Look at my impressive wingspan.'

I stood between Callum and the evil toy, holding up my arms.

Then it twitched threateningly again: '*I have a laser and I will use it.*'

The fucking thing was alive.

'Callum, quick! Run! Go down the alligator to Michael! L for lobby – go!'

There was an acrid, burning smell. The doll twitched even more violently, now knocking its head insanely against the wall like a mental patient in a padded room, and fixed me again with its hellfire stare. My first instinct was to run downstairs to Michael after Callum. Instead, I grabbed the coverlet off the couch and threw it over the now-berserk Space Ranger.

Knocking over the coffee table and everything on it, I scooped up the thrashing bundle and ran to the window. With one hand, I tried to lift the latch through the heavy new curtain. With the other, I tried to hold onto the crazed wild creature I'd just trapped.

I managed to part the curtain, but the window wouldn't

budge. And I was afraid to let go of the snarling, writhing thing in my other hand. I looked around for something heavy to smash the glass with. A chair? Too heavy. A book? Too light.

I ran back towards the hall. I grabbed the fire extinguisher off its hook and slammed the bundle hard into the wall next to it for good measure.

I jumped up onto the Esmeralda Sofa and bounced down to the end. I swapped the bundle to my left hand and swung the extinguisher back and up behind me like a golfer preparing to tee off.

I heard a sniffle: it was Callum – still cowering in the far corner behind the table.

'Don't yell me again, Daddy! I just sayed that you gotta play with me and throwed Buzz to you . . . But now he's not working proply.'

'Go-ooo!!!' I screamed, my voice trailing him as he ran crying and jabbering down the hallway and out the front door.

But then, just as I was about to extinguish the window, the bundle stopped moving.

Trembling, I held it up to my ear and listened. Nothing.

Buzz suddenly seemed to have lost all his frenzied energy. I stepped down off the couch and gingerly placed the bundle on the carpet and stomped my foot on it. Not a peep.

I got down on my knees, raised the extinguisher high up above my head and brought it down on the inert outline of the doll as hard as I could. The metal container bounced back into my forehead, almost knocking me out.

But the bundle still didn't move. Putting a palm to my throbbing head, I lifted the bottom of the bundle and tipped the thing out.

Buzz looked up at me with vacant, dead, cloth eyes. He was just a plain old doll again.

Malfunction or Mephistophelean?

I needed to be sure.

I raced to the kitchen and came back with the carving fork. I plunged it deep into the doll's chest as if it was some small astronaut vampire that required a stake through its solar heart to finish it off. I watched the fork swaying gently from side to side as I refilled my glass with shaking hands.

It was then I felt someone standing behind me. It was Callum – still shaking and whimpering – holding the hand of one of the Irish maids who serviced our apartment. She looked askance at the empty bottle of Jack, the scattered cushions and newspapers, the upturned coffee table, the skewered doll and the sweating, still-panting man on his knees keeping watch over it.

'Mr Russell?' she even stopped chewing her gum for a moment. 'What in the good lord's name is going on here?'

Love to Love Ya, Baby

The next morning, Bill dumped a bulky J.C. Penney bag on my desk.

Given my recent nine rounds with Buzz, I eyed it with a degree of trepidation.

'It's only books, man,' Bill said. 'Don't worry, they won't bite.'

I pulled the first one out: *Hostage to the Devil* by Malachi Martin.

'Although they may just hijack your soul and drag you straight down to Hell!'

I pulled out the next two: *The Exorcist* by William Peter Blatty and *People of the Lie: The Hope for Healing Human Evil* by M. Scott Peck, MD. Then there was *An Exorcist Tells His Story* by Father Gabriele Amorth and the final volume, *Beat the Devil: A Modern History of Exorcism in America* by Randall Maddox.

I looked dumbly at Bill. 'For your alleged novel, dummy!' he clapped his hands together. 'I thought you wanted to write the next *Omen*!'

Since we'd come back from Arcadia, I'd half-heartedly surfed the net for subjects such as 'demonic possession in children'. Bill had looked over my shoulder one early evening and declared, 'Typical copywriter: always researching – but never actually writing – his alleged novel.'

'Oh yes, sorry,' I said, picking up Father Amorth's book and turning it over. 'Of course. Thank you. Where did you get them all?'

'My father gave them to me last year when I went to visit him.' Bill replied. 'He was beefing up on his occult studies.'

'Well thanks. I look forward to . . . learning from them.'

Bill was flicking through *The Exorcist*. 'You know, my Dad once told me that William Peter Blatty once appeared on Groucho Marx's TV Show, *You Bet Your Life,* back in the fifties and won 10,000 bucks.'

The demon spirit featured on *The Exorcist's* cover looked just like an ultrasound photo.

*

'So how have you been feeling this week?'

I shrugged. She was being paid a king's ransom to enquire about my well-being, so forgive me for being a little dubious about her sincerity.

'A little anxious, I suppose.'

That was all she was getting. I really didn't feel like doing all this psycho-bullshit today.

'You know Freud said that anxiety is the only emotion that doesn't deceive.'

'Yes, but maybe he was lying.'

Blakely leaned back in her Mirra chair and rolled her hazel eyes behind her Tom Ford bifocals. 'Guy, we've spoken about this before: you often use harsh humour – and it's often directed against yourself – to mask how you're really feeling.'

'If you knew how I was really feeling, you'd crack jokes, too.'

She now looked directly at me. 'Draw me a picture of your family,' she instructed, thrusting a fat blue Pentel at me.

I couldn't believe it: today she really was going to ask me to draw a picture. I shrugged again. Drawing would waste some interrogation time at least.

'My new family or my old family?'

'Your old family.'

'I'm a writer not an art director, but anyway . . .'

I slowly completed my rudimentary family portrait, then handed the sheet back to her.

My faceless parents were either side of centre – about two centimetres apart – and my sister, Raine, was rocking back and forth in her own little world bottom right.

I could sense Blakely sigh a little.

'Anything wrong? I told you I wasn't an art director.'

She rubbed her forehead. 'There's no right or wrong, Guy. Some people draw their family as a unit; all together. Some don't. But I'd like to know where *you* are in this picture?'

I hadn't included myself. I hadn't realized I was meant to. Maybe it was a trick question?

'In my room probably. Trying to stay out of trouble.'

Outside, the sky looked all bruised and broken up. Clouds bunched together like dirty old men in raincoats while a water tower on top of the adjacent building loomed grey and grim – like a sarcophagus.

I looked back into the room. Dr Blakely had put her

fingertips together and was holding them up to her lips. She seemed to do that whenever I gave her something juicy.

'All right, so now draw me your "new family".'

But I was onto her this time. I drew Mia, Callum and me all standing happily together, smack dab in the middle of the page. I even drew a little smiley face on Mia's belly.

This time, Blakely looked perplexed. She pointed at the little face.

'What's happening here?'

'It's another joke, I'm afraid. Callum used to draw a smiley face on Mia's bare belly.'

Her headlight eyes were blinding me now. 'But Mia doesn't have that belly any more, does she, Guy? And yet you've drawn her as if she does?'

I really had no idea why I'd drawn Bubby. I wished she'd leave me alone with all her stupid fucking questions.

'Guy?'

I decided I didn't like her so much today. She'd done something different with her hair that didn't suit her. She looked a little tired.

Plus, I was in an evil mood and felt like she was baiting me.

'So what?' I growled.

She gave me a few moments.

'You know, Guy, anger is usually masking something else much deeper. Like grief or loss. That's why you need to work through it. To get behind the mask . . . '

She was still going on about 'getting behind the mask', as if I were holding something back.

Truth be told, I'd wanted to tell her about the incredible events involving Callum over the past few months – and which I'd almost been able to get my head around because things had appeared to settle down for a short period of time after Arcadia – but just hadn't been able to find the right way to broach the subject.

Maybe that was why I'd drawn Bubby – as some sort of subconscious strategy? Callum seemed connected to Bubby in some mysterious and malevolent way, and introducing her into the discussion was the lead-in I needed?

But in recent weeks my terrifying Callum experiences seemed to be gaining in momentum, and I was again unable to make any sense of these events – even to myself.

So I still couldn't go there.

From the couch to the shoot for our commercial.

'Mia's going home.' I told Lucy.

'Jesus, Guy! When?' Was there some barely disguised joy in her question?

'In about ten days. She's taking Callum with her.'

'Oh God. What are you going to do?'

Bill had a quiet word with our female director – a frizzy-haired, highly strung little firecracker – who then instructed the actor playing the head detective to bring the note up closer to his face, rather than holding it at waist-height to read it.

'Dunno. It's beyond me.'

The actor did another take. He was still holding the note too low. Lucy squeezed my hand. 'Maybe you two should try some counselling?'

'Been there, failed that.'

Two of the coolcams clients – the older, fatter VC and the twenty-something CEO – looked at me uncertainly. I'd laughed too loud. *They* were worried about their precious ad baby – so why wasn't their creative director? In fact, for a while now they'd all been acting somewhat distant toward me.

'Don't worry, guys,' I whispered. 'We'll nail it!'

'Quiet on set!' the director yelled again.

'Oh dear,' Lucy said through her shine-in-the-dark teeth.

The actor did it right. Then he did it even righter on the next take. And the next one. We finally had a coolcams commercial.

'That's a wrap!' The director slumped down in her chair and clapped. 'Congratulations, people.'

'In the can, baby,' Bill's voice cracked with fatigue.

People already had their coats on. The director's assistant was pouring mid-priced champagne into paper cups.

Lucy leaned into me in the darkness. 'Would a slow, comfortable screw make you feel better?'

Compared to Mia – even unpregnant, unencumbered, non-depressed Mia – sex with Lucy was sharp, fast and brutal. It had a quicksilver, electric quality to it that reminded me of the down and dirty sex I used to have in my twenties when I was coming down off speed or coke.

In fact, Lucy was a wildcat with a very healthy and vivid fantasy life.

She loved to turn all the lights off in her apartment, put candles out and fuck standing up, on the floor, on the edge of her bed or over a sofa arm. She loved to slowly strip to a cranked-up 'Closer' by Nine Inch Nails or Donna Summer's breathy fuck-anthem 'Love to Love Ya, Baby' as she groaned and gyrated around me. Sometimes purring, sometimes screaming, Lucy would willingly abandon herself to pure primeval lust.

She also enjoyed role-playing, blindfolds, handcuffs, collars, dildos, anal sex, and talking dirty. 'I want to be your dirty girl' was usually the way she began proceedings. She used to love it when I slung her wet panties around her neck like a bridle, pulling her head down to feast on my cock and calling her a 'hungry little whore'. On a number of occasions, she asked me to handcuff her hands to the legs of her dining table while she lay face up across it wearing a sleeping mask she'd purloined from American Airlines with her open, pleading mouth tilted backwards to meet me.

'Fuck me everywhere!' she'd stage-whisper.

She had no inhibitions that I could discern and I was more than happy to match her recklessness. She also liked to wipe herself with her panties afterwards and give them to me as a kind of titillating trophy that I could enjoy later.

In fact, the only thing she wouldn't do was missionary position, which she dismissed as 'male inferior'.

She handed me a joint.

'You know, Guy, it's funny but even though I live for my career, I'd like to have a baby, too, some day.' Her body was slick with sweat.

'Babies are cute,' I said, drawing back and coughing a little, 'but sometimes not strong.'

'I know, you poor thing,' she gently squeezed my foot. 'How are you going with your therapy round all that stuff?'

How did she know about my fucking therapy? 'Did Bill tell you I was seeing someone? That bald-headed arse-hole, he told me he wouldn't say anything!'

'Don't be angry with Bill – I made him tell me. He's worried about you, and so am I. And so is Anthony – when he has the time.'

I took another long, slow toke. The end glowed orange, black and white in the candlelight.

'Well, funnily enough, Madam Inquisitor doesn't spend much of her time on recent developments. She seems much more interested in what happened to me when I was a kid.'

'But that's good!' Lucy enthused. 'My aunt's a shrink in DC – boy do they need them down there. And she says that *everything* – the way we act, the people we choose, the way we respond to traumatic situations and life in general – all goes back to our early childhood development, even infancy. Maybe even *before* infancy.'

*

Callum's little blackboard was blocking my view of the TV. He was already in bed and Mia was staring dumbly at *Letterman*, doing a final lap of her Chardonnay. I leaned forward and swivelled the blackboard to the right with my toe and saw that something new had been drawn on the other side.

It was the figure of a man approaching the spread-eagled figure of a woman on a chair. Expertly rendered in different coloured chalks, the depiction was much more impressive than mere childish stick figures. There seemed to be a computer on a desk in the background and, now that I looked more closely, I could see the man was sporting an enormous erection. On the bottom right of the board, someone had chalked the words 𝐟𝐮𝐜𝐤 𝐲𝐨𝐮!

I blinked and then felt Mia staring hard at me over the rim of her glass. 'Are you fucking with me?' I asked her.

'What do you mean?' she said. She tugged at the ugly brown coverlet with the black moons that had once again slipped off the crest of the couch.

I punched the board hard. 'Still the frustrated artist, eh, Mia? Are you fucking with me?'

'Am. I. Fucking. With. You?' She repeated each word slowly for maximum sardonic effect. She stood up unsteadily, reached into the top pocket of her shirt and leaned towards me.

'Am I fucking with you?' she said again. 'No, Guy, I'm not fucking with you.' A spluttering Vesuvius approached Pompeii. 'But it certainly seems like you're fucking with SOMEONE!'

And with that, Mia flung Lucy's scrunched-up purple panties into my face and tipped the dregs of her wine over my bowed head.

The Idiot

At the end of the second week of May, my Australian friends Jim and Nadine hit Manhattan like a meteor.

I'd completely forgotten they were coming until Anthony stuck his head in my office on Friday afternoon and announced that 'Sid and Nancy' – as he called them – were cooling their heels out in reception.

Anthony had met Jim and Nadine a couple of times back in Melbourne, but they were never really destined for his Rolodex. Although Anthony could shoot the shit with almost anyone, Jim and Nadine were a little too edgy for him, a bit too rock 'n' roll.

'Can't wait to meet 'em!' Bill enthused for the very same reason.

Over his circuitous and endlessly entertaining career, Jim had been a soap opera actor, manager of a U2 cover band, a game show host, a Winnebago salesman and, more recently, a much-in-demand voice-over artist.

In his early TV incarnations, Jim was always the good looking but not-quite-good-looking-enough leading man's best friend. He was like a big, friendly bear. His speaking voice was as deep as a cave and his laugh shook you like an approaching avalanche. It was often prefaced by the warning rumble: '*Ya know what?* and ended with a loud 'HA HA HA!'

I first met Jim when I auditioned him for some radio spots for a new Australian beer brand I was working on. '*A really cool mate*' was the sign-off line he had to deliver, and that's exactly what Jim became when we went out for drinks after the session.

I'd known Nadine only slightly before she hooked up with Jim. After ten years of 'rooting around in the regionals', she had finally worked her way up to the exalted position of music director at one of Melbourne's top FM stations. '3 NNN!' she'd yell after a few champagnes and a line or two of white mischief. 'That's *Nadine, Nadine, Nadine!*'

To get ahead in what she described as an industry of 'big swingin' dicks and buckets of bullshit', Nadine had developed a powerful persona as self-defence: half sex kitten, half rabid bulldog. 'My bite is worse than my bark,' she was fond of saying. In honour of her star sign, she had a scorpion tattoo slinking down the middle of her back, with the sting strategically positioned near her tail. Jim sometimes called her Nasty Arse. Only Anthony called her Nancy.

'4 p.m. Friday: beer o'clock. Pens down and pucker up, Guysville!' Nadine lifted one high heel off the ground to reach up and kiss me on the lips.

Then Bill slunk out, rubbing his head as he did when he was shy – which never lasted too long. 'Hi, I'm Bill,' he said, extending his hands effusively. 'You must be Guy's carers from Australia. We're so glad you're here – did you have a good flight?' He patted my shoulder like a kindly psychiatrist and suddenly became very serious, shook his head and looked down at his shoes. 'Our boy Guy's made a lot of progress since he arrived here. But there's still so much more work to do.'

Jim and Nadine stared at Bill as if he was insane. Then they got it and began to laugh so loudly that two or three of our hard-working VPs stuck their heads out of their offices at the commotion. Terry the Terrible even held his finger up to his lips as if to shush us.

'Come on, Bill,' Nadine ordered, locking her arm round his. 'Let's get the party started.'

Unfortunately my other drinking partner, Lucy, had gone home early and wouldn't be joining us. She'd been feeling a little queasy.

A number of hours of drinking later, Johnny Cash chuckled his way through the final verse of 'A Boy Named Sue' and the jukebox suddenly cranked up a Richter point or two. The Village Idiot bar was now officially bursting its britches.

Before we'd gone inside, Nadine had spotted a dreadlocked drug dealer shivering on the corner in a natty three-piece suit and dragged us up a dangerous-looking alley, where we'd snorted fat lines of coke off the lid of a rusty old iron drum.

'Jet lag begone!' Nadine threw her head back and howled like a coyote. 'Just like the old Barbie Benders, eh, Guy?'

The edges of the lid were sharp and jagged. 'Yes, as long as we don't catch tetanus off this drum.' I took a deep hoover myself and immediately felt a glorious whoosh of narcotic relief: this stuff was certainly the real deal. The worries of the week, of my entire time in New York in fact, blew away in a nano-second.

Only Bill declined, saying, 'I prefer beer to coke these days: I have no need to turbo-charge my many anxieties and insecurities.'

Maybe I should have taken Bill's lead and stuck to beer. But then I thought: what the hell – maybe some reckless R & R with my decadent old friends could help me forget about life for a while? It was worth a try.

Now safely inside the Idiot, Nadine, Jim and I were still exchanging knowing, powder-powered smiles when a growing murmur went through the crowd.

'Uh-oh,' Bill said. 'This is where the interesting part of the night begins. Take a look at ole Tommy, will ya?'

Dressed like a lumberjack, the black-bearded, bear-like owner of the pub was shaking a can of Pabst furiously up and down and roaring along to the music. He then put the whole can in his mouth, crushed it with his teeth and chugged the entire contents. People cheered. So did we. 'But this is the real fun part,' Bill warned us. 'You better start singin'!'

It was a song I only vaguely recognized. 'What is it?'

'It's called "You Don't Even Call Me by My Name",' Bill advised. 'And you better sing up or Ten Ton Tommy might piss on you!'

It was true. A clearing had formed in the middle of the floor because Tommy was whirling 360-degrees with one massive hand aiming his chubby-looking penis out of his fly at anyone who looked as though they weren't sharing his passion for the song.

'You take us to all the best places, mate!' Jim clapped me on the shoulder.

'Shoot to kill!' Nadine cried, as she distributed another round of shooters. The song finished and Tommy clumsily zipped up his pants. The crowd breathed a collective sigh of relief and clapped the finale of his vulgar one-man show.

'So I don't have to do a "Tommy" myself, where's the Ladies in this place?' Nadine asked. 'In fact, is there even a Ladies?'

'It's not really a toilet – more a portal directly to hell,' Bill replied. 'Why do you think Tommy pisses out here? I strongly advise an elegant lady like you to deport yourself instead to the much more salubrious and hygienic facilities at Hungry Jacks three doors down. It's a lot, lot safer,' he pushed back his chair. 'Hey, maybe I'll join you. So to speak.'

'So how was your trip?' I asked Jim as the others left us.

'Shit music but great fun,' Jim said. 'Naddy was off her tree most of the time with her record company buddies – I don't think she ever saw daylight while we were there. In fact, she's probably still flying.'

'So how did you amuse yourself while she was out playing?'

'It was great, actually. Bit of windsurfing, and a lot of just sitting by the pool with my book.'

'What were you reading?'

'*No Logo* by Naomi Klein. You heard of it? It's a bit

negative about our day jobs, I suppose. Makes you feel a bit guilty. But it really makes you think.'

'No, I still haven't read it. I have a hard enough time at work as it is without having to hate myself for doing it. Mia's been reading it, though.'

'So how is the wife holding up after your ... disappointment last year?' Jim asked. 'And, just as important, how are *you* travelling, my fine feathered friend? Have you guys managed to settle in yet or what?'

'Oh, we have our ups and downs, like anybody. Just a few more downs at the moment.' I wasn't ready to go into any detail. 'So how are you guys getting on?'

'Us?' Jim leaned back, possibly relieved to move onto safer territory. 'Oh you know us, mate: extra-marital equals extra fun.'

Jim and Nadine had had an open sexual arrangement for years. They were allowed to sleep with other people if the situation presented itself. In earlier years, they even encouraged the experimentation so they could enjoy talking about the liaison together afterwards.

Jim sighed a little. 'Like anything, the novelty soon wears off. Now she gets more pissed off when I don't get jealous!'

'Lucky you,' I said. 'Mia's a bit more old-fashioned than that.'

I didn't mention Lucy.

'She's a good girl though, your Mia,' Jim said. 'She certainly helped get you back on the straight and narrow all those years ago.' He blew a crooked smoke ring. 'I really hope the ... baby thing ... is something you guys can get over.'

'Thanks, mate,' I said, standing up. 'We're doing our best.' Although, in reality, I felt as though my 'best' was a good four or five years behind me. 'Wish me luck – I'm going to brave the Idiot's facilities.'

'You idiot! I'll man the fort.'

Bill was right: the toilet was an absolute shithole. The stomach-turning stench, rotting wood panels and cracked mirror put me in mind of the makeshift latrine on Captain Olav's leaky old trawler. The graffiti was strangely serious and thoughtful, as if massive alcohol intake had helped certain patrons achieve higher levels of philosophical or transcendental awareness. The multi-coloured hand basin looked and smelled as though it also doubled as a second toilet for those looking for some quick relief, while the naked light above the mirror crackled and buzzed like a fat predatory insect.

There was no urinal (aside from the aforementioned basin), so I pushed open the broken saloon style door to the cubicle itself: the light switch to this foul, fetid chamber hung off the doorjamb by its twisted wires so you only had the outside light to navigate your ablutions by. There was no toilet roll holder, let alone paper. The handle end of a toilet brush was sticking out of the balsa wood wall at a 90-degree angle while there was no top on the empty cistern and no button to push even if you dared to. There were black, chubby leech-like things swimming butterfly in the rusty gurgling water in the bowl itself.

I unzipped my fly. As my torrent of piss joined the cesspool below, I heard strange whisperings from the 'bathroom' outside.

Make me a cuppa, ya lazy bastard.

Do I have to bloody do everything?

I miss your sister but I'd never miss you.

My piss kept flowing but my heart stopped.

I pushed the cubicle door open a fraction.

The electrical sockets above the washbasin were sparking and smoking as if they were about to explode.

Then they started smiling at me.

You're a disgrace.

You'll never be anything.

You're useless.

And then the whispers became hysterical screams of laughter.

I almost knocked Bill and Nadine over as I burst out of the Idiot's front door into the cold night air. I needed another drink desperately, but I needed to clear my head and escape even more.

Bill just presumed that I'd had second thoughts about using the Idiot's putrid WC. 'Uh, Guy, ya might want to do up your zip before you go down there, buddy,' he called after me, guffawing.

'Cos unlike here, they have hygiene standards at Hungry Jacks!'

Davy Jones' Lockers

Clubs

Hell or High Water

APT | Find Tickets
419 W 13th St (between Ninth Ave and Washington St)
Meatpacking District | Map
212-414-4245
Subway: A, C, E to 14th St; L to Eighth Ave | Directions
http://www.aptwebsite.com
Tickets: $20

Description

'Ahoy, me hearties!' and get down and dirty to everything from hop-infused sea shanties to bowdlerized Broadway ditties and turbo-charged pirate rock. The awesomely authentic ship deck dance floor throbs with beautiful buccaneers of both sexes – NB To gain admission, you have to dress 'pirate' – while the seriously sexy staff help create a swashbuckling ambience that actively encourages debauchery. (Though be warned: the basement area known as 'Davy Jones' Lockers' is only for the seriously adventurous . . . or truly 'sea sick'!)

This month's visiting guest jock from Maui, the tastefully top-hatted Sir Orpheus, brings a treasure chest filled with fabulous funk, Hawaiian voodoo, Brazilian and Latin beats, high-end house and torrid techno. As well as all the usual 'fucked-up' sea shanties. Go to aptwebsite.com for more info.

When Tomorrow from 11 p.m.

The Hell or High Water was cleverly fitted out like the deck of a Spanish galleon, replete with a full-sized mast, curved canvas sails, small side bars masquerading as long-boats, old rusty cannons, coiled snakes of rope, rum barrels, a massive self-turning wheel behind the dance floor, Jolly Rogers (with a Jagger tongue protruding from the skull's mouth) fluttering under hydraulic fans, and lithe semi-clad club staffers scampering across the rigging like so many sea monkeys on heat. There was a prow over-hanging the main bar and galley with an evil-eyed Medusa figurehead threatening to lash out at the revellers below. On a huge screen on the far wall, a breeched and booted Errol Flynn came swinging down on a rope like vengeance itself.

I looked up. In the crow's nest, there was a statuesque black woman wearing only white bikini bottoms and a scarf around her head, peering through a telescope at the heaving hordes below and gyrating to 'Pirate Love' by the New York Dolls. Standing next to her, Sir Orpheus, the top-hatted DJ, was grunting like a gorilla over the chorus.

'Where do ya reckon they keep the rum rations on this tub?' Jim shouted.

'Drinks ho!' Nadine pointed ahead to the bar with the rabbit ears of her blouse. 'Follow me, landlubbers!'

I managed to lose Nadine and Jim as we swam through the crowd. When I finally reached the bar, I bought a drink with my credit card and took in my surroundings.

Pirate theme aside, the dance floor thronged and thumped under the bouncing lights like a thousand others. But when you peered into the club's darker recesses, into the cordoned-off corners or behind the 'longbars', or peeked behind the skimpy velvet curtains of the 'private cabins' on the forecastle, there was a whole other world of libertine activity going on.

I drew back the curtains on one heavily cushioned cabin and saw two stunning topless girls – one Asian, one redhead – kissing enthusiastically as they stroked each other through silky red slave girl pants. I watched them trade tongues and fingers for a while. Then I checked out the scene in the next cabin, but there were two men in British naval uniforms and wigs cosying up in there so I sauntered on another cabin or two and spied on a curly-haired blonde pirate queen in a three-cornered hat and ruffled shirt on her knees blowing a big-biceped boatswain.

'She seems to have a pretty good handle on things, old Long Sally Silver,' I said, bumping into Nadine again.

'Good to her mates,' she agreed.

'Where's Jimbo?'

'Gone to the Buoys.' She pointed with her glass across the crowd to two neon signs on the other side of the club:

Buoys and Gulls. 'I've just been in there myself – they're just separate doors leading to the same bathroom. Funny, huh?' She rubbed under her nose. 'They even have a sign in there saying 'The Dispensary' and a dealer dressed up like an admiral selling 'gun powder' and a special barrel for sniffing it off. What a hoot!' Have you got any cash on you? We might need to top up later and I don't think the admiral takes credit card.'

Just then, a captain with bad skin and a fake moustache that looked like it was stuck on upside down bumped into me, sloshed his drink and scowled. I locked eyes with him but didn't feel up to a physical confrontation in my current state.

'Why don't we head upstairs where we can hear ourselves think?' Jim suddenly reappeared. 'I'll bring the next round of rums up.'

The Upper Deck was the club's designated chill-out zone: Gianni Versace channelling Joseph Conrad. Jim and Nadine fell together into a hammock while I rolled into the one opposite, each of us slopping some rum overboard in the process.

'So did you blast your nose off with the gunpowder?' Nadine wrinkled her nose at Jim like Samantha from *Bewitched*.

'Not me,' Jim said. 'You know I've been trying to live healthier lately.'

'Oh yes – on the "New Wonder Beer & Doughnuts Diet!" Nadine scoffed. 'Well maybe we need to up the ante a bit.' Nadine flashed her naughty schoolgirl smile. She tried to sit upright in the hammock, untying her blouse, which she'd tied pirate-style as we'd entered the club.

'I've already seen your tits,' Jim said. 'And I'm sure Guy remembers them from spas gone by.'

'Yes but you haven't seen these, smart-arse!' She extracted a small plastic packet from inside her leopard-skin bra. Inside there were a number of small hexagonal-shaped blue pills with the letters PHY stamped on them.

'Where did you get *those*?!' Jim threw up his hands and looked across at me for support. 'It's like living with fucking Keith Richards in drag!'

'I brought them back from Ibiza,' Nadine said coyly.

'*Brought them back*?' Jim was incredulous. 'As what, hand luggage?'

'No, *boob* luggage: in my *bra*!'

'In your bra? We could have been arrested and jailed! For years!'

'But we weren't, were we, darling?' She sprinkled three of the little blue pills into her palm. 'So just calm down and join me in a little phantasy! That's what the "PHY" stands for.'

'What does it do?' I asked, holding my hand out.

'It's two-thirds ecstasy, one-third heroin. They're meant to fire you up and chill you out at the same time. Keith Richards would approve, I'm sure.'

Jim reluctantly held his hand out as well. 'You sure they're not Blue Meanies?'

'*You're* the only Blue Meanie round here,' Nadine laughed. 'Loosen up a little, will you? We're trying to cheer up Guysville here, remember?'

A slow song came splashing over the bulwark as we each swallowed our little blue pill.

'"Dites-moi" from *South Pacific*!' Nadine squealed with delight. 'My mum used to love musicals!' She suddenly looked beatific in the ambient light; a fallen angel. 'So, Guy, *dites-moi* what the fuck's really been going on with you and Mia and little Callum? You said some strange shit has been happening since you arrived here?'

Bill had an early brunch planned the next morning with his new Japanese girlfriend so had excused himself from coming to the club with us. Without his manic energy distracting us, I could now talk to my friends more seriously if not soberly.

So I began to tell them about our first few weeks in New York. About working with Anthony and Bill – but not about Lucy. About winning coolcams. About how everything had seemed so wonderful and shiny and new. But then, with cold, clipped words, I told them about Mia's suicide attempt and how it related to that awful night at the hospital before we'd left Australia.

As I'd told them at the time, we simply 'lost the baby' without going into any of the murky details or my part in them.

'Oh God!' Nadine said, wiping her eyes. 'You poor things. It must have been just been awful!'

Jim just shook his head and stared down through the ropes. And then, as I started to feel my inhibitions peel away, I began to tell them about the wonderful world of Callum. About him constantly reminding me of Bubby, unwilling to let her memory go. About the foetus appearing on the TV screen at Arcadia while he was sitting right there next to me on the couch; about his unnerving drawing and his disturbing little sculpture. I started to tell them about his kamikaze Buzz Lightyear doll, but checked myself when Jim broke in and said, 'Yeah, losing a baby like that is gonna do some strange things to your head.'

I suddenly realized that in our current semi-coherent, quasi-euphoric condition, Jim and Nadine simply wouldn't get what I was trying to explain. That all the incredible Callum-inspired occurrences could be real and not imagined. It'd be as fruitless as a bunch of stoned, beaded hippies in New Mexico trying to convey the reality of a UFO sighting to the local redneck sheriff.

So I told them about Esmeralda's accident instead. At least that event couldn't be construed as something delusional or made-up.

'Your nanny fell and went into a fucking coma?' Nadine sat bolt upright, almost catapulting Jim out of their hammock. 'How, for Chrissakes?'

'A freak accident. She was adjusting the curtain.'

'Jesus,' Jim groaned, putting one long leg on the floor. 'You guys have really been through the bloody wringer.'

'And now you and Mia are having troubles – no wonder,' Nadine surmised, also stepping ashore. I looked down at the giant video screen. Peter Pan and Captain Hook were crossing swords as some shitty punk band that not even Nadine would recognize massacred Rod Stewart's 'Sailing'.

'It's like Sid Vicious doing "My Way",' Jim cringed,

unaware of Anthony's nickname for him. 'Let's go back to our place. This music's making me feel seasick.'

'OK, but I need to swing by the Buoys first,' I said, slipping out of the hammock. 'I'll meet you at the front door.'

The truth was that talking about everything that had gone on with Mia and Callum and Esmeralda had sent my mind spinning. I needed to take a psychic breather and be by myself for a bit, especially before the PHY started to kick in.

In the interests of cramped-cabin authenticity, the ceiling of the Upper Deck was sloped and low. As I stood up and turned around too quickly, I banged my forehead very hard on a serious crossbeam. It was exactly the same place I'd hit myself with the fire extinguisher.

Lucky I'd had a few drinks.

Apart from the couple fucking in the corner, the 'Buoys' and 'Gulls' was empty. But then, as I unzipped, in the mirror I saw the admiral that Nadine had mentioned walk in behind me holding a small wooden treasure chest. He resumed his station under the Dispensary sign, took a clear plastic bag filled with coke out of the chest and sprinkled long white lines out across the polished top of the powder keg.

As he straightened up the lines with a little gold dagger, he caught my eye in the mirror. 'Be lookin' for some gunpowder, sailor?' he asked with a wink. 'Fresh from the Spanish Main.'

*

On the three days a week that my grandmother took care of Raine, my mother worked at an illegal abortion clinic — they were pretty much all illegal back in those days.

Located in a separate dirty little building in the overgrown backyard of a suburban medical clinic, it was euphemistically called 'The Dispensary'.

Because that's what they did in there: they 'dispensed' with sad little lives.

I only went there once: my father dropped me there unexpectedly one day because he had to attend an urgent 'business meeting' that somehow involved the fishing rods and slabs of Melbourne Bitter hidden under the picnic rug in the back seat of his green FJ Holden.

I sat there for hours in that grey little waiting room — which wasn't much bigger than the sodden welcome mat — flicking through tattered copies of the Women's Weekly and TV Week and watching my mother walk weeping young women to the gynaecological gallows. A photograph of a rose-cheeked young Princess Elizabeth being crowned hung crookedly on the wall, as if giving her sad and tacit sanction to the unfortunate business she saw before her.

My mother wore a puce-coloured hospital apron and had her hair tied back in a hard little bun. She hit me with a rolled-up magazine whenever she wanted me to give up the chair to a new red-eyed admission and told me to shut up when I asked what the doctor — though in his careworn gabardine cardigan and scuffed Hush Puppies he didn't really look like much of a doctor — was doing to the yelping young woman behind the door.

Sometimes my father would come home smelling of infidelity and goad my mother with a voice thick with beer, dark with guilt: 'So 'ow were things down at the hatpin factory today, eh, Vile-et?'

He'd then point his bottle at Raine, rocking happily in the corner.

'*Looks like one of 'em got away.*' *And then turning the bottle to me like a rifle,* '*Maybe two.*'

Raine and I were related in his self-loathing repugnance for us: a girl without hope and a boy without heart.

'*Stop it,*' *Violet would say wearily.* '*Just stop it, Ray.*' *She'd start fiddling with my sister's hair.*

But this was just the preamble, not the kicker. The kicker was Ray grabbing the last beer out of the fridge, screeching the FJ backwards out of our driveway and disappearing for a few days.

Because that's when my mother would decide that it was high time she washed our hair.

'*Bath time!*' *she'd yell.* '*Get here now or else!*'

She'd always do Raine first.

My sister actually quite enjoyed it – she loved the water. And when my mother finally let her head up, she'd splutter and laugh at the fresh air, as happy as a porpoise. She thought it was a game.

But I knew it was no game. And I'd learned from bitter experience that hiding or trying to avoid getting my hair washed would indeed lead to a far worse '*or else*'.

Like having my hair completely shaved off. Or taking up Ray's spot in my mother's lonely bed.

Unlike Frank Sinatra, I didn't wake up in Carnegie Hall.

A couple of times I woke up in hospital with my mother peering at me with mock-concern through the grimy plastic of an oxygen tent.

''*e sometimes has asthma attacks when 'is father goes away,*' *she'd be telling some dim-witted doctor. And then she'd be smiling at me proudly like I was some kind of exotic fish in a tank.*

I used to wonder why she did it. Apart from washing away my

father's disdain, I think she liked the fact that she was killing children but then bringing them back to life.

Which was something that she obviously couldn't do at her work.

'Hey, mate, you were away with the fairies.' Fingers snapped in front of my eyes.

It was Jim. Someone had pencilled a curlicued pirate moustache under his nose.

Nick Cave was droning through the 'The Ship Song'. I was now standing outside the toilets. I had absolutely no recollection of how I'd got there. Or how long I'd been gone.

'We waited by the door for you, but you never showed up! Hey, you look a bit shaken up.' Nadine put her arm around me. 'You didn't go down to Davy Jones' Lockers, did you? Not after what Bill told us.'

According to Bill, the bowels of the club were 'dire', and only for the seriously perverted. Apparently there was a second and more expensive door charge to access the basement area, which was guarded by a dangerous-looking albino with a bandage over his eye – who traded in much more serious substances than were available from The Dispensary. Then, once you were in Davy's dungeons, any act, fetish or orifice became completely acceptable.

Most disturbing of all, there were rumoured to be cameras hidden in the walls that shot footage for execrable X-rated films that were later sold on the black market.

I looked at Nadine and shook my head slowly. But I really had no idea where I'd been for the last few minutes.

The last thing I could remember was the admiral offering me the gunpowder.

'You've probably been off thinking about you and Mia, haven't you, Guy?' Nadine said gently. 'Let's go back to our place,' she said, hustling me towards the front door of the club.

'Where are you staying?' I asked as Jim flagged a cab.

'Where else?' Nadine punched the air. 'The Chelsea!'

As we pulled away, there was an ambulance siren wailing towards the club.

I half-felt like calling one myself.

Shower scene

The phantasy crept up on you like a gorgeous harem dancer.

There was an overall sensation of lightness but not light-headedness. There was the expected expansive lovingness of the ecstasy and the blissed-out wisdom and knowingness of the smack. But in that exquisite area in between where they lay down together like lovers, there was an intense sensual pleasure that extended far beyond appreciative synapses to your whole way of being. It was like your soul got a hard-on, too. Although to describe it in merely sexual terms was to belittle the equally magnificent spiritual side of the experience. You became not just tumescent but omniscient at the same time – a walking, talking, orgasmic epiphany. So you saw things in a wholly new and more majestic light.

Jim was now a bona fide sun god, descended and temporarily slumming it on 23rd Street as he glided across the Chelsea's lobby. And God knows what the phantasy was doing to Nadine. 'Wow!' she kept repeating, 'Wow wow wow!' she chanted to the seen-it-all-before desk clerk as she sashayed towards the elevator, gyrating her arms up and down like a hyperactive back-up singer in an old Motown video.

On the wall behind the clerk, there was a battered old black-and-white TV with the sound down: Bill Clinton was giving Hillary a brotherly hug on the White House lawn.

Everything sparkled and glittered and shone, even your thoughts – *especially* your thoughts. That's what the naysayers never understood about drugs: sometimes they equalled love. And this one truly was phantastic.

Somehow we found the room. Third floor, end of the corridor. It was all pink inside, like a scallop shell. Although, if you tilted your head to the side, it immediately turned pale-blue or purple.

Jim had sunk deep into the couch's embrace, still wearing a supremely satisfied grin. He was obviously experiencing some glorious private nirvana that not even the twangy sappiness of Shania Twain coming from the radio could sully. Nadine had disappeared into the bathroom what seemed hours ago.

I hoisted myself out of the cosy womb of the cracked leather armchair and went to investigate. Pushing open the door, I walked into a cumulus of steam. 'Nadine? Are you in here? Or have I really died and gone to heaven?'

She parted the mist like she was doing breaststroke. She held a pink face cloth towards me and burst into hysterics.

'Hey, who's this?' She couldn't stop laughing.

I shook my head.

'Nancy *Sponge*-en!'

I laughed so hard it hurt my stomach.

'Hey, isn't this *gr-eaat*?' she asked, attempting her best country accent in homage to the background music. 'I had a shower and every single part of my body was like a pleasure zone. You should have one, too!'

I looked at her – it was hard not to. All she was wearing was a tiny pair of black knickers that matched her glistening wet hair. 'You look like a bit of a pleasure zone yourself,' I said.

It was then she noticed the bruise blueing on my forehead from the heavy bump I'd received on the Upper Deck. 'Oh, you poor baby,' she cooed and tenderly touched it. She bit her lip hard and touched it again and then ran a delicious finger all the way down to my lips. 'You poor, sexy baby.'

Nadine and I had shared a few moments of sexual tension years ago, but I'd always blocked them out because of my friendship with Jim. Tonight, however, the rules of engagement, the rules about everything, seemed open-ended. We *were* our desires, our ids, our pure animal selves. Any restrictive thoughts of right or wrong or morality had evaporated into the mist.

I lifted Nadine up onto the vanity unit by her gym-built buttocks, sweeping away the dusty little complimentary shampoo bottles and soaps. 'You are *so fucking sexy*,' I grunted. Every single word felt itself like a hungry, needy thrust, like my tongue was my cock.

Nadine felt it, too. 'Fuck me!' she moaned, spreading her knees with her jangly bangled hands and leaning back into the mirror. 'Jim won't mind. Just do it.'

It felt so good to talk. 'Oh yes, I *will* fuck you,' I promised, removing her black panties and lassoing them around her neck. 'But first I'm going to taste you.'

We continued swapping obscenities as I went down on my best friend's partner. It felt so safe and warm down there in the humidicrib of our lust. And given Jim's own splendid stupor on the couch, he seemed unlikely to intrude.

Nadine shuddered and shifted on her buns to open herself up even more to my hungry mouth. If I could have, I would have crawled up inside her. 'Oh wow,' she said dreamily. She tasted Moorish, smoky, exotic . . . like a delicious sweet and sour syrup.

But as she introduced some fingers, I paused to snatch a breath and looked down. There were a couple of strange red blobs spreading on the white tiles at my feet. They looked like little baby seals or dolphins.

Shiny little bleeding bath toys.

Nadine screamed with the insane pleasure of it.

*

'That's it, Guy, grab the towels.

'Now throw them in the sink.'

There are red bath towels and white ones.

The kitchen sink is filling up with cold water.

The water is turning pink because the red towels are bleeding into it.

My mother is still in her pale blue dressing gown. She's had a horrendous fight with my father earlier that morning and has been too distracted and upset to get dressed yet.

Janet Leigh in curlers.

She turns a knob on the oven. There's suddenly a funny smell and I feel a bit dizzy.

'Now grab the towels out of the water and put them along the bottom of the doors – like this.' Normally she would scream at towels dripping water onto the kitchen floor and the lounge room carpet.

'Why are we doing this, Mum?'

But she doesn't answer. She just continues sealing door cracks with the towels.

'Right. All covered? Good.' She does a quick, frantic final recce of all the doors of our brick veneer prison. She also checks all the windows to make sure they're shut fast, too. Then she prods me down the hallway. 'OK, Guy, now you go out the front door and go over the road to Nancy's.'

Our friendliest neighbour.

'Go!' she screams now, the last towel dripping in her hand to seal the door behind me.

My sister is rocking in an unusually agitated way behind her and humming quietly. My mother opens the door and pushes me out over the threshold. 'Goodbye, Guy.' She slams the door shut like a slap.

I sit on the front porch for a few bewildering moments, unsure of my next move.

It's a still Saturday morning and the sun is shining. 'A perfect day for the gee-gees!' my father had said before the argument with my mother.

I walk over the road to Nancy's and knock on her front door. A kettle whistles from somewhere behind her like a parrot squawking in a jungle.

'What is it, Guy?' she asks.

I must look upset. I'm only a kid.

'Umm, Mum's locked all the doors and covered them up with towels. A-a-and she's kicked me out of the house.'

I'm sort of embarrassed. And my head feels kind of woozy.

Nancy lifts her nose, squints through her glasses and looks across at our strangely silent, now hermetically sealed house.

A couple of minutes later, Nancy has recruited a red-headed man from a few doors down whom we hardly know. He smashes our kitchen window, lets himself in and the gas out.

He cuts his hands on the glass and leaves bloody handprints all over the sink and cupboards.

And drops little red bombs onto our shiny kitchen floor.

Chaos

I was going down.

I tilted my head forward and extended my tongue as wet, warm thighs kissed my ears. Trapped in a beautiful box canyon.

I squinted up along the lovely ridge of her body and tried to see her face through the shifting sierra of her breasts. But her chin was thrust upward and I could only make out the soft blonde epaulettes on her shoulders.

She moaned a little as I leant closer to her core and I heard a groan of pleasure escape my own lips.

But then my tongue felt something that wasn't part of her.

Something cold and clammy.

Something slick and greasy.

I opened my eyes.

There was something coming out of her.

A head.

A horrible slimy little head.

It looked up and our eyes met.

Then it smiled at me and licked its fishy lips.

I jolted awake on the bath mat, wearing nothing but a hard-on.

I pulled on my pants and noticed Nadine's clothes lying in an incriminating little bundle on the toilet seat.

The clock radio in the main room was still lachrymose with dreadful country dirges, only now at a much lower volume. The display told me it was 1:09, but I had no idea what day or meridian it was.

'Well it looks as though you two had a bloody good time.' Jim was looking up at me from the couch. But not like a best friend should.

'Hi, mate,' I said weakly.

He wasn't just looking daggers at me, but scimitars. 'Only Women Bleed, eh mate?' he said, swinging his big legs onto the floor. He stretched his arms upwards and grunted while his eyes grew colder. And then I understood. I bolted back into the bathroom and looked in the mirror. In colour counterpoint to the shiny new black and blue bruise on my forehead, my cheeks and chin were bright crimson with Nadine's menstrual blood.

I grabbed the face washer out of the shower and tried to scrub the crime off me. But it was difficult to see properly in the mirror. Someone had scrawled the letters c H a O s on it with lipstick. I walked back out, my face still stinging with shame. Jim was violently ripping open the heavy black velvet curtains. The sun smashed in and my eyelids snapped shut like clams. Jim turned up the radio just to make things worse and pretended to hum along. I sat back in the armchair I should never have strayed from.

Nadine moaned from the bedroom. 'Oh, for fuck's sake – turn the cunt-ry off!'

Jim turned it up even louder and flopped furiously back onto the couch. A few seconds later, Nadine came limping out of the bedroom wrapped in a sheet that had dried blotches of blood on it. Her smudged make-up gave her a ghastly Kabuki mask.

'Please . . . take my wife,' Jim said coldly.

'He did,' Nadine said, pulling the radio plug viciously out of the wall.

The socket glared at me knowingly.

'So what?'

'Ya know what, Naddy?' Jim replied. 'I know we still have our little "arrangement" and all – which always seems to work out better for you than me, by the way. But I didn't realize it included fucking my old best . . .' he paused and kept looking very hard at me '. . . friend. So how did you enjoy old Nasty Arse, eh, Guy? Worth the wait?'

'Grow up, Jim. It was a drug fuck. It didn't mean a thing, did it, Guy?'

Actually, it did. It meant fifteen years of friendship and trust were now all smashed and bloodied up.

'Just seems a bit unfair, that's all,' Jim sniffed at me. 'Or do I get to fuck Mia now?'

There was an excruciatingly long pause.

'Sorry, mate,' I finally said. 'We just got carried away, I suppose.'

Nadine ducked into the bathroom without making eye contact with either of us. 'Where are my fucking tampons? Hey, Guysville,' she called out much too lightly. 'Do you remember telling me about your "CHAOS Theory" last night?'

It rang a distant, disquieting bell.

Nadine stuck just her head out of the door. 'First you said that "CHAOS" stood for Cataclysm . . . Heaven – or was it Hell? Then Archangel . . . Oblivion . . . and . . . and . . . Symmetry!' She clapped her hands.

Nadine was silent for a minute. 'But then I think you said: "Callum . . . Has . . . Another . . . Older . . . Spirit." '

She wobbled back into the room in her black pants and bra.

'But then you said something even more freaky, Guy.'

She looked at me but still hadn't looked at Jim.

'You told me that what you meant by that was that you think your mother's spirit had something to do with the death of your unborn baby.

'And that she was now attacking you and Mia through Callum.'

*

I taxi-ed back to the Olcott alone.

As I was leaving the Chelsea, Nadine had issued a half-hearted invitation to maybe catch up for a quiet dinner later on, but Jim didn't second the motion. In fact, he didn't even say goodbye.

They were flying out midday the next day so that was that, I supposed.

I hung up my smoky jacket. My feet echoed down the empty hallway.

The place suddenly seemed much bigger. And quieter.

There was a letter propped up like a hand grenade against the yellow vase on the table.

Guy,

It seems that things have come to a sad, bad sort of head here. For me anyway. I just can't seem do this New York thing any more. Being here is tough for me but it <u>really</u> seems to have changed you. And not in ways I can happily relate to any more.

There's a distance between us that has been growing wider and wider for months now. And I've got absolutely no idea how we can ever start getting back to where we were, pre-New York.

I can't talk to you any more. But then again, I don't even really <u>feel</u> like talking to you. Anyway, I feel the smartest thing to do – and maybe the ONLY thing to do for <u>us</u> to have <u>any</u> sort of chance as a family in the future – is for me – and Callum – to head back home.

I'd love to leave today, if I could, but I've just found out that all of our stuff from Melbourne has just arrived and is sitting down on the fucking dock at Newark. I've instructed the shipping company to send it all back home – but it'll take a few days to be loaded onto another ship and then maybe nine-ten weeks for the return trip.

They're saying it'll arrive back first week of August, but they can't promise anything. In the meantime, I'm going away by myself for a while – Susanna's lent me the money because she thinks it's the best thing for me to do – so I can try to get my head together and when I get back become a good mother to Callum again.

But I just can't look after him at the moment – I can't even look after myself. I need to get away by myself and think and get better. Then I'll come back and get him and take him back home to Australia.

(Please don't try to find me, Guy, I don't want to see you for a while.)

So, short term, Callum is going to be staying – mostly – with Susanna and Anthony and Courtney. I think this is best given that you seem to have quite a few of your own issues at the moment (!!) and I'm not convinced that you're capable of looking after Callum properly either full time. Plus you still have your job, of course. (Though Anthony gave me a funny look when I said that??)

Anyway, I hope this arrangement doesn't cause you too many issues at work, but Anthony swears he is not taking sides and wants to support both of us. (Susanna is not quite so bipartisan – so be warned!) So if you want to see your son, how about you look after him at the Olcott (or wherever else you decide to move to??) Tuesday and Saturday nights?

That way you still get to see him a couple of times a week??? That's if you still have any interest in spending time with your so-called 'weirdo' son?? (I could say a lot of stuff here Guy about pots and kettles etc., but I'm not going to.)

Anyway, I'm sure Callum would love to keep seeing <u>you</u> – whatever strange ideas you might still be having about <u>him</u>.

I'm sorry it's come to this, Guy, I really am. And I imagine at some level, you are too. But then I'm not sure I know you nearly as well as I used to anymore.

Maybe – and it's a big maybe at this juncture – you could join us back in Melbourne when you're 'ready' and we could try to talk things through. Because I just can't talk to you here, Guy.

You seem like a completely different person.
I just feel so very, very sad.
Mia

PS I haven't given the tenants in Melbourne notice to vacate yet cos I'm not sure I'm/we're ever going back to our house. So they may as well keep paying us rent until we decide what to do with it.

PPS And it wouldn't kill you to go and visit Esmeralda sometime – she was your nanny too.

Although I'd only been gone a night, it felt like a million years.

Although I was tired beyond words, the floor seemed the only place I could be.

There was a miniature Jackson Pollock with a pickaxe busting up my brain.

The room was spinning slowly and a large black hole was opening up beneath me.

I spread out my arms, closed my eyes and simply tried to hold on.

3

Evel Knievel

Monday.

And I was already late for my own funeral.

I cocked an ear from behind the closed boardroom door:

' . . . and with coolcams' improved traction and recall coming through the TV, press and online modules, we can build off that solid base to explore other more innovative and daring extensions of the brand.'

'How about a reality TV show, for example? Remember our initial pitch TV concept? Why not produce a show where people send in all kinds of weird and wonderful real footage that they've captured on their own coolcam? Sort of like a home-made *Hard Copy*, where the coolcam owner gets to play director.'

'Sorry I'm late,' I said from the doorway.

My voice sounded strange, even to me. Like it was coming out of the blank TV screen.

Anthony, blue marker in hand, didn't – or couldn't – continue talking.

The director and the producer had apparently already shown the rough cut of the TV ad and were now sitting out the business end of the meeting out of politeness. The director scowled at me like I was a father who had missed the birth of our child. Her frizzy hair seemed to almost spark with contempt.

Bill looked at me like he didn't recognize me. Lucy looked down at her lap.

The coolcams clients, who had flown over specially from Frisco late the night before, blinked at me like security cameras and whispered something to each other.

Funny, now that I looked around at everyone I worked with, they all seemed like the biggest bunch of phonies.

Anthony hustled me out of the room and propelled me into the sterile, gleaming kitchen, shutting the door behind us.

'Guy . . . ' For once he had no idea what to say. The smile ran away from his face. He sat rigidly with his hands on both his knees, like a parole officer prepping a perp.

The electrical sockets behind him were laughing like bastards at me.

'Sorry I'm late,' I repeated dumbly. 'Callum must have done something to the clock radio.'

But the fact that I had still been up at 5 a.m. speed-reading Bill's Dad's godforsaken books and still had unabsorbed particles of Nadine's nefarious Blue Meanies scuttling around my cerebellum like turbocharged cyber-crabs hadn't made it easy for me to make the 8.30 a. m. Monday morning meeting either.

Plus, I hadn't shaved or showered since Friday. My suede jacket had ugly brown rum and Coke stains on it. Not to mention the bruise of the century I was sporting on my forehead. I must have looked a sight.

'Girly,' Anthony said again, reaching out but then pulling back his arm. It was shaking. 'You're not quite right at the moment. I think you need some help. I know you're already seeing someone, but maybe you need to ramp that up a bit.'

A ramp. That sounded like a good idea. Something I could fly a motorbike off into the wild blue yonder with. Like Evel Knievel.

'Now, Guy, I've got to get back to the meeting.' He was talking very slowly and repeating my name like I was a mental patient or something. 'It's all under control, Guy, so don't worry. They love the ad. Take some time off, I'll talk to Mia, and we'll work something out.'

'Mia's gone,' I said. But he already knew that. And I didn't give two shits about the fucking ad any more.

There was only one thing that really interested me this morning.

'Anthony?'

'Yes, mate?'

'Who wrote *You'll see* on the whiteboard?'

Baby, One More Time

Christ – when was she going to get some decent magazines for her fucking waiting room?

I picked up an antediluvian *People* with a strapping and hirsute Patrick Swayze dancing on the cover, then put it straight back down again. Then did exactly the same with the latest *Mind Monthly*: *the nation's most respected journal of psychotherapy.*

I finally unearthed a bedraggled *Scientific American* from the bottom of the pile and scanned the contents: it may as well have been hieroglyphics.

Truth be told, I was a complete science dunce. Which was also the reason why I'd avoided Terry's tricky satellite job for as long as I could. Not that it mattered any more. So I really had no idea about chaos theory or string theory or M-theory or multiverses or any of that heady Stephen Hawking stuff. God knows what I'd been dribbling on to Nadine about.

All I knew was that lately I felt like one of those accursed figures in an Escher drawing who are constantly on the move yet never actually getting anywhere because the planes of their existence keep shifting beneath their feet.

For a few moments, I couldn't even remember how I'd got to today's session. Had I walked or taken the subway?

And, bizarrely, I'd even temporarily forgotten Madame Inquisitor's surname.

I imagined there was a whole conference in that alone.

'With dissociative – or fugue states as they're sometimes called – often it's not one specific thing that causes it. More a combination of factors or events over a period of time colliding or interacting with the individual psyche of the patient.' She smiled as if to say: the more, the merrier. 'That's why some people handle traumatic or stressful events better than others.'

'I see.' But I didn't really.

'Sometimes "nothing" needs to happen in "real life" for the psyche to feel attacked or become distressed.'

I constructed my own fragile finger steeple. It wasn't the short, easy answer I was looking for.

'But that's because "real life" isn't really our real life. It's only our internal world that is truly "real".'

I looked at her blankly.

'OK then. So why have these "episodes" only started to happen to me now? Why didn't they start years ago?' Go on, answer me that, Ms Know-it-All.

Her brow furrowed into a knowing smile above her eyes. 'Well that's not to say that the psyche can't also be placed under extra stress through external or extraordinary "real-life" events. There may be a cumulative internal dysfunction building up over a period of months, years or even decades. And then something "happens"' – she parenthesized the air – 'in the everyday world that triggers a psychological crisis or meltdown.'

She fixed me with those punishing eyes. 'And that's when some patients "zone out", to use your term. In extreme cases, people can commit atrocious crimes while in a fugue state. Not long ago, for example, a man in Canada lost his job, then drove sixty miles through a blizzard to a farmhouse and murdered his in-laws for no apparent reason. Then he drove home again and carried on as if nothing had happened. Afterwards he had absolutely no recollection of the event.'

I wished I could have zoned out then and there.

A nice long drive through the snow might be fun.

'But that's an extreme case. Can you think of anything that may have triggered inner turmoil in you recently, Guy?'

'You mean apart from losing my wife, my son and now probably my job?'

Her pupils expanded slightly, ready for the kill. 'What about losing your unborn daughter?'

'Bubby – what's she got to do with it?'

'*Bubby*? I didn't realize you had a name for her.' She suddenly looked super-alert and dangerous. 'You haven't mentioned "Bubby" before, Guy?'

No I hadn't.

Because what could I possibly say that would make any sense.

Even to me.

*

It was Courtney's eighth birthday. I hadn't been invited to the party, of course, but since Saturday was one of my designated 'Callum Days', I was picking him up afterwards.

Estella the maid opened the door.

'Any news on—?'

But I already knew the answer before she looked down and shook her head. I'm sure Anthony would have had the decency to let me know if there'd been any improvement in Esmeralda's condition.

Estella looked tired. It was no wonder: she spent every day at the Johnsons', and most evenings by her second cousin's bedside. But they were much more than just relatives, of course. Esmeralda was an only child and her parents were both dead. She'd spent a lot of time with Estella growing up at her grandmother's house and then as young women the two of them had come to New York on a great adventure together.

Just like we had.

I followed Estella down the brightly lit hallway along a long, tawny tongue of Turkish carpet past a mini-gallery of Man Rays, Tannings, Smarts and Whiteleys. Mia had been openly envious of the Johnsons' small but significant Austral-American art collection.

Britney Spears *Baby, One More Time*'d from a speaker somewhere over a chorus of high-pitched screams and giggles. I heard Anthony laugh then snort like his wife, as he did sometimes after a few drinks. I found him sitting on a high stool in his gleaming, restaurant-sized kitchen with a champagne flute on the gold-flecked granite bench in front of him. He was talking to a Botoxed and bronzed East Side yummy mummy – presumably there to collect her snotty daughter.

'You look like shit,' he said under his breath, running a hand through his wheatfield hair.

'Maybe a champagne would help?' I hinted, when he didn't offer one.

'Uh, Guy, this is Sabrina.' The woman was as thin as an eight year old herself.

'Hi,' I said stupidly. 'I'm Callum's dad.'

As if she gave a flying fuck.

Susanna walked in the other kitchen door, holding an empty flute. 'You're late, Guy: I said three not four,' she said curtly before walking out with a refill.

'Jeez, love the bloody welcoming committee!' I said, moving back towards the hallway. 'Where is my son?'

'Down in the "zoo",' Anthony called after me. 'They're watching a clown.'

I manoeuvred past a couple more Moët-handed mommies in the main living area and went through to the jungle-themed rec room where the kids hung out. One of the girls was replacing Britney with Eminem on a huge ghetto blaster in the centre of the room.

'But I hate Eminem!' one of the other girls stamped her feet.

'I only like red M&Ms!' said a much bigger girl, cracking a gag. The others all laughed, perhaps in deference to her superior height and weight.

The white rapper's scatological chanting grated on my nerves: I was admittedly a little old for Eminem, but from the white trash words I was hearing, these girls were way too young for him.

I scanned the room. Crisps and cake. Cups filled with green and red fizzy drinks.

No sign of Callum.

I asked one of the now-rapping girls if she knew where he was, but the music was way too loud and she couldn't hear me. I walked towards Courtney's bedroom.

Bright plastic letters on the door spelt out 'COURT'; a befitting abode for a little princess.

I tapped twice, but then was almost bowled over by a clown running out in a slapstick hurry, frantically scooping up all his silly horns and squeakers and water pistol-flowers and shoving them – along with his matted platinum wig – into a big plastic bag resting against the wall.

And although I only caught a quick glimpse of his pancaked face as he ran out, there was something disturbing about it under the make-up. His red-ringed eyes were glassy like a fish's, his rubbery lips quivered like Jell-O and his bald head seemed way too small for his puffy sequined shoulders.

Gollum the Clown. He also reeked of cheap perfume.

I stepped into the dark room. The light was off and the curtains were drawn. The cheap perfume smell was in here, too. I turned on the light: Courtney was lying motionless on her bed. She was naked, with her underpants lying on the pillow beside her. Her jeans were on the floor.

'Fuck!' I said. 'Courtney – are you OK, honey?'

She moaned softly. Then turned her head and threw up some shiny green stuff.

I picked up her jeans.

'Courtney?' I said, tapping her pale cheek. 'Courtney?'

She moaned again just as I felt a presence behind me.

It was Callum. And Susanna.

I went to open my mouth, but then Susanna's shrieking completely drowned out me, Eminem and everything else.

Britney pouted accusingly at me in her tartan school dress from the poster above the bed.

While Callum now stood beside me: silent, his head turned upwards and his piercing blue eyes locked firmly on to mine; giving me that same unnerving look he'd given me in my office after that poor little bird had lost its head.

*

The cop patted me on the shoulder and lifted his moustache in apology. We'd been in the kitchen for what seemed like hours.

'Sorry for the mix-up, Mr Russell,' the cop said, closing his folder. 'The doctor says Courtney's fine. You obviously disturbed the perpetrator before he—'

Anthony patted my other shoulder, a little less convincingly. Susanna was still eyeing me suspiciously. According to the cop, the clown – one Barry Abbott – was a distant cousin to a big political family and a habitual child molester. While not blessed with the family's trademark charm, intelligence or good looks, his surname and money usually got him off the hook. All of which enabled him to keep popping up in variety of kid-friendly guises round Manhattan and the boroughs: magician, junior swimming coach, clown etc.

Four hours after he'd fled the party, he had been caught white-faced and red-handed near his apartment in Prospect Park in Brooklyn, shoving the plastic bag into a dumpster. He foolishly hadn't thought to wipe off his make-up yet.

'But I'm still not clear why *you* were in Courtney's room too, Guy?' Susanna had said, even after the cop had eventually cleared me.

'I told you: I was looking for Callum.'

'But Callum was right here with me here in the kitchen. I was getting him a glass of water.' She still seemed convinced I was implicated in some way.

'Well he wasn't in the kitchen when I looked in here, was he? He must have come in through that second door after I walked out.'

Unlike Lee Harvey Oswald, I wasn't feeling as cool as a cucumber.

I looked tiredly at Anthony for verification.

'That's right,' Anthony said. 'Guy's a lot of things, but he's not—' The shocking thought didn't bear completion.

Anthony and Susanna looked at each other. Then Susanna started to fill a glass of fruit juice for her daughter and Anthony gave me a 'what are you gonna do?' shrug.

I walked slowly back down the Turkish trail to the front door with Callum in tow.

But I was too petrified to hold his hand.

What the policeman had said may have been enough of an explanation for Anthony and Susanna, but I couldn't shake the clear sense that whatever maleficent force

Callum was channelling was now growing stronger by the day.

And that force had just tried to frame me for a heinous crime.

And it was beginning to now impact on innocent people too, rather than just attacking and torturing me.

As I stepped off the tongue of the rug, out of the front door into the dark New York night, I felt like I was walking straight into the mouth of doom.

The little people

In a vain attempt to block out my fears, I got into the habit of hanging out at the Hell or High Water most nights till dawn.

I'd read in the *Post* that there'd been a murder at the club the night I'd been there with Jim and Nadine: the reason for the ambulance we'd heard as we were leaving, no doubt. But the crime didn't seem to have kept the revellers away.

I'd get there round midnight, do a quick lap of the sex cabins, then head down below to buy some of whatever the one-eyed albino had going.

Then I'd buy a couple of beers at the Medusa Bar, head upstairs to the 'Jim and Nadine Memorial Hammock' and sway there till they turned the lights up.

One night after the club, I came home and rearranged the furniture to make more room for my growing stockpile of reading material. As well as Bill's father's occult titles, I was also steadily working my way through a fast-growing collection of Kennedy assassination books, essays and videos.

Like Oswald stacking textbooks at the Depository, I now had plenty of time to kill.

I pushed the main couch out – the end where Mia used to sit.

Underneath the couch on the floor, I found the old Madonna/Rupert Everett *Vanity Fair* magazine she used to flick through all the time, now coated in dust. One of the pages was folded back to mark her place. Funnily enough, the article was about Nadine's pleasure playground, Ibiza.

The apocryphal tale was about a promiscuous young American girl who was holidaying on the island back in 1970. While taking a heap of drugs and having sex with all and sundry, the young woman (not surprisingly) became pregnant. Upon hearing of her situation, she decided she wanted to have an abortion. However, when she saw a doctor, she was informed that her pregnancy was already four months advanced and that it was therefore too late for them to perform a termination.

The woman had no idea who the father was, yet was equally certain that she was going to name the baby either Alice (after *Alice in Wonderland*) or Peter, as in Peter Pan.

A party was organized on the highest house in the Old Town to celebrate the impending arrival. Local musicians piped flutes and strummed guitars while the expectant mother was festooned with veils and a turban like an Ottoman harem girl in an *Arabian Nights*-style tent.

But while the welcoming well-wishers were all stoned or tripping out of their heads, the baby boy was born with a head the size of a golf ball.

His tiny body was almost transparent – like a jellyfish's – apparently because his mother had ingested so much LSD.

Those present immediately took the baby to the

doctor, who advised them to return him to his mother, because he wasn't going to live much longer anyway.

The doctor was right: poor little Peter Pan survived only three more days.

They dressed him in a soft, white cloth, laid him down on a piece of wood, lit a candle for him and pushed him out to sea.

After that, his mother was no longer popular on the island, and the people who had once been her friends soon made it clear that it might be best if she too sailed away.

I folded back the dog-ear and carefully placed the magazine on the top shelf.

*

'So which room did he have?' Michael was twirling a striped straw in his Fluffy Duck. Enriquo was spit-polishing glasses.

'I can't tell you that, Guy. That's classified hotel information. I could tell you . . .' Elmer Fudd took over, '. . . *but den I'd have to kill you – eh eh eh.*'

'Well what floor did Mark David Chapman stay on, then? You can tell me that at least, can't you?'

Michael sucked his straw. 'He stayed here for a few days in the November, lost his nerve and flew back to Hawaii. Then he came back to New York a few weeks later, checked into the Y on West 63rd, then the Sheraton, and then he shot Lennon.

'What I *can* tell you is that he was as nutty as a fruitcake.

He had this whole imaginary world going on where there were thousands of little people living in his living room with their own little government and ministers and committees and shit. And Chapman was their president!'

'And did these little people tell him to murder Lennon?'

'No. Apparently his little cabinet was actually horrified when he told them his plan. They advised him strongly *against* any violence.'

'Well why did he do it then?'

'Satan.' Michael said, twisting the straw. 'Satan sent Chapman two personal demons called Lila and Dobar to give him the courage to kill John Lennon.'

Lila and Dobar? They sounded like exotic dancers who might appear down at the Hell or High Water.

Michael slurped the duck's entrails. 'Apparently when Mark David Chapman was interviewed by psychiatrists, he spoke to them in the demons' voices, which were completely different from his own voice.'

I changed the assassin, if not the subject. 'By the way, my friend Bill told me that when Lee Harvey Oswald was a teenager he washed dishes here at the Olcott after school. Before he went into the Marines. Have you ever heard that?'

Michael looked at his watch and shook his head. His break was over.

'That was a kid called Oswald Lee, not Lee Oswald. That kid was Chinese. Got his own restaurant down in Chinatown now, I believe.'

*

Mr Guy Russell
Hotel Olcott, #901.
27 W72
NYC, N.Y 10032
6.15.00

Dear Guy,

After due consideration and due to the recent unforeseen economic downturn, I regret to inform you that your position as Creative Director at Brave Face has been made redundant – effective immediately.

You will receive a cheque for four weeks' pay in a separate letter at the end of the current pay period and your Blue Shield health benefits will remain valid until 7/15/00.

We thank you for your contribution to Brave Face and wish you well in your future endeavours.

Yours sincerely,

Anthony Johnson
CEO
Signed: A Johnson

CC: S. Chandran, CFO.

'But if I missed the last session, why do I still have to pay for it?'

Money was getting extremely tight. There wasn't going to be any cash coming in any more, apart from rent from the tenants back in Melbourne. And that was being paid directly into our monumental mortgage back home: money I couldn't access without getting Mia's signature, too. Plus, if it came to legal push and shove, I imagined Mia would end up with the house anyway.

Blakely gave me the standard psychobabble answer. 'Because I set that time aside for you, Guy. I keep it free for you and nobody else.'

Somehow I'd lost a whole day and missed a scheduled dose of shrinkage.

I think I slept through most of it.

I probably did some reading.

Went for a run.

Something.

'Well, what did you do in my regrettable absence? Did you make notes? Is there a dossier on me that you updated? Can I see it?'

She smiled that infuriating smile. 'We have a contract, you and I. For some reason, you chose to break our contract and not attend the last session.'

What contract? I hadn't signed anything for her apart from Visa bills.

'Do you want to *talk* about your anger? Do you feel that I somehow wasn't here for you, even though you made it impossible for me to talk to you by not even turning up?

'Not to mention what we've already discussed many

times before, Guy. About you being not willing or pre-pared to open up to me even when we're sitting down here and facing each other.'

I looked out the window. Like I always did.

'And just so you're prepared, I'll be away from the 27th for two weeks. You might wish to discuss your feelings about that as well?'

*

It was the last week of June, I think.

'What?' I couldn't hear what he was saying. The music was pounding in my temples.

'Uh, Guy, you're dripping onto my counter.' Michael shouted, giving his desk a wipe with a little Olcott hand towel.

I was collecting my mail. Another letter in a Brave Face envelope – my final meagre payout, no doubt. An eviction warning notice from the Olcott. And a letter from *Reader's Digest* addressed to a Mr M. Balsam.

I pulled the sweaty little plugs out of my ears. 'Riders on the Storm' made me feel incredible. 'Sweet Child o' Mine' made me invincible. 'Heroes' immortal.

'You've been running a lot lately,' Michael noted. 'Looks like you've lost a few pounds.'

I wiped my brow on my forearm and checked my watch: the reservoir and back in less than thirty-five min-utes. Not bad, considering I'd been up all night again.

Twenty minutes later, I climbed into Callum's bed for my afternoon nap.

The running helped me to sleep. My foot hit something hard: Callum's Etch-a-Sketch was hiding under the blanket. I looked at the glowing screen.

There was a series of uneven ovoid shapes or circles.

And a single word that looked like BuB.

I kicked the toy onto the floor and pulled the pillow tight round my ears.

I'm in the belltower, looking out.

First Mia falls past me screaming.

Then Callum.

Then Bubby falls but stops right in front of me.

Hovering in the air like a bat and giggling.

And then a man in a grey flannel suit slams down right on top of her and they scream obscenities at me as they hurtle out of sight.

Hemingway on ice

I'd given Dr Blakely one of my stories to read while she was away.

She'd been pestering me for a writing sample for some time. No doubt part of her ongoing strategy to get me to 'open up more'; to help her 'break down my wall' as she so annoyingly put it. So I printed one off the floppy disk I kept all my stories on in the vain hope that I might resurrect my stillborn writing career one day. Yeah right.

I made sure I chose a story that had nothing to do with me personally. Something so far removed from me and my real life that she'd never be able to draw any of her cutesy, sophomoric conclusions from it.

I thought of it as a sort of 'Cold man's Hemingway'.

Pound of Flesh

By Guy Russell

It was about five to five when The Kid locked me in the Big Fridge.

Every second Friday we move most of what's left in the Big Fridge into the cool room. Sides of beef, legs of lamb, sausages, pigs' trotters, the odd chook – whatever's left. Then, Monday afternoon, the boys from the abattoir arrive and restock the fridge for the following fortnight.

We call it the Big Fridge, but it's really a freezer.

About twelve by twelve with an eight-foot ceiling.

Inside there's two huge stainless steel racks with three shelves on each. The aisle between them is about five foot wide.

There's a footstool at the far end of the aisle.

I should have sussed The Kid.

He's been acting funny all afternoon.

At first I thought he was just sooking on account of what happened at lunchtime.

He was sitting behind the counter out the front reading one of those motorbike magazines that he always reads and scoffing those disgusting cheese and banana sandwiches that his Mum makes for him.

O'Malley our boss was at the bank.

I was sweeping up.

The Kid's got a real bad case of pimples and today he's got a bump the size of a pinball right in the middle of his forehead.

'Hey, Pus Head,' I says. 'Looks like ya brain's trying to escape again.'

'Piss off, Clefty,' he says, pullin' up his top lip to pay me back.

Now if there's one thing that sets me off, it's when someone takes the mickey out of me scar. So I swings around with the broom so hard I damn near knock his head off. He falls to the ground, pretending he's hurt. I give him a good kick up the arse to go on with and waddya know? He spits out a bloody tooth!

'Musta been a rotten one, Pus Head,' I laughs. 'It'll save ya a trip to the dentist, anyhow!'

Like I said, he had his funny ones on all afternoon after that. He goes all quiet but still has that mad dog look in his eye that he sometimes gets. He didn't dob me in to O'Malley of course. He knows better than that.

Anyways, O'Malley pisses off just after 4.30 to go fishin' for the weekend.

So The Kid and me start to empty out the Big Fridge.

We'd been goin' about twenty minutes.

'Any more?' I calls out.

I don't expect him to answer on account of his mood.

But he yells back from the cool room: 'Just bring the cutlets!'

So I goes back into the Big Fridge and waddya know?

The door slams shut behind me, the light goes out and I hear the lock click.

The little bastard's locked me in.

I had ta laugh. I'd fallen for it.

Hook, line and sinker.

'Good one, Kid!' I shout.

'Now let me out and I'll give ya a lift home!'

There's no answer. He can't hear me.

The door to the Big Fridge is four inches thick.

I sits down on the little stool.

I wait.

He's smarter than I give 'im credit for, The Kid. I spose he thinks I give 'im a hard time. But he don't know what a hard time is. When I was 'is age I got picked on much worse.

'Oi, Clefty – *what's wrong with your mouth?*' they'd all laugh, pulling up their lips. The Kid don't know he's alive. His skin's gonna clear up one of these days, but I'll always look like this. I give 'im the occasional hiding. So what?

It's gettin' cold now.

Come on, Kid – a joke's a bloody joke.

The Big Fridge is set at twelve below. It's black as the grave.

I press the light button on me watch: 5.17 and the glass is starting to frost over.

I'm shivering like a bastard.

The footstool feels like a block of ice.

So I get up and start jogging on the spot and hugging meself.

All I've got on are a pair of slacks, a T-shirt and me apron.

Me gloves are out in the cool room. I know that there's no extra clothes kept in the Big Fridge. But there's always a big pile of plastic sheets, some rubber bands and a pricing gun down the far end. We use these for wrapping and pricing the offal and pet mince.

I slowly feel me way down between the big metal racks.

The Kid was telling the truth about the cutlets anyway. About halfway down the aisle, me left hand lands on a tray of them on the second shelf.

I pick one up and snap it in half.

It takes a good three or four hours to freeze meat properly.

About the same time it takes to defrost it.

But that's dead meat.

I wonder how long it would take to freeze a live animal in the Big Fridge.

I find the plastic sheets at the end of the rack.

I take out me filleting knife and cut the plastic into different shapes and sizes.

Two long rectangles for me arms and hands and a big square one for me head.

It's harder to get the head one right. I end up having to put a whole sheet over me head and then cut a hole out for me mouth.

I know the plastic won't keep the cold out. But it might help protect me skin from frostbite. I'll just have to be very careful when I peel it off that I don't peel half me face off with it.

Doing it in a warm bath would probably be the best bet.

I wrap some lacka bands round my neck and wrists to hold the plastic in place.

I scrape the ice off me watch: 6.01 now. Because me hands are shaking so much, it's taken me an hour to do what would normally take five minutes.

I mean, The Kid and me once cut, bagged and priced 100 bags of lambs' livers in less than an hour. Easy.

I make me way back to the stool like one of them Arctic explorers in the olden days. I'm shivering so hard now I nearly fall over.

I don't feel cold any more. More sort of high than anything.

Like when I used to sniff them aerosol cans when I was a kid.

But I feel me legs are gonna break if I keep trying to run on the spot. And there's sort of an ache growing in me chest.

And there's an awful cold stinging feeling on the tops of me legs where I've pissed meself.

I remember seeing a TV show one time about hypothermia.

They reckoned your blood pressure drops and your breathing slows right down. Till you eventually pass out.

I check me breathing again: about one breath every eight seconds now.

Tick . . . tick . . . tick . . .

My life is freezing away, second by second.

The TV show also showed these smartarse surgeons who'd deliberately frozen people so they could operate on them. They said it was quite safe as long as ice crystals didn't form in the tissues.

What else did the bastards say? Oh yeah, the only other thing I can remember is that when you're cold, shivering is the body's way of getting your body temperature back up.

In fact, when you're shivering to the max, the body can produce five times more heat than it can normally.

It's when you stop shivering that you're in trouble.

I sit meself back down on the stool. I'm feeling very lazy now.

When I was The Kid's age, I often thought about bumping meself off. Jumping from a building, shooting it out with the coppers, playing chicken with a train – somethin' schmick. But this was something much better than I could ever have thought up.

You had to give the bloody Kid credit! An '*accident*'?

It was perfect.

That's what he thinks! I pulls out me filleting knife and start to scratch a message into the wall. I can't see what I'm doing in the dark so I use big, long strokes. It seems to take even longer than it took to put the bloody plastic strips on. But I'm much tireder now so it's hard to compare.

I finish.

I check me work with me watch light:

THE KID DID IT
8:19

I've stopped shivering.

O'Malley walked in on the Monday morning with an Esky full of flathead and found him on the floor.

Stiff as a board.

There was a $3.99kg price sticker stuck to the back of his head.

They charged The Kid with Murder One. But the jury let him off.

Because the coroner placed the time of death at approximately 11.00 p.m. on the Friday night.

And that was at least five hours after The Kid had snuck back to the Big Fridge and turned it off.

THE END

From the records of Dr Jennifer Blakely

Guy Russell story: 'Pound of Flesh'

'fridge' = tomb-like/womb-like maternal coldness/hostility

and/or disapproving/unforgiving super ego.

Locked in !!! Terror of infantile helplessness.

Feelings split off and 'frozen over' for self-preservation
False self-development

'The Kid' – bullying played out and reversed, psyche in revenge mode = fragmented/split off – no real empathy

narrator's cleft palate – cf. Guy's own inability to speak up, unable to defend himself & therefore persecuted by the id

paranoid/persecuted – primitive/aggressive defence mechanisms

suicidal ideation but homicidal tendencies more prominent – wants to kill the bad, rotting part of himself which has been projected into the other

e.g. price sticker = worthless piece of meat

– possible psychotic tendencies

Story told in first person – authorial sublimation?

Florida

On the last Sunday in June, Susanna called me at 5.00 p.m. She said that Mia had instructed her to retrieve Callum back from me by 4 p.m. on Sunday afternoons, so where the hell was he?

'Do you know where my lovely wife is?' I countered. 'And, more importantly, who she's with?'

There was a beat at the other end. 'Guy, she's by herself. And you know I'm not going to tell you where she is, so please stop asking me.'

Secrets of the sainted fucking sisterhood.

'So when are you bringing Callum back?'

'Why would I bring him back?' I said, swigging on my Bud. 'He's my son, too. If Mia's not here, then he should be with me.'

I had recently decided that I needed to keep Callum near to me, under close surveillance. Without me there to monitor his every movement, who knew what could happen? I'd sit and watch him for hours, looking for the slightest aberration or change in mood. It was getting very tiring, but I couldn't relax for a moment.

If I had to go on an errand or a run or to see my shrink, I'd park him downstairs in the office with Michael for a couple of hours.

There were two unused sockets under the fire

extinguisher in the hallway: one was yelling 'Fuck off!', the other was yelling 'Whore!'

I drained the rest of my beer. 'Thanks for calling, Susanna,' I said, hanging up.

As well as food, I'd also run out of beer. Callum was watching *Scooby Doo on Zombie Island*. His new favourite.

He wrinkled his nose as I sat next to him on the couch. 'Ew! You stink, Daddy!'

'OK, I'll have a little wash and then when Scooby's finished, let's go down to the Dallas and have us a drink and some nachos. Then we'll go shopping and buy some nuffins. And some more Cheerios.'

'I love nuffins!' he said. But then he looked suddenly pensive.

'Daddy, when's Mummy coming to get me?'

It was a good question. Mia's farewell letter was still propped up against the piss-yellow vase. The centrepiece to our disintegration.

'You know how you and Mummy like those animal shows on TV? With the lions and tigers and panthers and pumas and stuff?'

He nodded.

'Well, she saw this really good show about alligators on the Discovery Channel the other night. So she's gone down to Florida to check 'em out. She'll probably take a whole lot of cool photos of 'em and bring them back to show you.'

Since I had no idea where Mia actually was, Florida was probably as good a guess as any.

*

Every now and again when things got too much, my mother would need a 'little rest'.

Especially in the winter.

Violet – her name slyly omitting the 'n' near the end that revealed her true nature – would retire to her bed with her dildo and her Serepax for anywhere between twenty-four to seventy-two hours.

Meanwhile, Raine and I would happily watch TV for whole days and feast on Cheerios.

We had no choice really: our mother would lash us to our chairs with the long curtain cord that otherwise lay curled along our lounge room wall like a cobra waiting to strike.

She'd slip newspaper underneath us in case nature called during these enforced TV marathons.

I'd always do my best not to soil today's headlines, however, because that would necessitate a really good dunking in the bathtub later on.

But sometimes fate was kind.

If my father happened to come home earlier from his 'trip' than expected, he would leave his zonked-out wife in bed and take us kids down to the front bar of the Black Rock Hotel.

The pub was home to cantankerous fishermen, lazy tradesmen and alcoholic retirees. The soggy pool table tilted thirty degrees and there were cracked old photos of ships and yachts and fluorescent seventies sunsets hanging crookedly on the walls.

My father seemed to revel in the seediness of it. He would buy beer after beer for himself and I would try to match him with ginger ales as we watched the toy boats skating across the grey slate of Port Phillip Bay through the wide salt-flecked window.

Raine liked to draw faces on the window.

She also liked to scratch her arms and face with the hooks poking out of the tackle boxes under the fishermen's tables.

Sometimes she would tear up a beer coaster into one long strip and ignite the end of it with my father's lighter.

I loved to sit and watch the snake of fire burn down into nothingness.

America's bouncing baby boy

A couple of days later, during the first week of July, Bill dropped over one afternoon to see how I was doing.

I'd been watching an old black and white British film called *Dead of Night*. One of the best parts of the film – it was broken into five separate little vignettes – was the final story, about an evil ventriloquist's doll who controls his master. Bill watched the dangerous little dummy for a few seconds and smiled with recognition.

'Did you happen to know that a bunch of British cosmologists were watching this movie together one day in the forties and because of the movie's clever "portmanteau" construction' – he made quotation marks with his fingers like a university lecturer – 'they suddenly hit on an alternative to the Big Bang called the Steady State Theory of the universe?'

It was a strange thing to say. Even to me.

'UCLA course: British Films 1945–1960,' he smiled nervously. 'Did you like that other vignette in this movie where the guy looks in the mirror but sees a completely different room from his own in the reflection?'

Truth be told, I'd been rewinding and fast forwarding between the ventriloquist and the mirror vignettes for the last seven hours straight. But I didn't feel like discussing what they meant with Bill at that particular moment.

He turned away from the screen, surveyed the catastrophe I now called home and scratched his head. As usual, I had the curtains drawn. He wrenched them open and the sun seared my eyes. A fat family of flies took off from the windowpane.

'Hey, I love what you've done to the place . . . it's kinda . . . ' he picked up three empty Coors bottles, took them out to the kitchen and tried to stuff them in the already overflowing bin ' . . . Bowery chic.'

He looked towards the corner of the room. I had by now dumped all of the shitty old hotel books into a pile on the floor and used the bookcase to organize Bill's father's books and all my new Kennedy assassination stuff into a kind of mini reference library next to the TV. It was the one neat area of the apartment.

'You know, buddy, maybe you should get out more? Get some fresh air.' He took some more bottles and mouldy Chinese food boxes out to the kitchen, whistling 'Strangers in the Night' softly to himself.

'Oh I run every day,' I said. 'Sometimes twice.'

'Yes, I can smell that,' he laughed. But it wasn't his usual Bill laugh.

He went into the bathroom, then came out again quickly, looking pale and wrinkling his nose. 'Uh, Guy, I think you should take the "Do not disturb" sign off the front door. Or at least get the maid to clean your bathroom. Callum's written a strange little message on the wall in there. What does 'r' 'a' 'i' 'n' 'e' mean? "*Rainy*"? As in a shitty weather forecast? And when I say shitty, I mean that literally cos I don't think he used a brown crayon to write it.'

'Kids.' I said. 'Full of surprises.'

I hadn't actually been in the bathroom for a few days. I tried to avoid it. Because as well as my aversion to the little white screaming electrical sockets, I sometimes saw an old woman's face in the mirror. And, once when I was drying myself with my eyes closed, I thought I even felt her cold, angry hands reach out and grab me. So it was just easier not to wash so often.

Bill couldn't wait to leave. 'Why don't we go downstairs to that Tex Mex joint you told me about and have us a beer? Talk about the good ole days.'

Standing at the jukebox, I looked back across the Dallas BBQ at my other old ex-partner. It was the only time I'd ever seen him not happy sitting behind a drink. I dropped a quarter into the slot and it reverberated like a steel door slamming.

After Bill left and I got back upstairs, I saw that Lucy had forwarded me an email from her father, and along with that had asked me to meet her in the park that weekend. I suspected this rendezvous was the real reason Lucy was getting in touch with me, as her father's email was dated from a couple of weeks previous.

*

From: jtate@texasnet.com
Date: 14 June 2000 4:59:32 PM
To: ltate@usbraveface.com
Subject: sinatra/ruby/oswald

Well hey there my Lil Lucette!

Why you wantin to dredge up these bad things that are best forgotten?

Anyways in response to your request, according to my highly suspect memory (!) here's the order of events as I was told them by a VERY reliable source from the Dallas PD who I sold a warehouse to in Houston back in 66/67. I've written it in point form cos you could go on for ever with the whys, wherefores and whatevers of the Kennedy thing!

When you comin down to visit us anyhow? Your mother misses you and I could stand the sight of you for a day or two too.

Love Dear old etc . . . oxox

In the meantime, here you go:

1 J Edgar Hoover & Bobby Kennedy have both warned JFK to stop fraternizing with Sinatra due to his unsavoury Mafia connections. Then in March 62, JFK stays at Bing Crosby's house in Palm Springs instead of accepting an open invitation to stay at Frank's pad out there because Frank has allegedly also had mob boss, Sam Giancana, as a frequent house guest, and it wouldn't look good

for the president to be staying at the same holiday pad as 'Sam the Cigar'.

Frank is livid: he's gone to a lot of expense to have his Palm Springs ponderosa fitted out like a 'western White House' for the president's convenience: extra guest rooms for the Secret Service guys, phone lines, etc. – he's even built a helipad for the presidential copter. He goes out and smashes the helipad to pieces with a sledgehammer after hearing of the snub.

And from that day forward, Frank vows vengeance against JFK for his ingratitude & disloyalty.

2 Sinatra recruits Ruby – who used to supply the friendly ladies for him up at his Cal-Neva Lodge & Casino on Lake Tahoe – to organize his revenge.

3 Ruby recruits Oswald – who he first meets at the Sports Drome Rifle Range outside Dallas doing target practise. Ruby needs the money, Oswald wants to kill someone famous: he's already tried unsuccessfully to pop off General Walker in Dallas a few months earlier.

4 Ruby and Oswald stake out the 6th floor of the Depository. Oswald helps Ruby get in the building without being seen. Oswald takes the eastern-most window looking out onto Houston, Ruby the western-most window overlooking Elm and the grassy knoll.

Ruby also has two other snipers positioned down on the knoll. One is indeed lurking behind the stockade fence – standing on the bumper of a car as many conspiracy theorists have claimed – except, instead of being right at the corner of the fence like 'Badge Man', he is 10 feet to the west, towards the Triple Underpass. The other sniper is hidden on top of the tool shed behind the white cupola closest to the Depository.

5 Ruby is planning to shoot Oswald at a secret location after the president has been killed and make it look like suicide. In his pocket, Ruby has a forged suicide note written by Oswald explaining all Oswald's crazy reasons for killing JFK and then himself.

6 But Oswald loses his nerve just before the motorcade is due to swing by. He bolts down five flights of stairs – cos the freight elevators are on different floors – to the 1st floor lunchroom. Where he sits quietly in a booth finishing his chicken sandwich.

He feels safe for a while because he knows Ruby can't shoot him out in the open. Then Oswald goes up to the 2nd floor to grab a Coke out of the machine and to strengthen his alibi, has a very quick exchange with a cop and the building superintendent, is verified as a Depository employee and then vamooses safely out the front door of the building.

7 Back upstairs on the 6th floor, Ruby is torn between chasing after Oswald or still doing the hit. He decides he better do the most important job

first. Oswald was meant to take the first pot shots up Houston St as the motorcade APPROACHES the building but Ruby is flustered so decides to stick with HIS original target of the president moving AWAY from the building, westwards along Elm towards the knoll.

8 Bang! Bang! Bang! Between them, Ruby and the knoll snipers hit the president . . .

Then Ruby immediately throws on a big fur and a blonde wig belonging to one of his strippers from that sleazy club he owns, the Carousel, leaves Oswald's rifle out in the open but throws HIS rifle way under the open floorboards, where it's probably still lying to this very day – it's not well documented but they were laying new boards on the 6th floor that week.

Ruby then bolts down the stairs and out the back door of the building. He sneaks across the top of the knoll through the pergola – you can see him (her!) in certain photos – and jumps into a POLICE CAR (there were some DIRTY COPS in on it, too) parked just on the other side of the Triple Underpass.

9 Ruby radios Officer Tippit to find Oswald and kill him because he knows that Oswald will blab. BUT Oswald has taken a bus then a cab (Oswald can't drive) to his rooming house and gets HIS revolver BEFORE Tippit can get to him. And then when Tippit finally does spot Oswald out on the street near where he lives – Oswald shoots HIM first.

10 Oswald runs a few blocks and then gets arrested in the Texas Theater.

So then Sinatra calls up Ruby and tells him he STILL better shut Oswald up and that he should lay the blame for JFK on LBJ – if he knows what's good for him!

You know the rest . . . Ruby plugs Oswald two days later on national television in the basement of the Dallas Police Station, gets arrested himself and then dies of cancer three years later at Parkland Hospital (where Kennedy and Oswald both also died), still fearing the long deadly reach of Sinatra.

And the moral is? Never cross a lounge singer with a mean streak.

(And visit your father more often!)

Love Daddy x

So poor old Lee Harvey Oswald was really just the MacGuffin?

And Jack Ruby was no gem.

The great white hope of Hyannis Port, little Jack Kennedy had been America's bouncing baby boy.

But they terminated him.

While Sinatra howled with glee under that 'Old Devil Moon'.

It was certainly an interesting theory.

And no less plausible or unsavoury than anything that had happened to me, or I had had to endure, lately.

Or long ago, for that matter.

I hear a scrubbing, scratching noise from the room I share with my little sister, Lorraine.

I push open the door and there is a shocking smell.

It almost knocks me out.

My mother is on her hands and knees with a soapy bucket beside her, scrubbing my sister's shit off the wall. Her cot is also caked brown with it while Lorraine herself is over in the corner rocking and humming and rubbing shit all over herself.

'Guy – get out!' my mother barks. A squadron of flies are dive-bombing her.

I stand dumbfounded – and suddenly nauseous.

My sister rocks and laughs and draws a shitty smiley face on the wall.

'Get outtttt!' my mother screams, throwing a filthy rag at me.

Despite a quick, desperate rubdown, little pieces of the shit remain on my shirt and my schoolbag and when I get to school that day, the class clown pinches his nose in an exaggerated manner and stage-whispers to all the other kids:

'Phew ,Guy! What did you have for breakfast this morning? '"Snap, Crackle, Shit"?'

The Well-Tempered Clavier

It's a drizzly Sunday lunchtime.

Early 1970s.

We pull up in my father's old green FJ Holden. He turns the radio off. 'Happy Together' by The Turtles.

It's been a long drive.

Leaves, papers and mosquitoes litter the big stagnant puddles in the pebbled car park and the grounds have obviously seen better days and not enough gardeners recently.

I look up and take in the biggest, weirdest looking building I've ever seen.

To my nine-year-old eyes, it looks like the Brothers Grimm have designed it.

Blood-red bricks. Shuttered windows like rows of closed eyes. A bent weathercock on the roof, listing into the wind.

We're here all because of a pissy yellow vase.

My grandmother's vase.

My mother's favourite.

My friend Timmy and I are horsing around with my second-hand Sherrin football in my lounge room after school.

It's where my mother sits to smoke her Winfield Blues and listen to Shirley Bassey and Roy Orbison and cry into her Cinzano Bianco when my father goes away on his 'work trips'.

Her grandmother's vase sits on the middle of the mantelpiece: pride of place.

Why we're even in that fucking room, I'll never know.

Anyway, the inevitable occurs – doesn't it always? – and suddenly the vase lies in a thousand screaming pieces.

'Don't worry,' I tell Timmy. 'I'll say Raine did it. She breaks everything anyway.'

My sister's name is Lorraine.

We call her Raine.

And so here we all are at the living hell known as:

BONNIE BROOK:
INSTITUTION FOR THE INTELLECTUALLY &
PHYSICALLY DISABLED.

Saying goodbye to my kid sister, Raine.

Actually, my father doesn't even say goodbye. He is leaning against the curved bonnet of his car, rolling a cigarette, facing away from the building.

He is now whistling 'Happy Together', but very slowly.

Raine kicks and screams as my mother drags her by her hair across the car park and up the steps. My special little sister gives me a final 'how could you do this to me?' look before she's swallowed up by the big, red nasty building. The clouds clash their cymbals and rain starts to fall like giant panes of glass smashing.

It's the last time I ever see her.

A few weeks later, my father drives away in his beloved green machine and never comes back either.

I had to see Dr Blakely immediately.

I had to tell her about all this stuff really, really badly.

'I'm sorry, Mr Russell,' her PA kept saying. 'I can't help you. The airline strike is still going on in Bermuda and she can't get back till next week at the earliest.'

Next week?

The world could change a lot in a week.

It could change in a New York minute.

*

Saturday 5.35 p.m.

I was giving rock and roll a rest and enjoying Bach's *The Well-Tempered Clavier*, tapped out by Glenn Gould, when there was a loud rap at the door.

Bill had once mentioned to me that Lee Harvey Oswald's mother's maiden name had been Marguerite Clavier. Pity she hadn't produced a better tempered son.

'And apparently she was a real piece of work, too,' Bill had gone on. 'Some psychiatrists around at the time suggested that Oswald killed Kennedy just so he could get away from his crazy, interfering old mother!'

There was a second loud rap. I wasn't meant to collect Callum from Michael until six, so I tiptoed grumpily down the hallway, dodging the rubbish bags, newspapers and stray toys. I opened the door.

UNIDENTIFIED MURDER VICTIM
NEW YORK CITY, NY
May 12, 2000

Victim – Jane Doe

DESCRIPTION

Age:	22 to 30	**Hair:**	Brown
Sex:	Female	**Eyes:**	Hazel
Height:	160 cm	**Race:**	White
Frame:	Small	**Weight:**	55kg

DETAILS

The intact body of the victim, a white woman aged between 22 and 30 years, most likely 23 to 26 years old, was discovered in Lower Ground Level Room #4 in the 'Hell or High Water' Night Club, 419 W 13th St, NYC at approximately 2.10 a.m. on May 12, 2000. The victim was nude and – subject to autopsy results – appears to have been strangled with her black underpants.

A reward of $5,000 is available to anyone who provides information that leads to the arrest and conviction of the person or persons responsible for the death of this unidentified victim.

Anyone who has seen or has information pertaining to the identity or death of this Unidentified Murder Victim, please contact Detective John Winslow at NYPD Precinct 6 at 233 West 10th Street (212) 741- 4811 or your nearest FBI Office.

'Ever seen her before, Mr . . . ah . . .' Detective Angelo Barino licked his thumb and flicked his notebook back a couple of pages. ' . . . Russell?'

No. But I felt like I'd seen his face a thousand times before: on *NYPD Blue*, on *Law and Order*, on *Homicide: Life on the Street*.

He was perfectly cast: the dirty grey-brown moustache, deep pockmarks and yellow teeth were all very convincing.

Detective Barino and his partner were standing in my living room waving an artist's impression of a pretty girl under my nose.

Barino's partner – a skinny younger cop with freckles and a crew cut – picked up the base of the broken vase. I'd sticky-taped Mia's note to it for good measure. He was turning it over in his hands, trying to read it.

'No,' I finally answered. 'But what's her name, and tell her if she's free next Saturday night, I'm not doing anything.'

'At the moment, her only name's Jane,' Barino growled. 'And she'll be spending this and every other Saturday night with some maggots in her dirt-brown bed.'

His breath smelled like the ashtray at an all-night poker game.

'Oh, sorry,' I said, genuinely remorseful. 'I only looked at the picture, not the words.'

I noticed Barino's hands were shaking a little. And his skin seemed sallow. Yellow and liverish. His partner noticed the shaking hands too and seemed a little embarrassed by them.

Barino walked over to the window, pulled open the curtain, looked down and sighed.

'Would you like a drink, detective? I was about to have one myself.'

He sat down heavily in an armchair. 'Speaking of drinks, Mr Russell, this woman was murdered at the Hell or High Water Club in the Meatpacking District a few weeks ago. We know you were there that night because we've got your credit card details and got you on cameras on both the ground floor and the Upper Deck.'

'Poor girl,' I said. 'I do remember hearing an ambulance as we were leaving that night. I was with some Australian friends.'

Barino flicked his notebook again. 'Ah yes: Mr Jim O'Leary and Ms Nadine Prior. They were staying at the Chelsea and flew back to Australia two days later.'

He'd done his homework all right. I hoped there were no cameras in the rooms at the Chelsea.

He continued. 'Anyway, this girl was killed in the base-ment section of the club. In the area they call Davy Jones' Lockers. Did you happen to visit that downstairs area on the night in question?'

Me vs. the human bulldog.

'Not at all,' I said. 'I didn't even know there was a down-stairs section.'

Barino squinted at me like he was lining me up through a gun sight. 'Well the thing is, they have hidden cameras in those rooms down there. And whatever sick things hap-pen there, they turn them into tapes and sell them to sick fucks who like looking at other sick fucks doing sick fuck things. They even got an asshole albino down there with an eye-patch selling drugs.'

There were little beads of sweat glistening on Barino's moustache. His partner, meanwhile, was taking a keen interest in my reference library.

'We're getting very close to recovering the tapes from that night. So if you did happen to be down there, we'll soon know all about it.'

I sat down myself. I could really use a drink now.

'But why do you think I have anything to do with it?'

Barino laughed like a pig and leaned forward aggressively. 'Oh, no particular reason, Mr Russell. Just routine and all that. But rumour has it that you recently lost your job because you'd been acting strangely at work. "Unstable" was how your friend Terry there described you.'

Terry the fucking Terrible.

'And your wife has left you, and even left the country. And she's moved your son over to your boss's house for safekeeping.'

'Not true. Callum still spends at least two nights a week here with me. He's downstairs right now watching TV. The desk clerk will be bringing him up in a few minutes.'

'And you still seem to be spending an awful lot of time down at the Hell or High Water.'

He was smiling like a madman. I was surprised he hadn't blamed me for Esmeralda's coma as well.

'What have you got to say about all these things, Mr Russell?'

I swallowed spit. The beer was calling my name from the kitchen.

'I'd say you've got yourself a really hot new screenplay

idea: you should write it up and make a million dollars, Detective Barino.'

Barino shook his head in disgust. He snapped his notebook shut and stuck the bitten-down pencil back behind his ear like a cheap cigar.

He waggled a chubby finger at me. 'I'll be seeing you again very soon, Mr Russell,' he said as his partner snapped a photo of me.

'You can bet your life.'

After the cops left, I went up to the roof to suck down a Stuyvesant.

Barino was right: things seemed to be going in only one direction for me. And I could hardly deny that the situation was escalating.

Maybe the tide was turning at last.

Maybe the time for swimming around in circles was over.

Maybe, to put an end to all this, I would have to become a Big Fish after all.

I would have to show some heart.

If it's to be, it's up to me.

I'd done it before, long ago.

*

What the bloody hell have you been doin' out there?

You're a disgrace.

You'll never be anything.

You're useless.

I can't stand you.

I step forward with a great big smile.

What are you——?

But before my mother can get her very last question out, I've lassoed the towel round the backs of her fat purple-veined legs and pull it towards me in one fierce, swift action and with all my might.

Her legs slip out from under her and she goes down like a nine pin, bashing her head on the stained tile wall and then again on the edge of the bath on the way down.

Perfect.

She's now lying motionless, but face up on the bottom of the bath with a small but powerful geyser of blood from the back of her head spurting vivid jets of red into the otherwise murky water. Her head and hair are covering the plughole so hardly any of the water is draining out.

Perfect.

These are delicious, exquisite moments. I want them to go on for ever.

Eventually, I lift her head up out of the water, grab a flannel and shove it into her gloriously silent mouth.

I wait till her face and neck are blue.

'By the way, Violet,' I say in case she expires before I get the chance to tell her, 'Raine never broke your fucking vase. It was me.'

She waves one of her arms like a lunatic and tells me with her eyes that she has one last thing to say. She can't seem to move anything else.

I remove the flannel from her mouth and she fountains up a gutful of alcohol. I bend down to the edge of the bath, still careful not to get too close.

I cup my ear down to hear her last wheezy words as I force her head on its side and turn the taps back on.

'You'll . . . pay . . . for . . . this . . .'

She gives a final vengeful snicker before I submerge her one final time.

'. . . You'll see.'

The Omen

Sunday lunchtime in the park.

I looked at Lucy's rosy cheeks and soft red lips and wondered where all those lovely, warm 'Love to Love Ya, Baby' feelings had gone.

Because I could tell: she didn't seem to like me so much anymore.

'You look pale, Guy, and there are bags under your eyes – have you been sleeping?'

She scrunched up her little snub nose. 'And you smell a little . . . ripe.'

It was a gorgeous day but there were big black clouds approaching like zeppelins.

'And how are you today, Mr Callum?' Lucy asked gaily, sipping her fruit juice. She handed him her bagful of breadcrumbs. 'Would you like to feed the ducks, honey?'

We had arranged to meet at the Central Park Lagoon. Last time Callum and I been here, it had been stuffed with skaters. But now the homecoming ducks were the only ones coasting over the clear cobalt surface.

'Guy, I'm pregnant,' she whispered just out of Callum's earshot.

She reached out to me, but I withdrew my hand like a snake slithering to safety.

'I know this is not necessarily great news for you given

what you've been through. But I wanted you to know because . . . Well . . .' she paused uncomfortably.

I stared at her.

' . . . because I'm going to keep it.'

Lucy's dream had always been to take the diplomatic corps by storm. Become the next Madeleine Albright. How did a new baby possibly fit into that equation?

'I love kids, as you know. I spoke to my Mom about it and she offered to help raise it for me while I keep working.'

'For Anthony? In New York?'

'No, I'm leaving advertising. There's a big, important chapter of the UN down in Austin and I've got an interview there next week for a position as a translator. It's not much, but it's a start. A good place to learn. And close to my family.' She threw a ball of breadcrumbs towards the water.

She reached out again for my hidden hand. 'Guy, you don't have to have a single thing to do with this baby if you don't want to. But maybe you could come visit us once in a while.'

She tried to read my face. 'And don't worry, I haven't told anybody it's yours.'

Callum walked up to us with his hands outstretched. 'Daddy, the ducks need some more bread.' He looked down at Lucy's hands covering her midriff. It was how Mia used to sit when she was pregnant.

'Have you gotta Bubby in your tummy?' Callum asked hopefully.

'Wow – is he psychic?' Lucy whispered.

I looked around. There were small groups of people right round the lagoon. Walking their dogs, cycling, enjoying the summer sunshine. It was steamy and tropical around the edge of the water. A chopper was scything the sky above and I was reminded of the wonderful joy flight I'd taken that first weekend we arrived.

I wondered what advice my former self would have given me if he could look down and see me here now.

A parrot shrieked from somewhere far behind us as a little remote-controlled boat putt-putted through a jungle of fronds.

Its leisurely arc described a large, rippling 'C' in the water.

Then it changed course; coughed, spluttered and double-backed, making what looked like a sharp 'V' within the 'C'.

My Olcott key was biting painfully into my hand. 'Thanks for telling me,' I said to Lucy. 'But I've gotta get Callum home now.'

'Guy?' I could hear her calling out to me as I spirited Callum away. 'Wait! Is that all you have to say? Gu-yyyy?'

I'm squeezing Callum's hand very hard as we cross the park, lifting him off the ground.

'Ow, you hurting my hand, Dad!' he cries.

But I don't say a word as we power along the poplared walkways. Past the fat-fingered Chinese masseuses, past the summer-lovin' ice cream hawkers and stars-and-stripes balloon salesmen, past a squeal of schoolgirls, past the ponytailed poodles and the rabid roller-bladers, past the ever-twinkling Tavern on the Green, past the never-ending John Lennon wake at Strawberry Fields, past the endlessly muttering bag lady.

Not a single, solitary word do I utter.

Suddenly there's a crash above us.

The mime artist at the 72nd street entrance to the park looks up at the angry clouds with a silent scream and holds his hand up above his face like a swooning damsel in a silent film.

Then the dark, dangerous sky above starts shooting hot silver bullets of hail down on the blameless throng below.

When we got back to the Olcott, I made Callum a nice big chocolate milk and mixed in some ground-up Valium tablets.

I needed to keep him quiet and I needed to keep him weak.

Then I plonked him down in front of *Scooby Doo on Zombie Island* and told him I'd be back in a few minutes.

I needed some time to think. And I couldn't think if Callum was there.

Because I now knew, without any doubt, that if Callum was there, then Violet was never far away.

I went up to the roof.

I lit a cigarette and considered the great big 'C' I'd just seen in the pond at the park. Followed by the sharp, nasty 'V'.

It was a sign.

An omen.

It was *the* omen.

'*You'll "C"*.'

Violet's dying threat to me all those years ago.

And indeed, I *did* see it all too clearly now: because I now knew for sure that my dead mother's evil, vengeful spirit was behind almost every single bad thing that had happened to me – and us – since that fateful night we'd lost Bubby back in Melbourne last September.

It was a growing, gnawing fear I hadn't ever fully been able to eject from my mind, even during those infrequent calmer times when I'd almost managed to convince myself that the threat couldn't possibly be real.

But what did it all mean?

Maybe she had played a role in Bubby's death?

Or maybe she hadn't been involved in Bubby's death at all, but because she'd initially been planning on coming back *as* Bubby, she had then had to make alternative plans once Bubby was no longer an option?

Maybe she showed me – through Callum – all those shocking things that initially only I could see to isolate me from Mia? And then everybody else.

And perhaps she worked her evil wiles on Mia at the same time so our family would inevitably implode?

But why wait till now? Why hadn't she simply come back when Callum was born?

Was it because she needed a new female host from the newborn stage?

Like Bubby?

Maybe that was why she could only channel and show things *through* Callum or the objects or people around him?

She needed a new little girl.

'*You'll "C".'*

What if it wasn't just a reminder, but a brand-new threat?

What if Violet was now planning on making Lucy's child her new incarnation?

Perhaps there was one upside to that devastating thought: because she'd no longer have any use for him, at least Callum was now going to be safe?

Who knew?

It was time to eat my logical hat. Because these were questions, suppositions and theories I had no rational answers for – in any universe.

I peered over the edge; the laneway below beckoned: a churning, sulphurous chasm.

For a split second, I pondered diving into it.

Head first.

But that was the coward's way out.

Hemingway blew his own brains out and left other people to pick up the pieces.

He wasn't a shark. He was a minnow.

I had to think really hard about what I could do to protect myself – and others who got in her way.

There was no telling what the mother from hell would do next.

I went back down to the apartment and washed down a couple of Valiums myself with a nice cool Coors.

The *Zombie Island* video had finished and Callum was now peacefully dozing with his head on a cushion.

I lay down on the couch next to him and drifted off nice and slowly.

I really needed a rest.

It felt good to close my eyes against the world for a while.

The coin rolls into the slot and Frank starts whistling the soundtrack.

I can see it all in gorgeous Technicolor:

I'm in the back of a long black car that's half Honda Passport, half Lincoln Continental.

A Chinese version of Lee Harvey Oswald is sitting beside me, radiant in Jackie Kennedy's hot pink Chez Ninon suit and pillbox hat. Twisting his foot-long Fu Manchu moustache between his spidery fingers, he waves his other white-gloved hand to the adoring crowd like a magician about to perform a trick.

But suddenly I realize that the presidential motorcade is driving up Elm Street towards the Texas Schoolbook Depository, instead of down Elm Street, away from it.

It's the Zapruder Film in reverse.

I tap the driver on the shoulder to find out what's going on.

Detective Barino turns around and smiles knowingly. His skin is weeping like stigmata.

We chug under the Triple Underpass and on my left, I can see Dr Hill crouching behind the stockade fence with a machinegun trained on the waving well-wishers on the grassy knoll. The end of the gun is attached by a cord to a foetal monitor that groans and moans like an old woman dying in agony.

As Hill opens fire, I can see my family sitting picnic-fashion by the left-hand curb. My father raises his beer can in silent salute. My mother is watching Raine, who is rocking happily back and forth under the shady protection of Umbrella Man.

The dead girl from the Hell or High Water is sitting on a seagrass rug next to them singing harmony with Frank, with her hair up in a bun like Kim Novak's.

Then, just before we reach the back of the Stemmons Freeway sign, a single ear-splitting report from a bolt-action rifle rings out above the machine-gun fire and Barino slumps forward onto the wheel. The horn keeps blaring under his weight and we begin to careen across the right-hand lane of Elm and onto the south side lawn as people scatter willy-nilly.

The famous long-coated spectators, Jean Hill in red and Mary Moorman in black, dive either side of us like synchronized swimmers. Moorman drops her Polaroid camera and we crunch over it.

Babushka Lady – a fatter version of Susanna Johnson – waddles away grumbling like a penguin hungry for fish.

Two more deafening shots ring out through the box canyon.

The wind is screaming now, but even louder than that is the sound of a thousand wings beating in unison.

We mount the curb, thump over the black epileptic thrashing and frothing on the pavement and smash into the low wall of the reflector pool right up near the corner of Elm and Houston.

Lucy's father takes off his Stetson and scratches his head. He looks just like Jimmy Stewart.

I look up at what I now understand is the Olcott Schoolbook Depository – a dirty amalgam of grey and orange bricks.

On the entry steps below, Mia is looking up, too, and pointing frantically at the watch on her wrist, like the White Rabbit imploring Alice to hurry up. On cue, two long, bony hands hold a plastic bag filled with water out of the sixth-floor sniper's window and let it fall.

Mia hops out of the way at the very last second and disappears into the building as the bag shatters onto the pavement into savage red and yellow glass shards, like a stained glass window smashing.

They look like pieces of Callum.

I can see a shadowy figure in the window but I can't make out who it is.

Somebody with bright-blonde hair.

And as I slowly rise above the adjacent Dal-Tex Building with my myriad baleful eyes, I get a bird's eye view of Lee Harvey Oswald washing his suit in the pool below, trying to wring the blood out of it.

His pillbox hat is floating on top of the water, bleeding pink.

He curses in Cantonese.

And as I look down on the crashed presidential limousine, I can now see that it's not me in John Fitzgerald Kennedy's brain-spattered Cardin shirt and single-breasted Savile Row suit after all.

But Bubby.

And half her little head has been blown into smithereens.

Weather: fine. Track: fast

When he'd come over to visit that day, Bill had slipped an envelope stuffed with twenties into my jacket pocket.

I'd only just discovered it.

Go crazy. Love Bill he'd written on the outside.

It was now Tuesday and Callum and I were heading out to the gee-gees to see if we could win some money for the next few months' food and rent.

I'd tried to study the Belmont form guide in the paper, but my mind had been galloping even faster than usual since my meeting with Lucy some forty-eight hours before.

There was so much to think about.

I had a whore's bath in the kitchen sink and donned my best racing outfit: a pin-striped navy-blue suit and a red tie with little white carousel horses on it.

Belmont Racetrack, here we come, doo dah, doo dah . . .

It was funny, but I wished my father could have seen us.

Callum hadn't been on a New York bus yet and this morning he was begging me to take him on one.

Can we go on the bus, Daddy? Can we go on the bus? he kept repeating.

Late morning, clouds lifting.

Weather: fine.

Track: fast.

I lifted Callum up the two big metal steps of the bus and nodded to the female driver. Late fifties with curly blonde hair that made her look a little like Harpo Marx, she chewed gum with her mouth open while tapping the cigarette pack in her breast pocket – as if her fat yellow fingers enjoyed smoking as much as her puffy red lips did.

There were already some older people on board with shopping bags and newspapers, a couple of punks rocking to the noise in their headphones and a small group of schoolkids aged seven or eight with a 'Bellerose Elementary' crest on their schoolbags. Their early thirties female teacher was telling them there wouldn't be any more excursions to Manhattan if they didn't sit down in their seats and start behaving themselves immediately.

I let Callum push a few quarters into the machine for our tickets. We sat halfway down, near the rear exit doors. Callum stared straight ahead without expression, waiting for the trip to begin.

The doors hissed shut and we lurched out of the terminal, throwing a couple of the still unseated schoolkids together in the aisle, who laughed at each other in surprise. 'Sit *down*, I said!' the teacher repeated. 'You're not the only ones on this bus – think about it!' Her eyes bulged through her glasses. The teenage punks smiled at the young miscreants, no doubt reminded of their younger selves.

As the bus picked up speed, trees and telephone poles blurred past. Wind whistled in through the windows. We were going pretty fast. And we seemed to be getting faster.

After a couple more kms whizzed by, one of the old

men with a string shopping bag and a walking cane stood up and reached up for the cord. 'She's going too fast!' he complained, shaking his head. 'She's going to go right past my stop!' He yanked hard on the wire twice with his cane but the bus just kept right on going. 'Stop!' he yelled at the driver. 'Stop!' He began waddling down the aisle, buffeted from side to side by the bus's increasing velocity.

Some of the other passengers craned their heads for a better view as the two standing schoolkids stepped out of their teacher's reach and followed behind the old man to see what would happen next.

There was a scream of brakes from both sides of the intersection as we accelerated straight through a red light.

I felt Callum's body lean into me.

One of the teenage punks unhooked his headphones and frowned at his ghetto blaster: his hip hop radio station's frequency must have been bumped and now 'I'll Come Back as Another Woman' by Tanya Tucker suddenly flooded the bus.

I suddenly understood what was going on, but wished with all my soul that I didn't: we were suddenly all expendable extras in a murderous set-piece orchestrated by Violet Russell.

'Stop!' I echoed the old man. I was already halfway down the aisle. 'Stop!'

I could now see Violet in the rear-view mirror, smiling evilly under her electric Harpo hair.

She even slumped her shaking arm onto the horn like the mute Marx Brother.

'Stop!'

I bundled the two kids behind me with big butterfly strokes, then bumped the old guy over to a seat on the left, grabbing his cane.

There were now screams inside the bus, rising above the horns and screeches of metal outside. A siren outside somewhere began howling in pursuit.

Three more steps and I was up by the driver's seat. She turned to me and scowled, suddenly taking her hands off the wheel and clapping them together, applauding her own wicked ingenuity.

I smashed her head with the willow cane, then wrapped the end of it around her wretched neck and yanked it as hard as I could. She came out of the seat surprisingly easily, hit her head on the passenger rail, then slithered into a heap on the floor.

The bus slowed down a little now her foot was off the pedal but started to veer dangerously over to the left, across the opposite lane of oncoming traffic. I jumped into the driver's seat and stamped my foot first on the accelerator by mistake, then on the brake.

We thudded to a stop.

When I finally looked up from the wheel, I saw that we had mounted the curb outside a fire station.

At least something had gone right.

Some of the firemen walked out scratching their heads and one of them explained how to open the pneumatic doors.

We made the six o'clock news.

But when I looked at the screen later and saw the man

and his son sitting by the side of the road, I couldn't recognize them.

The driver's official cause of death was given as 'cardiac arrest'. Some of the passengers claimed that I had struck her with the cane for no good reason. Others – like the punk kids – claimed she'd had a heart attack at the wheel and that I was a hero who had saved all our lives.

The fire chief mentioned something about a possible medal.

Sitting on the curb next to Callum, I watched the schoolkids walk quietly away behind their quietly sobbing teacher. They kept turning round to look at me, as if I might suddenly spring up and hit them with a cane.

Callum had looked completely wrung out when I'd carried him off the bus. As if he had drowned and been resuscitated.

We'd just survived a bus crash, but were still travelling down an impossibly dangerous road.

Because Violet's objective was, and had always been, to destroy me and those I loved.

The dead bus driver marked the second occasion I was aware of where she had taken over the body of another adult woman.

Because, of course, it was now obvious to me that Violet had been responsible for Bubby's death: she'd been there hiding in plain sight all along – inside that cruel, cold nurse in Mia's room at Cabrini.

'You'll see,' she'd promised after she'd squeezed Mia's shoulder.

Then that same chilling message delivered to me in writing on Bill's pad straight after I'd received the awful call from Esmeralda about Mia being in Mount Sinai.

And then again on the boardroom whiteboard when the coolcams clients had come to town:

you'll see

Constantly channelling herself through people, objects – but mainly Callum – as she became stronger; endlessly torturing me.

Trying to make me lose my mind.

Like the real-life horror movie she'd produced – and that only I could see – at Arcadia: the TV screen; the drawing; the episode in which she actually revealed herself, reaching out of Callum's chest and pointing her finger at me.

All this was her way of showing me that she was the evil inside and that I would be totally powerless to make anyone else believe me.

And to drive our family even further apart, all the time working on Mia behind my back – appearing to Mia in her perverse birth dream at Arcadia. And the cruel symmetry of Mia's suicide attempt and Violet's own gassy endeavor to abandon me when I was a child.

Part of Violet's sick genius was that I could never be totally sure it was really her pulling the strings until it was too late for me to act and stop her.

Callum would become a nice, normal little boy again,

like that short period of time after we returned from North Fuck – not because we'd returned to normality or I had 'come back to reality' or whatever Blakely might call it – but because Violet was now elsewhere, working on Mia or simply lying low to make me doubt what I'd experienced and question my own sanity.

Or perhaps she *hadn't* been deliberately torturing me all those months? Perhaps she was simply growing in strength as time went on? And then as she became stronger, other people around me also began to experience her insidious influence.

Esmeralda had witnessed the omen of the deer; Bill the portent with the bird; our maid had been seconds from seeing me being attacked by Callum's Buzz doll and had seen the destruction that this left behind in the apartment.

While poor Courtney may be forever tainted by Violet's unsuccessful attempt to frame me on her birthday.

And, on top of this, and all along, there was the one thing that Violet knew I would never be able to rationalize.

The sockets.

Speaking through Callum, uttering that chilling warning: 'Stay away from the sockets, Daddy!' that morning in the Olcott hallway all those months ago, was her way of letting me know there was something I simply couldn't explain away, no matter how hard I tried.

And now, today, Violet had tried literally to drive us to destruction.

For me to be so stupid as to think that Callum might

now be spared because Violet had set Lucy's baby in her sights.

How had I been so naïve? Believing what I wanted to believe, pretending that my son could just become my son again and that any of us could ever possibly be safe?

No. It was crystal clear that whatever plans for the future Violet was harbouring, she was also prepared to do absolutely anything to get rid of me – right now.

Even if that meant taking the lives of innocents.

But the one thing she didn't plan on had happened.

I had survived.

So I now had one last chance to stop her.

I had to stop her once and for all.

Because this was about more than just me now.

Whatever it took, I had to do it.

I'd done it before.

I could do it again.

By the next day, I have my plan in place.

The MacCallum

I really want Callum to enjoy this special morning with his Dad.

So after a nice big bowl of Cheerios, I take him over to the park and we visit the little zoo where we haven't been since that very first weekend we arrived.

We marvel at the micro-antics of the tiny battalions swarming the ant colony. We play peek-a-boo and duck the fruit bats in the indoor rainforest. We laugh at the dinner-suited comedians in the penguin house and feel sorry for the polar bears sweating it out by the pool.

I have a very strong compulsion to let all the animals out.

Then we leave the zoo and walk through one of those acrid-smelling tunnels towards the carousel. I stick Callum on a big brown horse and watch him blur past as a creaky 'Campdown Races' wheezes out of the speaker.

Then I buy him a strawberry ice cream and a little *I love NY* T-shirt.

He wants to know if his real heart is the same size as the one on the shirt. He spills ice cream on his chest and the flies start to follow him.

Finally it's time to go home. It is time to put a stop to the evil, once and for all.

It's time for our big race.

*

'Olcott Races, Daddy's Day, doo dah, doo dah . . . Olcott Races, Daddy's Day, oh–the-doo-dah-day . . .'

'Again!' I yell at Callum. 'One more race!'

'I too tired, Daddy,' he groans.

'One more!' I yell. I do a quick final scan of the corridor: dead and deserted both ways.

Callum leans, panting, against the wall near the corner. He bends down to roll up the bottom of his pants as I sprint towards him and scoop him up with my right hand.

'Uggh,' he says, as I knock the stuffing out of him.

I have to move very quickly in case Violet cottons on to what comes next.

Round the corner, just a few more paces and we fly past room 901. The stairwell door yawns wide open with the small bin I've propped against it.

I watch him sail gracefully over the rail.

It was just as Mia had dreamed it all those months ago.

For an eternal second, his angelic little face looks up at me in cartoon confusion as he desperately flaps his arms.

Then he disappears into the soulless fluorescent void.

Of course I felt terrible – what father wouldn't?

But there was a lot more at stake now than just Callum or me: I was on a life-saving mission for the greater good.

Like a modern Abraham, I had been forced to make a horrible sacrifice.

And I'd just made it.

But then the unbearable thought slowly dawned on me: what if Violet had tricked me again?

What if she'd just convinced me to kill Callum – her cosy little home all these months – so I'd presume she was gone for good . . . when in fact she had *already* moved into her new abode?

Callum was just the bagman, the decoy, the ticking suitcase.

The patsy.

The MacCallum, if you like.

I ran back into the apartment for my remaining half-packet of albino powder and Nadine's last two Blue Meanies.

Most importantly, I was going to need my sacred sword.

Because what goes around, comes around, doesn't it, Violet?

The Stranger in the Night

They'd cut off the phone at the Olcott and I'd had to give my cell phone back to Brave Face before they'd pay me out.

So I fumbled for some coins and called from a payphone outside the same seedy bar on 8th Avenue where Anthony had kept company with me after Mia had tried to kill herself.

I wondered how Mia was. I wondered where Mia was.

It had been a while now since I'd seen her.

An eternity, in fact.

Someone finally picked up at Brave Face. Rosemary was at lunch. So it was actually Terry the Terrible who told me where Lucy was.

'She's at home, throwing up.'

*

'Guy? What are you doing here?'

She blinked at me in a black leotard.

I'd got to Lucy's apartment pretty fast. The running was really paying off.

It looked as though she had secreted a small round cantaloupe or coconut beneath the tight fabric under her plumper-looking breasts. There was a red yoga mat on the polished floor next to her crimson couch, and ocean wave breathing exercises were lapping gently in the background.

It seemed the only thing Lucy had really been throwing up that morning was her supplicant arms in a 'salute to the sun'. Her body was glistening like a tantric goddess; she'd never looked more supple and radiant.

'It must be a hundred out there?' The air conditioner clicked up a gear in confirmation as Lucy was walking away, not looking at me, towards the kitchen bench.

'Get on the table,' I ordered her.

'Oh no, Guy. I'm in no condition for games today,' she said, her voice cracking a little. 'I'm not feeling well.'

'It's no game.' I opened the escritoire drawer and removed the handcuffs.

A little bell chimed. The water she'd been boiling in the pot for her herbal tea was ready.

Once I had her cuffed to the table legs like the good old days, I stuffed her old purple panties into her mouth.

'Bye bye, Lucy.'

She could still make a surprising amount of noise. I turned the ocean waves up so they crashed a little louder.

'Bye bye, Bubby.'

I held the carving fork aloft.

Lucy's eyes rolled back into her head as if she couldn't bear to look.

'Bye bye, Violet.'

There was a flyer sitting on top of the escritoire.

Baby Benders
Yoga for yummy mummies

The YWCA on 53rd and Lexington.

I looked at Lucy's limp figure on the table. The slow-flowing crimson rivulets matched the couch beautifully. She suddenly spasmed and rattled as if voicing her aesthetic approval.

I knew that Lucy attended the gym at the Y.

Maybe she'd swung by the yoga classes for pregnant women and checked them out for future reference?

Maybe Violet was still one move ahead of me?

I couldn't afford to take any more chances.

4 p.m.

'Excuse me, Sir!' the large bespectacled woman behind the desk was waving her paperback at me. 'But this is a women's only class.'

I removed my earplugs: U2's 'Beautiful Day' was humming quietly out of the radio behind her.

'Sir!' she protested like an irate school ma'am. 'Sir, you *can't* go in there – it's for pregnant ladies only!'

I snatched the key from the outside lock and pulled the door gently shut behind me.

The carving fork felt like a double-headed cobra in my hand.

Twin nine-inch nails.

I pulled it out like Lancelot drawing Excalibur. The long, tapered handle felt white hot in my hand.

I walked into the cool womb of semi-darkness and for

some unknown reason self-consciously dropped to my knees into the combat stance that a personal trainer had once demonstrated to me back home.

There was a stubby row of candles flickering on the floor and incense smoking in little golden bowls.

It smelled like napalm.

I was the Stranger in the Night.

There were eight more bulging bellies in that room.

So many places for her to hide.

So much more work to do.

*

I staggered blindly out onto Lexington screaming in pain, my arms outstretched like a ludicrous Frankenstein charade.

'Murder! Death! Bodies! Blood!' the receptionist was wailing behind me like a siren. 'Murder! Death! Bodies! Blood!'

A musclebound security guard from the Charles Schwab next door truncheoned me into submission and made a beanbag out of me till the blue and white cavalry arrived.

I sustained second-degree burns to my face from the coffee urn water that the receptionist had thrown at me after she'd found the master key and burst through the door.

My eyes were fried, too.

But nobody worried too much about calling an ambulance for the crazy burning man.

Just for the now four dead ex-mothers, the three

wounded ones, and the one that had gone into hysterics and couldn't form any recognizable human words.

They jabbed me with some sort of sedative.

I have a vague memory of Detective Barino appearing on the way down to the station and asking me some really stupid questions.

But maybe it was just the Blue Meanies talking.

And when I eventually came to, no matter how many times they asked me, I stuck to my original statement:

'Read Beat the Devil, it's all in there.

The Kid Did It.

I'm just a pastry!'

The Post — and all the other tabloids — immediately and lazily dubbed it *The Yoga Mommies Massacre.*

They were equally unoriginal with my moniker: I instantly become known as *Australian Psycho.*

Christ, one hack even christened me *Guy Forks.*

The fucking media — they're even worse than ad agencies.

They're positively evil.

FIJI CENTRAL POLICE STATION Joske Street, Suva Tel: +679 3311222 Fax: + 679 3304805.

Case #: H 28/07/00/3462 (ex USA).

Incident:

Multiple homicides: Bowden, Fuhr, Hammond, Khan

Attempted homicides: Hobbes-Nevinson, Duella, Ling, Mulvey

Location of incident: YWCA, Room 7: Cnr 53rd & Lexington, New York City, NY USA

Date of incident: 28/07/00

Reporting Officer: Sgt. Ranjit Singh

Date of interview: 01/08/00

At about 10.40 hours on 1st August 2000, I met with Ms Mia Giancarlo, wife of the accused at Central Station, Suva.

Ms Giancarlo had previously been convalescing on Castaway Island, Fiji, before I summoned her to an interview.

Ms Giancarlo became profoundly distraught upon hearing of the confirmed death of her son, Callum Russell (aged 3 years, 11 months), and the arrest of her husband, Guy Raymond Russell – who has been charged with the homicides and attempted homicides listed above in New York City on 28/07/00, as well as the homicide of their son, Callum, earlier on the same day and also in New York City.

(Such was her distressed condition, I had no opportunity to also inform Ms Giancarlo of the separate homicide investigation involving Mr Russell's work colleague, Ms Lucille Emily Tate – also deceased on 28/07/00.)

Before being medicated and taken by ambulance to CWM Hospital in Brown Street, Suva, Ms Giancarlo was able to inform me that apart from one 'rough sex' episode during her pregnancy, her husband – from whom she had recently separated – had never shown any previous violent tendencies towards her – or other women – that she was aware of. She did, however, indicate that she believed he had been conducting an affair with a work colleague – Ms Lucille Emily Tate as listed above.

Ms Giancarlo also declared that her husband had never demonstrated any violent tendencies towards their son, Callum. Although she did say that she believed her husband had become increasingly 'unhinged' in recent months following the death of an unborn child, that he had been fired from his job and that he had come to believe that Callum had been 'possessed' by some sort of malevolent force.

The only violent incident involving her husband and son that she could recall was in February 2000, when she discovered her husband had been sleepwalking one evening in their bedroom in the Olcott Hotel, shaking his son frantically and screaming the phrase 'Stay away from the sockets' repeatedly.

Ms Giancarlo stated that she had – and still has – no idea what this phrase meant, and had not had the chance to question her husband about its meaning the following morning, as he left the hotel before she woke up to catch an early flight to San Francisco. Due to her growing feelings of depression at that time – and the fact that her husband often talked in his sleep – the incident went out of her mind.

(Ms Giancarlo informed me that her husband experienced a second sleepwalking episode, which he was made aware of afterwards, a few weeks after the first, during a family vacation to Long Island, but there was no direct physical contact with his son on that occasion.)

However, after requisitioning Mr Russell's records from the Australian police, it appears that the aforementioned phrase may have had something to do with the fact that, in 1973, his younger sister Lorraine died from electrocution as the result of inserting a carving fork into an electrical socket in a kitchen – at the institution where she had been committed as an eight year old.

The Australian police records also confirmed that Mr Russell's mother, Violet Russell, died accidentally in 1979, having slipped in the bath, sustaining serious head injuries, which – along with a significant amount of alcohol in her system – caused her to drown in the bathwater.

Mr Russell, then sixteen years of age, was the person who found her body and reported the incident to the police.

Upon her release from CWM Hospital, pending a positive evaluation from Dr Albert Pillai, Consultant Psychiatrist at St Giles Psychiatric Hospital, Suva, Ms Giancarlo will return to Melbourne, Australia, where she will need to make the necessary funeral arrangements for her son, Callum.

Should any further police interviews be required with Ms Giancarlo, she can be contacted from 24/08/00 via Victoria Police Homicide Squad, 412 St Kilda Road VIC 3004 Australia (613) 9865 2770.

Fiji Central
16:40 –3/8/00
Ranjit Singh (2306)

My new office

The Shawshank Redemption is a lie.

There are no kindly Morgan Freeman types in here.

There are no free men at all.

No secret tunnels to paradise and certainly no hope of redemption.

As I sit writing these notes I look out my high barred window and try to remember more open skies.

Nine is my lucky number. At least it used to be.

I believe nine used to be John Lennon's lucky number, too. (October 9 was his birthday.) Except he was also gunned down on December 9 1980 (1+9+8+0 =18: 1+8 = 9) Australia-time, on W72 (7+2 = 9) by an assassin obsessed with Chapter 27 (2+7=9) of a famous book.

Anyway, nine years is how long I spent at the Kirby Forensic Psychiatric Centre on Wards Island, Manhattan.

Before they transferred me here six years ago.

To my new office.

A lot can happen in fifteen years:

The Crocodile Hunter is dead.

The Powerpuff Girls were cancelled after six seasons.

And Patrick Swayze is now dancing in the dirt.

In fact, although I don't have access to a television, and

nobody ever visits, it's surprising just how much one can find out inside about the outside.

Detective Barino sometimes tells me things.

I still see him from time to time.

He's been here longer than I have.

It was Barino who killed that poor girl down in Davy Jones' Lockers that first night at the Hell or High Water club.

I'd even come across him that very same night: the captain with the bad skin I'd collided with as I staggered to the restroom.

A sharp-eyed doorman had recognized him when he paid an early evening visit to the club in August 2000, flashing his police badge and waving my photo around.

As Barino talked with the club's manager, the doorman had had a quiet word with Barino's partner – the same officer who'd accompanied him on his visit to the Olcott – about the 'regular customer with the terrible skin.'

One Detective Angelo Barino.

You see, Barino hadn't realized there were secret cameras in the basement rooms until he started investigating his own case. Which is why he had been so desperate to get his hands on the tapes.

Barino's wife had left him. He'd started drinking heavily and shooting speed.

In fact, he'd become one of the 'asshole albino's' best customers.

To this day he claims the devil made him do it.

*

I'm reading another one of Naomi Klein's books.

It's called *The Shock Doctrine: The Rise of Disaster Capitalism*.

It's about how certain supposedly 'democratic' governments use natural and sometimes even manufactured disasters to push through unpopular and unjust policies while their citizens are still in a state of shock:

The War on Terror gets outsourced to private companies with close political affiliations, conveniently affording them vast economic gain.

Hurricane Katrina destroys public schools in New Orleans that are then replaced by new, private ones.

Fishing villages swept away by the Southeast Asian tsunami are 'remodelled' by wealthy international resort developers.

Our world gets carved up and monopolized by criminals masquerading as patricians and politicians.

They cash in on chaos.

Intervention via illusion: the most dangerous MacGuffin of all.

*

I try to keep busy during the day.

It's the nights that are hardest.

That's when Callum comes to see me.

He still looks all bruised and broken up.

Other nights, it's four faceless women with their bellies gaping red.

But they never say anything.

If only they'd let me sleep.

*

Esmeralda appears in my dreams, too, sometimes.

Truth be told, I'd never meant to hurt Esmeralda.

But when I'd subwayed back to the Olcott that morning to retrieve a pad on which I'd scrawled some important campaign ideas and saw her fiddling with that curtain cord again, for one short, sick moment I saw my mother instead.

I lashed out at her in a moment of madness.

She fell and hit her head hard on the windowsill and then even harder on the floor.

Just like Violet had all those years before.

I panicked.

Callum was asleep in the bedroom, and I was sure no one had seen me enter the building; the lobby had been empty – as it so often seemed to be – when I'd bolted in.

So I took the stairs back down and the fire exit out to the alley that ran along the side of the building.

Within forty minutes of leaving, I had been back in my office.

Once she eventually regained consciousness in late 2000, Esmeralda was able to recall the last moments prior to her fall, and made a statement to the police.

Shortly after that, Estella informed her of what had happened to Callum, Lucy and all the other women, and I hear Esmeralda almost lost her mind with grief.

*

Sometimes there's another voice in my cell.

A voice so vile that I sometimes can't stop it coming out of my own mouth.

That cunty, carping, wheedling, needling, emasculating, enervating, never-ending voice.

Make me a cuppa, ya lazy bastard.

Do I have to bloody do everything?

I miss your sister but I'd never miss you.

When the voice starts up, I have to press my palms into my ears, squeeze my eyes shut and sing 'Olcott Races' really, really loudly.

From where I sit, if I crane my neck I can make out half a water tower on top of the next cell block.

It looks Zen-beautiful as the early evening sun disrobes behind it.

The blackbirds seem to like it, too.

But here's the thing: the tower's not operational anymore since the warden had it all sealed up.

A prisoner hid in there one time and they didn't find him until the smell gave him away.

Acknowledgements

I started writing this book back in the dim, dark days of late November 2003.

I could not have possibly stayed the course without the benefit of the kind hearts and/or sound minds of the people below:

To Shoba Purushothaman for financing what turned out to be an intensive twelve-month New York research trip in year 2000.

To my razor-sharp young editor at Quercus London, Richard Arcus, and his far-sighted boss, Jon Riley.

To my uber-agents in Los Angeles, Alan Nevins and Eddie Pietzak; and before that to Anthony Mattero who deserves a LOT of credit for this book.

To my friend and now well-known screenwriter, Terence Hammond, who demonstrated through actions – not just words – that 'never giving up' is really the only viable option.

I'd also like to thank Mark Lucas, Nikki Christer, Cecily Maude, Isobel Dixon, Carson Reeves, Katherine Finemore, Mark Farrelly, Graham Smith, Simon Lord, Andrew Joy, Martine Shrives, Kim Burns, Mark & Emma Merton, Jacinta Di Mase, Adena Graham, Annie Condon, Paul Paxton-White, Tim O'Leary, Terry Comer, Andrew & Libby Hicks, Alan Baldwin, Josh Hunt, Flip Shelton,

Dominique Hanlon, Stephen Gault, Brad Felstead, Liz Burgess, Kate Langbroek, Noble Smith, Michael Payne, Dan O'Brien, Christine Elmer, Mathew Hehir, Greg Foyster, Diana Thornley, John Fuhr, Serge Guala, Rudolf Buitendach, Gary Ravenscroft, David Rawlinson, Robert Stock, Chris Bilby, Peter Leckey, Linda Clark, Seb Rachele and Doc Johnson for their reading, counsel or encouragement.

To my real 'old family' – Jo, Geoff, Louise and Danielle – thank you for always being there, even before I started writing this book.

And finally, I'd like to especially thank my long-suffering wife, Moira, who will tell you that the real nightmare is living with a writer.

(Seconded by my sons, Louis and Flynn, who have had to put up with an oft-distracted Dad . . .)